Chris...

Passion
&Proposals

Three brand-new, irresistible,
festive romances from bestselling,
beloved authors

CAROLE MORTIMER
JANE PORTER
CATHERINE GEORGE

Presents,
Passion
&Proposals

Carole
MORTIMER

Jane
PORTER

Catherine
GEORGE

Harlequin Mills & Boon Limited, Eton House,
18-24 Paradise Road, Richmond, Surrey TW9 1SR

PRESENTS, PASSION & PROPOSALS
© Harlequin Enterprises II B.V./S.à.r.l. 2010

The Billionaire's Christmas Gift © Carole Mortimer 2010
One Christmas Night in Venice © Jane Porter 2010
Snowbound with the Millionaire © Catherine George 2010

ISBN: 978 0 263 88827 0

009-1110

Harlequin Mills & Boon policy is to use papers that are
natural, renewable and recyclable products and made from
wood grown in sustainable forests. The logging and
manufacturing processes conform to the legal environmental
regulations of the country of origin.

Printed and bound in Spain
by Litografia Rosés S.A., Barcelona

The Billionaire's Christmas Gift

Carole
MORTIMER

Carole Mortimer was born in England, the youngest of three children. She began writing in 1978 and has now written over one hundred and fifty books for Harlequin Mills & Boon. Carole has six sons, Matthew, Joshua, Timothy, Michael, David and Peter. She says, "I'm happily married to Peter senior; we're best friends as well as lovers, which is probably the best recipe for a successful relationship. We live in a lovely part of England."

Look for an exciting new novel from Carole Mortimer, *Jordan St Claire: Dark & Dangerous*, available from Mills & Boon® Modern™ romance in January 2011.

Dear Reader,

What a wonderful time of year this is! A time for the giving and receiving of gifts but most of all a time for caring and sharing and being with those we love.

I love to read books with a seasonal flavour, but I love writing them even more! It is an absolute joy for me to write a book with a Christmas setting and to indulge my love of the holiday season by having two of my characters fall in love with each other. I hope you enjoy reading this story as much as I enjoyed writing it!

Merry Christmas!

Carole Mortimer

CHAPTER ONE

NICK glowered through the windscreen from inside the warmth and comfort of his heated car as the rain and sleet fell heavily outside, in no hurry to find a gap in the slowly moving vehicles that would allow him to edge back into the morning rush hour of bumper-to-bumper traffic. Having dropped his daughter Bekka off at school for the day, he was too immersed still in the memory of their last conversation before Bekka had climbed, sulking, out of the car.

'It's not fair, Daddy! Just because my birthday is on Christmas Day… Why can't I have someone over on my birthday like the other girls do?'

'Because—'

'Because "everyone is busy with their own families on Christmas Day,"' Bekka parroted—a reminder that this was the excuse Nick had been giving her for the past week.

'I'm taking you and three of your friends bowling and then out for a meal on Saturday instead—'

'I want to invite someone over on my actual birthday,' Bekka had maintained stubbornly. 'It's just one little guest, Daddy. Just one,' she wheedled.

'But—'

'And I already know that Mrs Morgan isn't busy on Christmas Day with her own family because she doesn't have one!' Bekka had announced triumphantly.

Why couldn't his eight-year-old daughter be totally consumed by self-interest, as most of her friends seemed to be? Nick now fumed inwardly. Why did it have to be his daughter who took in all the abandoned kittens, stray dogs, injured birds—and now widowed schoolteachers—whom Bekka knew happened to be spending Christmas alone?

He and Bekka did okay together, didn't they? Nick questioned with a frown.

Bekka had lived with her mother after Janet and Nick divorced three years ago, and Nick had been trying to be both mother and father to Bekka since Janet had died ten months ago. To be there for Bekka as much as he could when business interests already took up so much of his time. And he tried—even if he didn't always succeed!—to spend the weekends doing things that Bekka wanted to do.

Surely he didn't have to give up the peace and quiet of his Christmas Day, too, in order to entertain an elderly, probably bewhiskered widow, so bereft of family and friends no one else was willing to invite her to join them for the holidays?

No, of course he didn't.

Nick's heart sank again as he remembered Bekka's last petulant shot. 'Mummy would have let me do it!' And then she'd slammed the car door and disappeared through the rain and sleet into the school building. Seven words. Seven little words guaranteed to guilt Nick into agreeing to whatever hare-brained scheme Bekka had come up with this time. Seven little words that meant Nick now possessed three thoroughly spoilt cats who thought they owned him, rather than the other way around, and an anti-social dog who more often than not tried to keep him out of the house rather than intruders. Plus a hamster one of Bekka's friends had had to get rid of because she was allergic, and, of all things, a rat that Bekka had literally saved from the jaws of one of the spoilt cats.

Add in a goat and some ducks and they could open up a damned petting zoo!

No, he had to draw the line somewhere, Nick decided firmly, and, whether Bekka liked it or not, inviting an elderly widow—a complete stranger, to boot—to join them next week on Christmas Day, was going to be it!

Having settled that situation to his satisfaction, Nick pressed his foot gently down on the accelerator to manoeuvre out into the traffic so that he actually reached his office some time this morning after all.

At that exact moment a huddled pedestrian chose to step off the pavement in front of his car!

The first indication Beth had that the car parked at the end of the school driveway was now actually moving came as she stepped off the pavement, hunched down in her duffle coat, the hood pulled low over her face to keep off the worst of the rain and sleet, and felt the slight bump of impact against her hip!

It wasn't a painful or hard bump, but it did succeed in knocking Beth off balance, causing her to stagger slightly as she tried to prevent herself from toppling over. A battle she totally lost as the heel of one of her boots slid on the icy surface of the tarmac.

She fell down on her bottom—hard. Straight into one of the deep puddles that had formed at the side of the road.

Great. Not only was her outer clothing soaked through, but now her trousers and underwear were awash too!

'Are you okay?' demanded a gruffly concerned disembodied voice from amidst the blinding weather.

'Apart from my injured pride, you mean?' Beth muttered, her cheeks flushed with embarrassment.

'Yes, I'm absolutely fine,' she assured the man ruefully.

'What the hell did you think you were doing, stepping off the pavement in front of me like that?' His shock at the near-disaster obviously assuaged, he obviously took this as an invitation to vent his own emotions. 'Damn it, woman, I could have killed you!' he added accusingly as his firm grasp on Beth's arm pulled her easily to her feet.

'I find that very hard to believe, when you were only driving at about five miles an hour!' Beth drawled dryly, halting her attempts to wring the worst of the rainwater from the hem of her coat as she finally looked up at the man from beneath the wet bangs of her dark auburn hair.

And then looked again.

As any woman with red blood in her veins would have done!

Even on a winter morning, with the sleet and rain continuing to fall down relentlessly, soaking her even more than she already was, and with her dignity in tatters.

Well, if she was going to be knocked down, Beth decided fatalistically, it might as well be by a man so gorgeous he should have one of those sexy calendars dedicated just to him! He was certainly ruggedly handsome enough to play the lead in one of those action movies Beth enjoyed so much.

He was probably aged in his mid-thirties, and at least a foot taller than Beth's diminutive five feet two, with slightly overlong dark hair curling damply about chiselled features of such hard masculine beauty they were mesmerizing: pale eyes—blue or grey? Beth couldn't tell—a long and aristocratic nose, high cheekbones, and a sensual mouth above a sculptured jaw.

As for his hard and muscled body...

She was soaked through. Had been hit by a car and had fallen down in the road, which was undoubtedly going to make her late for work. Yet still Beth couldn't help but admire the ruthless good looks of the driver of the car that had knocked her down!

What did that tell her?

That it was time her self-inflicted solitude came to an end, probably...

'Look, I've assured you I'm perfectly okay,' she said briskly, at the same time extracting her arm from that firm grasp. 'You, on the other hand, are getting very wet.' Beth frowned as she realised that the man wasn't even wearing an overcoat, and that his dark and expensively tailored business suit was now as wet as her own clothing. 'Please get back into your car—'

'We'll *both* get in my car,' Nick decided impatiently, and as he once again took the woman's arm with the intention of pulling her towards his Mercedes.

A move she instantly resisted. 'I make it a rule never to get into the car of a man I don't know!'

Nick turned back to her, taking in her appearance at a glance; the hood of the blue duffle coat was pulled over dark auburn hair that lay in wet tangles about a pale face dominated by huge blue eyes and freckles and all her clothing was absolutely soaked through—including the sodden black boots on her feet.

'Will you just get inside?' he asked impatiently as the woman still hung back once he had wrenched the passenger door open. 'It may have escaped your notice but we're causing a traffic jam!' he added, with a pointed glance at the row of cars lining up behind his.

This man might be handsome as sin, Beth acknowledged as she reluctantly slid onto the passenger seat, but—that brief concern for having knocked her over aside—his manners certainly left a lot to be desired.

It was a deliciously warm and dry car, she realised within seconds of having the door slammed closed behind her. Warm, dry, and spaciously decadent, with pale blue leather upholstery and walnut veneer.

Although it seemed slightly less so once the darkly frowning driver had climbed in behind the wheel!

'There really is no need— What are you doing?' Beth voiced her alarm as he restarted the engine.

'I'm getting us off the road and out of everyone else's way, of course!' An icy grey gaze raked over her scathingly before he turned the car round in the driveway and pulled over to the other side of the road, parking, and allowing the row of cars behind them to move out into the crawling traffic.

Of course. Obvious, once she thought about it. *If* she'd thought about it. Which Beth hadn't.

She was surprised she could still function at all when she felt so numbed from walking to work in the icy rain and sleet for the past fifteen minutes!

Beth repressed a shiver as she pushed the wet hood of her coat back off her hair. 'I really am okay, you know. Wet and cold, obviously, and my dignity is certainly bruised. But otherwise I'm unharmed.'

'I doubt it's only your dignity that's bruised...' her reluctant rescuer drawled wryly.

Beth turned to give him a frown; was this man— now that he was assured of her well-being—actually laughing at her?

Nick could see exactly how wet and cold the woman beside him was now that the hood of her coat no longer hid her face; her teeth were chattering and her cheeks had taken on a slightly blue tinge. 'I'll drive you home so that you can take a hot shower and change into some dry clothes,' he offered briskly.

'That won't be necessary, thank you,' the woman refused primly. 'I'm going to be late for work as it is—'

'Aren't we all?' Nick muttered, knowing there was no way that he was going to make his nine-thirty appointment now. 'But you can't possibly go into work like that—'

'Of course I can,' she dismissed as she pulled the hood back over her hair—only to give a grimace at its uncomfortable dampness. 'I have some dry things I can change into once I get into school.'

'You work at St James's…?' Nick eyed her sharply as he reassessed her appearance.

She was young, probably in her early to mid-twenties, and wore little or no make-up. Small gold studs in pierced earlobes. The clothes he could see— blue duffle coat, black trousers, black boots—looked serviceable rather than fashionable or designer label. Her gloveless hands were long and slender, the nails kept short, the fingers completely bare of rings.

Probably one of the catering staff. Or perhaps she helped out in the classroom, Nick decided. If it was the former she no doubt had a kitchen uniform she could change into while her own clothes were drying on a radiator somewhere.

'It's your call.' He nodded abruptly, checking there was no traffic behind him before pulling out to drive back down to the entrance to the main school building.

This whole incident could have been so much worse, Nick acknowledged gratefully. He had been too distracted by the memory of that earlier unsatisfactory conversation with Bekka to even notice this woman stepping off the pavement in front of his car. Until he'd heard that telling thump, that was.

He glanced at the woman beside him briefly. 'I'll give you my business card—just in case you suffer any ill-effects from the accident later on today and need to contact me.'

Beth eyed the man beside her uncertainly, eyeing the expensive cut of his suit and the gold watch on his wrist bearing a discreet but very distinctive crest. The air of wealth made her wonder if he was a parent of one of the pupils at the school. She liked her job at St James's. Enjoyed working at the private school for girls more than she would ever have believed possible when she had reluctantly accepted the position almost a year ago.

Having grown up as an only child of loving parents in a small village in the east of England, and having been educated at that same village school, Beth's experience of private schools had been nil when she'd decided to make this move to London just over a year ago.

At the time Beth had thought she needed to get

away—that after all that had happened a complete change of scenery was called for. She just hadn't realised how completely different London was going to be from the village life she had known.

Her previous job had been at a large mixed middle school in the town nearest to her village home. It was attended by almost one thousand pupils, and she had been pleasantly surprised to find that she enjoyed the intimacy of working in a school with only three hundred girls.

The only drawback Beth had found was that parents tended to be more involved in a fee-paying school, and that the school and its staff were answerable directly to the governors, who were in turn answerable to those parents.

If the man sitting beside her, in his top-of-the-range Mercedes, really was the wealthy parent of one of the girls attending St James's, then Beth knew she was going to have to tread carefully. 'I really am completely unharmed, you know,' she reassured him lightly. 'If anything was to blame for the accident then it was my own carelessness in stepping out into the road in that way without looking!'

This woman really was quite beautiful now that she was drying out a little, Nick realised abstractedly. The blue of her eyes was a deep clear periwinkle, and she had a light dusting of freckles on the bridge of her nose, along with a slight flush in her creamy cheeks.

What colour would that dark auburn hair be once it was dry? he wondered. Red, of course. But would it be a bright carrot-red or—?

He was finally going quietly out of his mind…!

Ten months of trying to be both father and mother to Bekka, as well as juggling the demands of his extensive business interests to fit in with that dual role, must finally be taking their toll on him if he was starting to think the dripping wet waif and stray now sitting in his car—probably ruining his upholstery in the process—was in the least attractive!

He straightened abruptly to take his wallet out of the breast pocket of his damp jacket; unlike the woman beside him, Nick *would* have to go home and change into some dry clothes before going to his office. 'Here.' He pushed his business card into the woman's hand. 'I expect you to call me if you have any repercussions from your fall,' he explained impatiently, as, instead of taking the card, the woman looked at him, questioning.

Beth gave the man at her side one last inquisitive look before glancing down at the card he had thrust into her hand, frowning as she read the words embossed in gold in the centre of that card: 'Nicholas Steele, Steele Industries', and both a landline and mobile number printed beneath.

Nicholas Steele…

CHAPTER TWO

BETH knew the name Nicholas Steele, of course. Didn't everyone? The man probably owned or had developed half of London, and he had even merited special mention by Miss Sheffield when Beth attended her initial interview. The headmistress at St James's explained that the daughter of Nicholas Steele was a pupil at the school, and that, 'Mr Steele is on the board of governors and also our most influential parent.' For 'influential' Beth had known she should read wealthy!

This man was Nicholas Steele?

Rebekka Steele's father?

Incredible!

Rebekka was such a lovely little girl, very warm and open, whereas this man— Well, he might still be as gorgeous as sin, but the last few minutes had also shown Beth that he could be arrogant, and there was a definite edge of ruthlessness to those sculptured lips.

'There won't be any repercussions,' Beth declared firmly as she carefully placed the card on top of the dashboard before turning to open the passenger door.

Nicholas Steele's hand on her arm prevented her from actually getting out of the car.

Beth turned to look at him irritably. 'Yes?'

The perplexed frown between his brows deepened to a scowl before he slowly released her arm. 'If you're sure you're okay…?' he muttered gruffly.

She gave an abrupt nod before scrambling quickly out of the car, slamming the door behind her and hurrying into the school building.

'The bell rang for the start of lessons some time ago, Mrs Morgan.' Miss Sheffield's voice rang out disapprovingly across the cavernous hallway.

Beth turned reluctantly to face the middle-aged headmistress. 'It really is an awful morning, isn't it?'

The other woman's mouth tightened. 'I'm pleased to say that all of my other members of staff seemed to take that fact into account by leaving home earlier than usual to ensure that they arrived on time!'

Maybe so, but then none of Miss Sheffield's other members of staff had been delayed because they'd been knocked down by the school's 'most influential' parent!

* * *

'Am I speaking to Mrs Morgan?' Nick prompted tersely when his telephone call was finally answered.

The two days since Bekka's initial request for her biology teacher to be invited to their home on Christmas Day—correction, on Bekka's birthday, which just *happened* to be Christmas Day!—had been decidedly uncomfortable ones for Nick, as his daughter had brought the subject up every time the two of them were together. Initially wheedling and cajoling, Bekka had soon become whining and tearful as Nick had steadfastly refused to give in to her pleas.

The frosty drive in to school this morning, the last day of term, had been the final straw as far as Nick was concerned. To the extent that Nick had eventually decided to at least telephone the woman; with any luck the widowed Mrs Morgan would have the good sense to refuse the invitation!

Whatever the outcome of this telephone call, Nick knew his Christmas was already shot to hell. Forced into being polite on Christmas Day to some old lady he didn't know—and didn't want to know, either!—if the woman accepted. Or given the silent treatment by his daughter if this Mrs Morgan turned down the invitation—because Nick had absolutely no doubt who Bekka was going to blame if her teacher refused to join them!

Wasn't eight a little young for his daughter to be entering the terrible teens? Or perhaps Bekka was more like Janet, her petulant mother, than he had previously realised...

'Speaking,' Mrs Morgan suddenly confirmed gruffly.

And slightly familiarly, Nick recognised with a frown. Had he met Bekka's biology teacher before? Perhaps during one of the numerous school events he had been expected to attend since becoming a governor of the school two years ago?

'This is Nick Steele,' he explained tersely. 'Bekka Steele's father—'

'I know who you are, Mr Steele. Although I'm curious to know how you acquired my private mobile number?' she prompted suspiciously.

She's paranoid, Nick decided irritably. Paranoid, with a deeply husky voice that made Nick wonder if she actually *did* have that moustache and whiskery chin to go with it!

'Your headmistress very kindly gave it to me—'

'Miss Sheffield did?' That soft voice sounded dismayed now rather than suspicious.

'Once I had explained the reason for my call, yes,' Nick answered with rising impatience. Really, he didn't have time for this. He still had several meetings to get through today, before he would be able to leave his office just after lunch so that he could attend

Bekka's Nativity Play this afternoon—thankfully the last school event before it closed down for the holidays.

Which, with his parents flying to America to spend Christmas with his sister, and so not able to help look after Bekka as they usually did, was going to provide Nick with yet another headache.

How had Janet managed? Nick wondered, for what had to be the hundredth time. Although their divorce three years ago *had* resulted in Janet being more than adequately provided for. Enough so that she didn't have to juggle a job as well as motherhood, in the way that Nick was trying to juggle his business interests and recently acquired single parenthood.

Get over it, he instructed himself impatiently.

This was just the way it was.

The way it was going to remain.

Nick had no intention of ever remarrying. Things might be hard now, with a constant juggling act of Nick's time, but Bekka wasn't going to be with him for ever, whereas a second wife would be!

Hiring a nanny was the obvious answer, of course, but Nick had already tried that—twice—when Bekka had first come to live with him after Janet died. Both those nannies, for different reasons, had been a disaster.

The first nanny, a woman in her fifties Nick had thought would be a perfect surrogate grandmother-type, had turned out to possess the disposition of a drill sergeant. The second, much younger nanny, had been waiting for him naked in his bed when he'd returned late home from work one evening!

As Bekka was actually at school most of the time, and his parents had always been willing to help out with Bekka whenever they could, Nick had decided, after those two disastrous attempts, to dispense with the nanny idea altogether.

'And exactly what is the reason for your call, Mr Steele?' Mrs Morgan spoke slowly now.

Get it over with, Nick, he instructed himself impatiently. Ask the woman, make polite murmurings at her refusal, and then just hang up. 'Bekka would like—Bekka and I were wondering if you would care to spend Christmas Day with the two of us…?'

There was complete silence on the other end of the telephone line. As the woman tried to think up an excuse for refusing, Nick hoped.

'Are you being serious, Mr Steele?'

Nick scowled darkly as he detected the tone of disbelief. 'Of course I'm being serious, Mrs Morgan. Christmas Day also happens to be Bekka's birthday, and she—Bekka and I,' he corrected again through gritted teeth, 'would love you to spend the day with the two of us.'

There was another loaded silence. Finally, there was a gruff reply. 'Let me see if I've understood you correctly, Mr Steele. You knocked me down with your car two days ago. I've had the most dreadful cold as a result of the soaking I received. And now you're inviting me to spend Christmas Day with you and Bekka...?'

Nick reeled from the absolute shock of realising that paranoid and old Mrs Morgan was, in fact, the definitely *un*-paranoid and very young red-haired woman he had accidentally knocked over with his car two days ago...!

CHAPTER THREE

'HAVE I understood the situation correctly, Mr Steele?' Beth repeated as she stood in the privacy of the corridor outside the teachers' staffroom, talking on her mobile. 'Mr Steele…?' she prompted sharply as he still made no reply.

It had been a struggle for Beth to come into school at all for these last two days of term, after she had woken on the morning following that disastrous meeting with Nicholas Steele with a debilitating cough and a sore throat.

She was actually feeling a little better today, but not enough to deal with the lethally attractive and—as one of the school governors and the parent of one of her pupils—potentially dangerous Nicholas Steele!

Her fingers curled tightly about her mobile. 'Mr Steele—'

'You can't possibly be the same Mrs Morgan

my daughter talks about all the time!' he burst out disbelievingly.

Beth frowned slightly. 'Obviously I have no idea whether or not Bekka has been boring you by talking about me, Mr Steele, but I assure you I am indeed your daughter's biology teacher, Bethan Morgan.'

'*Mrs* Morgan?' he bit out harshly. 'The *widowed* Mrs Morgan?'

Beth felt a familiar ache in her chest at the description: 'the widowed Mrs Morgan'.

The accurate description.

Her name *was* Morgan, and she *was* a widow.

Only twenty-six years old, and already a widow.

Shockingly.

So much so that Beth still sometimes had difficulty in believing it herself. In accepting that all of Ben's incredible happy-go-lucky life force, along with that of Beth's parents, had been wiped out in a single moment. Gone for ever, when Ben had crashed the car he had been driving the three of them in two years ago.

She and Ben had been the same age. Had grown up together in the same village. Attended school together. Gone off to university together. Become engaged, and then married once they had both attained their degrees—Beth in teaching, Ben in economics.

Losing both her parents *and* Ben in that sudden

way had been as painful for Beth as she imagined having a limb severed might be.

She certainly didn't appreciate having Nick Steele—a man who had been less than sympathetic after knocking her down two days ago—call and invite 'the widowed Mrs Morgan' to spend Christmas with him and his daughter. As if Beth were some sort of charity case. A lonely widow in need of his pity!

Beth might spend a lot of time alone, might be lonely on occasion, but it was a loneliness of choice; she had spent the past two Christmases alone because she wanted it that way, not because she had nowhere else to go. She had plenty of aunts and uncles, grandparents too, that she could have spent the holidays with. She had just chosen not to—too aware, still, of their sympathetic glances, the awkward omissions in conversation of all mention of both her parents and Ben.

'Bethan...?' Nick prompted when the woman's silence became uncomfortably long. 'Look, I'm sorry if I seemed less than polite just now, but—' He broke off with an impatient shake of his head. 'Surely you can understand my surprise at discovering that Bekka's teacher, Mrs Morgan, and the woman from two days ago are one and the same?'

'I perfectly understand, Mr Steele,' Bethan Morgan came back softly. 'I also accept, given the circumstances, that Bekka must have somehow forced you to make the invitation for me to join the two of you on Christmas Day.'

'I rarely allow anyone to *force* me into doing anything, Mrs Morgan!' Nick cut in; he preferred to think that Bekka had coerced rather than forced him!

'I— Excuse me.' Beth broke off as she was beset by a sudden fit of coughing.

'Have you seen a doctor about that?' Nick frowned at the realisation that this woman's spill onto the icy wet road two days ago was probably responsible for the cold she had now.

That her huskily sore throat was the reason Nick hadn't immediately recognised her voice on the telephone a few minutes ago...!

'Believe it or not, I feel a lot better today,' she dismissed gruffly once the coughing had ceased.

'Look, I'm coming to school later this afternoon to attend the Nativity Play.' Nick frowned his impatience, aware that the minutes were ticking by; he hadn't expected this telephone call to take as long as it was. 'Perhaps we could discuss this again then...?'

'I assure you there's nothing more to discuss, Mr Steele,' Beth said hoarsely. 'I'm aware of the honour you're bestowing by issuing the invitation, of course, but—'

'Honour?' Nick echoed sharply. 'What is that supposed to mean?'

Beth gave a weary sigh, longing to get back to the hot cup of tea she had left in the staffroom. 'Bekka is a lovely little girl, with a kind heart, and I like her tremendously.' In fact she still found it hard to believe that Bekka was this particular man's daughter! 'But those things don't change the fact that your invitation is completely inappropriate.'

There was a brief, chilling silence. 'In what way "inappropriate"…?' Nick Steele finally snapped.

'In that it's totally unsuitable for a teacher to spend Christmas Day at the home of one of her pupils.'

'I also happen to be one of the school governors,' he pointed out impatiently.

'Exactly,' Beth said with feeling.

'Miss Sheffield, your esteemed headmistress, thinks that your joining Bekka and I for Christmas Day is "a charming idea"…' Nick Steele drawled derisively.

Beth gave an inward groan. 'You *told* her the reason you needed to speak to me?'

'I told you I had,' he said irritably.

'But—' Beth gave a dazed shake of her head. She might have more of a problem getting out of this if Miss Sheffield already knew that one of the school governors, and the school's 'most influential parent', was asking one of her teachers to join him and his daughter for Christmas Day. 'You had absolutely no right to do that, Mr Steele.'

'Bekka assured me that you don't have anywhere else to go on Christmas Day, but maybe she was wrong…?'

Beth bristled. 'My plans for Christmas are none of your concern, Mr Steele.'

'Look, Mrs Morgan, I have several meetings I have to get through this morning so that I can be free to attend the Nativity Play later today. Why don't you come out with Bekka and me for a meal afterwards and we can—?'

'No, Mr Steele,' Beth cut in firmly.

'Why not?'

'Again, it would be…inappropriate.'

'I'll let you pay the bill if you think that would make it more appropriate,' he came back mockingly. 'Or maybe you imagine that this invitation to dinner is just a preliminary to my trying to get you into bed…?'

'Really, Mr Steele!' Beth gasped.

'Don't tell me that I've actually succeeded in rendering you speechless!' he taunted.

'You're being utterly ridiculous—'

'No more so than the reasons you've given for refusing my invitation to join Bekka and me on Christmas Day,' he retorted.

Perfectly legitimate reasons as far as Beth was

concerned. Besides, she didn't *want* to spend Christmas Day with Nick Steele—

She didn't want to spend Christmas Day with *Nick Steele*…? Not Bekka, but specifically Nick Steele?

He unnerved her, Beth realised. All that forceful energy and sexual magnetism disturbed her in ways she couldn't explain. In ways she didn't want to explain!

She straightened impatiently. 'I'm not some sort of charity case, Mr Steele—'

'My invitation has nothing to do with charity. In fact, you would be doing me a favour if you agreed to come,' he continued heavily. 'This will be our first Christmas since Bekka's mother died of cancer, and—' Nick broke off with a self-disgusted grimace; he was starting to sound as wheedling as Bekka now!

Damn it, he hadn't even *wanted* Bekka's biology teacher to spend Christmas Day with the two of them. He'd been protesting against that happening for days now.

When he had believed he was having a complete stranger foisted on him…

When he had thought Mrs Morgan was an elderly and possibly bewhiskered widow.

Instead she was a young woman in her twenties. A young and beautiful woman in her twenties.

A very prickly young and beautiful woman in her twenties…!

'And…?' Beth prompted as Nick's continued silence began to stretch awkwardly between them.

'And having a third person around may just make it less of an ordeal for both of us,' he finished.

Beth moistened dry lips. 'I hadn't realised your wife had died so recently.'

'Ten months ago. And Janet and I had been divorced for over two years before she died,' Nick Steele explained stiffly.

It didn't sound as if it had been an amicable divorce, Beth recognised ruefully. Even so, it would still have been a shock to Nick, as well as to his young daughter, when Janet Steele died.

Was Beth allowing the sudden and painful death of Ben and her own parents to emotionally draw her in…?

If she was, then it wasn't on Nick Steele's behalf but Bekka's, Beth told herself firmly. The arrogantly forceful Nick Steele was a man who gave every indication of being well able to take care of himself. And his emotions. If he had any…

She was being unfair now, Beth recognised irritably. Allowing her own prejudice towards the man to colour her opinions; Nick obviously loved his young daughter very much if he was willing to put up with having a stranger in his home on Christmas Day in an effort to make it as pleasant as possible for Bekka.

Beth had preferred it when she had just been able to think of Nick Steele as being impossibly arrogant!

'I suppose I could go out for a meal with the two of you this evening—'

'That's settled, then.' Nick cut briskly across her tentative acceptance. 'I have a meeting to go to now, so we'll sort out the details later this afternoon,' he dismissed, before ringing off abruptly.

Leaving Beth feeling slightly dazed as she stood alone in the corridor, staring down at her mobile as if it were all the inanimate object's fault that she now found herself in this uncomfortable position!

'I have to stay here and make sure none of the girls forgets anything, and then help tidy away before I'll be able to join you and Bekka,' Beth told Nick after he had sought her out backstage once the school Nativity Play had ended.

Her shoulder-length hair, now it was dry, was a deep rich auburn, Nick noted admiringly. A deep rich auburn that was a perfect foil for her pale complexion and those blue eyes surrounded by thick dark lashes.

Eyes that somehow managed to avoid looking directly at Nick as he leant casually back against the wall, well out of the way of the crowd of excited and chattering girls as they came out of the dressing room before hurrying off in search of their parents.

No doubt about it. Tiny and slender, in a fitted pale blue sweater that outlined small firm breasts and a flat abdomen, and tailored black trousers that did the same for the rounded curve of her bottom and slender legs, Bethan Morgan was a delicately lovely young woman.

She certainly bore little resemblance today to that bedraggled waif and stray that Nick had met two days ago!

'Mr Steele…?'

Nick's gaze narrowed to icy indifference as he realised he had been staring at her for too long. 'As we're going to be spending the evening together I think it might be better if you called me Nick.'

Beth continued to keep her gaze on the level of Nick's perfectly knotted tie, totally flustered by his presence backstage. And totally aware, after her first brief glance at him, of how elegantly attractive he looked in a dark business suit and pale blue silk shirt that emphasised the width of his shoulders and chest, and tapered waist and long muscled legs.

'Bethan…?' The amusement could be heard in Nick Steele's voice.

Beth flicked an irritated glance up at that too-handsome face. And instantly wished she hadn't as she found her attention captured by amused grey eyes set in a hard and yet sensually magnetic face. A face guaranteed to set a woman's pulse racing.

Including her own?

Unfortunately, yes!

Strangely—because this man was the complete opposite of the blond-haired, blue-eyed and totally uncomplicated Ben...

Or the young man she'd had a noncommittal dinner with a couple of months ago—her first date since Ben had died.

During that first year after Ben and her parents had been killed Beth had been too numbed by their loss to do any more than simply function on a day-to-day basis. She had been an only child from a close-knit family. And she had loved Ben all of her life. He had been her best friend as well as her husband.

But once Beth had got over the shock, accepted that her parents and Ben were really gone, she'd had to get out of the place she'd grown up in and where she and Ben had made their own home after their wedding.

London—its sheer size, and the amount of people who lived here—had been hard for Beth to cope with at first. But slowly she had been drawn into the pace of life here, making several friends amongst the other teaching staff, and occasionally joining them on visits to the cinema or out for a meal. A couple of months ago she had accepted the dinner invitation from the

young man who came into school twice a week to
teach the girls how to play the guitar. He had proved
to be a nice, pleasant man, with whom Beth felt comfortable, and although she had refused any more of
his invitations the two of them remained on friendly
terms.

In sharp contrast to Nick Steele, who made Beth
feel decidedly *un*comfortable!

She certainly didn't want to feel this disturbing
physical awareness of him!

There was an air of challenge about Nick Steele,
a dangerous edge that told Beth she should steer well
clear of him. That *comfortable* wasn't a word used
in connection with this man's company!

She straightened. 'I think, for Bekka's sake, it
might be better if we stick to Mr Steele and Mrs
Morgan.'

'In case you haven't noticed, Bethan, Bekka isn't
here.' Nick regarded her with narrowed eyes.

'I prefer Beth,' she corrected distractedly. 'And
Bekka will be out in just a few minutes, so—'

'Are you always this uptight?' Nick frowned; the
woman was as tense as a skittish horse getting ready
to bolt!

Irritation glittered in her deep blue eyes as Beth
looked up at him. 'I told you—I've had a cold, and
the end of the Christmas term is always hard work,
and—Melanie, you've dropped your wings,' she

called out helpfully as she noticed one of the angels had dropped her tinsel wings in the middle of the hallway. 'I'm afraid you'll have to excuse me, Mr Steele,' she told him distractedly. 'As it's the last day of term I really do have to ensure that the girls remember to take everything home with them.'

'And I'm preventing you from doing that?' Nick drawled with interest.

'You're…distracting me, yes.' A frown marred her creamy brow at the admission. 'If you tell me the name of the restaurant you're going to I can meet you and Bekka there later,' she added briskly.

Nick looked at her intently. 'Why do I have the feeling you have no intention of meeting us there later…?'

Probably because that was exactly what Beth had planned!

Seeing Nick Steele again, realising how much his ruggedly handsome presence disturbed and unsettled her, Beth had decided it might be better if she just conveniently 'forgot' the name of the restaurant as soon as he told it to her. Then, if Nick decided to call her mobile, to see where she had got to, she could always claim her cold as an excuse for not joining him and Bekka.

A plan Nick had seen through easily, it seemed!

'Don't be ridiculous, Mr Steele.' Beth snapped her

irritation. 'As I told you, I simply have to finish up here first before I'm able to leave.'

'Then Bekka and I will wait outside for you in the car.'

Beth's hands clenched so tightly that her nails dug into her palms. 'I am perfectly capable of getting myself to a restaurant!'

'It's no trouble at all for Bekka and I to wait in the car for you.'

His silver-grey eyes openly challenged her now.

Remembering the comfort of this man's car two days ago, Beth was sure it wasn't any trouble. 'Very well,' she agreed tightly. 'I should be able to join you in about fifteen minutes or so.'

A mocking smile curved those sculptured lips. 'I'll look forward to it!'

Beth stared after Nick in frustration as she watched him greet the excited Bekka with a hug. The little girl was as dark-haired and grey-eyed as her father, and the two of them chatted warmly together as they went outside.

Beth felt hot and bothered by this most recent encounter with Nick Steele. Flustered. Agitated. Her heart thumping. Her palms damp. Her legs trembling slightly.

And, as much as Beth hated to admit it, she knew

she was feeling all of those things because she was
going to be spending the evening in the company of
the disturbing Nick Steele…!

CHAPTER FOUR

'DADDY is taking me and some of my friends bowling tomorrow afternoon, Mrs Morgan, would you like to come with us?' Bekka invited excitedly once she had finished eating her dessert.

To Nick's surprise the evening at Bekka's favourite Italian restaurant had gone surprisingly smoothly. Of course that could be because Beth had very no-ticeably—and deliberately?—addressed very few remarks directly at him, Nick acknowledged wryly. Instead she had confined the majority of her conver-sation to Bekka, and the two of them were obviously getting on well together.

Well enough, it seemed, for Bekka to issue an invitation for Beth Morgan to join them tomorrow!

Nick grimaced. 'Mrs Morgan has been so busy at school with all of you that she probably needs to go out and do her Christmas shopping tomorrow afternoon, Beks.'

His daughter turned to her teacher in disappointment. 'Do you?'

Beth had just been quietly congratulating herself on how well the evening had gone—how little she'd actually had to even acknowledge Nick Steele's presence when Bekka was quite happy to do most of the talking. And now this!

Of course Beth didn't have to go out Christmas shopping tomorrow afternoon; she had already given presents to the friends she had made at the school, and family presents had been sent in the post.

But the fact that Nick Steele was obviously as reluctant to have her join them as Beth was to go was certainly less than flattering!

She shot him an irritated glance before answering Bekka. 'I *do* have some shopping to do tomorrow afternoon,' she confirmed; she was going food shopping not Christmas present shopping.

In sharp contrast to the family and friends that had always filled her parents' festively decorated home at Christmas, Beth would only need enough food to get her through Christmas Day. Which should amount to one very small chicken, a seasonal vegetable pack, and a single portion Christmas pudding with a small carton of cream.

And she wouldn't even need that if she decided to accept Nick Steele's invitation to spend Christmas Day with him and Bekka.

She wasn't seriously thinking about accepting, was she?

It might be worth it just to see the look on Nick's face!

Perhaps not…

'But I'm sure that your father will ensure that you and your friends have a lovely time,' she answered Bekka lightly.

Nick wasn't conceited enough to believe that every beautiful woman he met found him attractive, but at thirty-five, with one failed marriage behind him, Nick wasn't naïve or inexperienced either, and he knew exactly how and when a beautiful woman responded to him.

A response Beth was obviously determined not to feel…

That skittishness she had demonstrated towards him earlier certainly hadn't gone away. If anything, Beth had become even more noticeably distant towards him as the evening progressed.

Irritatingly so…

He looked at her now from behind slightly lowered lids. 'Perhaps Mrs Morgan doesn't bowl, Bekka.'

'Of course I bowl.' Beth frowned her irritation.

He shrugged. 'Then why not do your shopping in the morning and join us at the bowling alley in the afternoon? It's Bekka's pre-birthday treat,' he added.

Beth eyed Nick with a frown, knowing too well from his taunting expression that he didn't really want her to change her plans for tomorrow and join them. That he was just playing with her—like a predatory cat toying with a mouse.

'I think it's time we left, don't you?' She lightly changed the subject. 'It's been an exciting day, and I think someone is ready for bed,' she added in a teasing voice as Bekka tried to stifle a yawn.

'Oh, do we have to, Daddy?' Bekka turned to her father in appeal. 'Mrs Morgan hasn't agreed to join us for my birthday on Christmas Day yet.'

And Beth knew, much as she might have enjoyed Nick's discomfort, that she wasn't going to agree, either!

A single evening spent in Nick Steele's company was enough to tell her that she didn't want to repeat the experience. That she wasn't comfortable with the way she felt in his company. That she didn't like the way he made her so totally aware of her own femininity. That she would much rather have continued to remain in ignorance of that body-tingling awareness, too…!

She and Ben had loved each other, had enjoyed making love together and been totally comfortable with each other physically.

Nick Steele's innate and nerve-tingling sensuality continued to unnerve her!

As if aware of that discomfort, Nick drawled. 'Come back to the house for coffee and a chat, and I can drive you home later.'

'No!' Beth's heart had jolted in her chest. 'I mean...' She gave a slightly flustered shake of her head as she saw the unmistakable laughter in the depths of those silver-grey eyes. 'I couldn't possibly allow you to leave Bekka alone in the house while you drive me home.'

'I wouldn't be leaving Bekka on her own. I have a live-in housekeeper, Beth,' he explained mildly.

A mildness completely at odds with the challenging gleam in his eyes.

'Even so...'

'It's civilised to sit and drink coffee together after a meal, Beth.' Nick signalled to the waiter to bring him the bill.

'It also keeps me awake if I drink it late at night.'

'Really?' Nick arched a mocking brow. 'I'll make sure I remember that...' he murmured throatily—and had the satisfaction of seeing the blush that instantly brightened Beth's creamy cheeks before he had to turn his attention to paying the bill.

Nick couldn't deny that he found Beth intriguing. She could only be in her mid-twenties, but in those few short years she had been married and widowed. Which meant she had to be physically experienced.

And yet she blushed at even a hint of flirtation from him...

What had her husband been like? Nick wondered as he escorted Beth and Bekka from the restaurant. Young, presumably. Perhaps her first love? And no doubt the man she had assumed she would spend the rest of her life with, only to have him cruelly taken from her?

Nick couldn't help wondering how many lovers Beth had had since her husband's death...

Beth was too nervous, as she waited for Nick Steele to come back down the stairs after putting Bekka to bed, to sit down on the gold brocade sofa in the elegantly furnished sitting room of the three-storey London townhouse. A room dominated by a lavishly decorated Christmas tree with dozens of foil-wrapped parcels beneath that made her own meagre pile beneath the small tree in her apartment look slightly ridiculous.

As ridiculous as the idea of her spending Christmas Day here!

As ridiculous as her being here now.

Not that Nick had given Beth any choice in the matter; he had just driven straight here, Beth's earlier refusal obviously completely forgotten. Or just ignored.

Most likely the latter, Beth accepted irritably. As

she already knew, this man was a law unto himself—a man who refused to take no for an answer. Arrogance personified, in fact.

Well, Beth didn't appreciate being manipulated in this way, and she would tell Nick so as soon as he returned from putting Bekka to bed.

In the meantime, Beth couldn't resist walking over to look at the numerous photographs that adorned the top of the shiny black piano standing in the bay window that looked out onto the now moonlit garden. Dozens of photographs. All of them featuring Bekka. From babyhood to now.

Nick was easily recognisable in a lot of the photographs. His hair had been slightly longer when Bekka was a baby, his expression more relaxed then too, not as hard and cynical as it was now.

Several of the photographs also showed a tall and beautiful blonde-haired woman. Obviously Bekka's mother, Janet Steele—short blonde hair surrounding a face dominated by pale blue eyes, a short, perfect nose, and full and pouting lips above a slightly rounded jaw.

'I see you've discovered the rogues' gallery,' Nick rasped behind her.

Beth gave a guilty start as she turned to face him, frowning slightly as she saw the laden silver tray he carried. 'I told you I don't drink coffee this late at night.'

'Which is why I made you tea,' Nick said as he placed the tray down on a low coffee table in front of the sofa before straightening.

He had removed his jacket and tie and unbuttoned the top two buttons of his shirt, the open neckline revealing the start of the dark hair growing on his chest, Beth noted with some alarm. Just as she noticed the way the pale blue silk shirt was fitted to the muscled width of his shoulders and the flatness of his abdomen and tapered waist.

Dear Lord, this man was gorgeous!

Nick's dark brows quirked as he saw Beth Morgan's obvious discomfort. 'Would you like to be mother…?'

She swallowed hard. 'I—yes. Just one cup, and then I really have to go,' she muttered awkwardly. As she moved to sit on the sofa to pour coffee and tea, a beautiful marmalade-coloured cat curled up on the cushion beside her.

'No cream or sugar for me, thanks,' Nick dismissed as he eased another cat aside, so that he could drop down into one of the armchairs to study Beth from a distance. 'And are you? A mother?' he enquired as she pushed back that silky curtain of auburn hair to look across at him questioningly.

'I—no.' She turned away. 'Ben and I had decided to wait for a while before starting a family, and—

No,' she repeated abruptly as she crossed the room to hand him the cup of coffee.

Nick took the cup. 'Ben was your husband...?'

'Yes.' Her face was slightly pale as she moved to sit back on the sofa, absently stroking the marmalade-coloured cat as it stretched lazily beside her.

'Just push him away if he's being a nuisance.'

She looked startled. 'What...?'

'The cat,' Nick replied. 'Bekka has collected a menagerie of pets in the last ten months. The insane dog is shut in the kitchen.'

Beth shrugged narrow shoulders as she continued to stroke the purring cat. 'I like animals.'

'You must have been very young when you married...?'

She frowned as Nick reverted to the previous subject. 'Twenty-one,' she acknowledged stiffly.

'Were you married for long...?'

'Three years.'

'When did your husband die?'

'Two years ago,' she answered tersely. 'Look, Mr Steele—'

'Did you still love him when he died?'

Beth stood up abruptly. 'What sort of question is that?'

'A valid one.' Nick Steele shrugged those broad shoulders. 'Janet and I were married for seven years—by the end of it we could barely stand the sight of each other!'

'Oh.' Beth wasn't quite sure what to say in response to that remark. 'Bekka seems to have adjusted well since her mother died…'

'She has, yes,' Nick acknowledged indulgently. 'I, on the other hand, am still floundering around in the dark, trying to be both mother and father to her,' he acknowledged ruefully.

'Then maybe you should stop trying…?'

'Sorry?' Nick gave a perplexed frown.

'Maybe I'm interfering, but—'

'Oh, by all means interfere, Beth,' Nick invited.

She chewed on her bottom lip with small white teeth as she formulated her reply. 'You can't actually *be* both mother and father to Bekka,' she finally murmured softly. 'And I'm not sure you should even try…' She gave a rueful grimace. 'At the moment Bekka is still a lovely and adorable little girl, but—'

'But she may not continue to be so if I don't stop trying so hard?' Nick finished.

'Exactly.' Beth Morgan looked deeply relieved that he had understood what she was trying to say without her actually having to say it.

And what she had to say *did* have merit, Nick realised. Bekka was becoming more and more demanding, rather than less so, as the days, weeks, months passed. A fact Nick had noted himself only two days ago, and had attributed to Bekka being more like Janet than he had realised, when his young daughter had slammed out of his car when he'd refused to invite her biology teacher to join them for Christmas Day.

He looked across at Beth Morgan in consideration. 'That's a very wise observation for one so young...'

'Sometimes it's just easier to see something looking in, rather than being involved in it yourself.'

Nick stood up slowly to cross the room and stand only inches away from Beth, his gaze searching as it rested on the fragile beauty of her face. 'And you don't get involved, do you...?' he said slowly.

'What...?' Beth felt completely unnerved by Nick Steele's close proximity, by the warmth in that pale grey gaze as he looked down at her with such intensity.

That nervousness turned to liquid, burning heat as he slowly raised his hand to move his knuckles in a light caress against the heat of her cheek...

CHAPTER FIVE

'I— WHAT do you think you're doing?' Beth had wanted to sound indignant, dismissive. Instead her voice was husky. Breathless.

'I'm sure you already know the answer to that, Beth,' Nick murmured throatily, looking down at her as she swallowed hard, her cheek hot against the back of his hand.

She moistened her lips with the pink tip of her tongue. A totally sensuous caress that caught and easily held Nick's attention. He felt the urge, the need, to run his own tongue across those soft and slightly parted lips before kissing her. He wanted to take her in his arms and mould those slender and delicate curves against him.

Beth couldn't move, held captive by the sudden darkening of Nick's gaze as he looked down hungrily at her mouth, unable to do more than groan low in her throat as his arms moved about her to draw her slowly towards him.

God, his body was so warm. Hot. And hard. His chest against her breasts feeling like steel encased in velvet, and his thighs—

Beth raised her panicked gaze to his. 'I don't think we should be doing this, Nick…!'

His eyes were dark and smouldering. 'Why not?'

Because Beth could feel herself reacting, responding to the sheer intimacy of having Nick's body moulded against hers. Her breasts felt full and heavy, the tips ultra-sensitive, and there was a fluid heat between her thighs, a swelling moistening of those delicate tissues.

She didn't want to feel this way! Didn't want to have this response to Nick Steele, a man far beyond her reach in physical experience!

'We both know how ultimately damaging any relationship between the two of us would be!' she reminded him.

'But we already have a relationship, Beth…'

Beth stiffened. 'What…?'

He gave a slow, seductive smile. 'You're Bekka's teacher, and I'm her father.'

'Exactly!' Beth managed to push her hands in between them, against that warm and velvet-hard chest. 'Let me go, Nick!' she insisted. 'You have to let me go now.' Tears stung her eyes as she looked up at him pleadingly.

Nick's gaze narrowed as he saw the tears on Beth's lashes. Those tears were a complete contrast to the way her body had melted against his seconds ago. 'How long has it been for you, Beth…?' he probed softly.

She stilled. 'Has what been for me…?'

'Hell…!' Nick gave a groan as the truth of this situation suddenly hit him. 'There's been no one for you at all since your husband died, has there…?'

She blinked. 'In what way?'

In *any* way!

Anyone looking at Beth Morgan could see that she was beautiful, with a body that was ripe for physical arousal. But those tears balancing so precariously on her lashes also told Nick that there had been no other man in her life—or her bed—since the death of her husband two years ago.

He had been utterly faithful to Janet during the years of their marriage, but since their separation and divorce there had been numerous women to briefly share his bed. Contrary to what he might have thought—hoped—the same obviously wasn't true of Beth!

He gave a firm shake of his head and dropped his arms back to his sides before he stepped away from her. 'I can't be that man for you, Beth,' he rasped harshly.

'What man?' She looked slightly dazed.

'*That* man,' he said again pointedly, his expression grim. 'The man you will want to fall in love with. That you would want to fall in love with you.' He should have realised sooner—should have known—

'I didn't start any of this—'

'No, I did,' Nick accepted. 'And I have nothing to offer any woman except a casual relationship.'

'Aren't you being conceited in thinking I would want *any* sort of relationship with you?' Beth glared her indignation at him.

Nick searched her face for several seconds, knowing by the flush in her cheek, the slightly wild glitter in her eyes and the hard swell of her breasts, that no matter how Beth might deny it, wish it wasn't true, she had been as aroused by their closeness just now as he was.

'I apologise.' He nodded abruptly. 'You're right—it is time I drove you home now.'

It was a relief, now that Beth no longer had Nick's body pressed so intimately against her own, to be able to breathe again. To think coherently. To realise how close she had come to having Nick Steele kiss her. To allowing him to do so much more than just kiss her...

What was wrong with her? How could she have allowed herself to respond, to feel desire for Nick, when she already knew exactly how wrong he was for her?

Nick was sophisticated, handsome, rich and powerful, and experienced in ways Beth couldn't even imagine—in ways she didn't *want* to imagine. She certainly didn't want to be the next in the long line of women in Nick Steele's life. Or his bed!

Then why did her body still tremble from that near-kiss? Why could she still feel the imprint of his hard body pressing against her own? Why did her breasts still ache for the touch, the caress, that hadn't happened?

She would be an idiot, a fool, if she allowed herself to see Nick as anything more than a governor of the school she worked at and the parent of one of her young students.

'Ready?' he prompted, not waiting for Beth's reply before striding out into the hallway, already holding the front door open for her to leave by the time Beth joined him there only seconds later.

As anxious to be rid of her now as she was to go, Beth thought.

Not surprisingly, the drive to her home was completed in strained silence. 'Thank you for a lovely evening,' Beth murmured quietly, once Nick had parked his car outside her apartment building.

'Very nicely said,' Nick drawled, and his hand came out to grasp her arm to stop her from getting out of the car. 'Can I take it you've definitely decided *not* to come bowling with us tomorrow?'

Beth turned back with a frown, her face appearing very pale in the moonlight. 'Nor will I be joining you and Bekka for Christmas Day.'

Nick's eyes glittered in the semi-darkness. 'Or setting eyes on me ever again if you can help it?' he guessed easily.

Her mouth firmed. 'No.'

He gave an impatient shake of his head. 'Nothing really happened tonight, Beth, so stop beating your-self up.'

She chewed briefly on her bottom lip. 'I don't know what you mean...'

'Liar,' he replied as he turned fully in his seat to face her. 'If I had to guess, I would say you've only ever had one lover in your life—'

'That's none of your—'

'A man who died two years ago,' Nick continued. 'Two *years*, Beth!' he repeated incredulously. 'Isn't it time—past time—that you moved on?'

Her chin rose defensively. 'By having an affair with you, I suppose you mean?'

'I thought we had already agreed that probably isn't a good idea.' Nick gave a hard smile. 'You did nothing wrong this evening, Beth—nothing you have to feel guilty about.'

'I don't feel in the least guilty!' Beth assured him.

'I would call you a liar again, but twice in one evening may be once too many!' he said sceptically.

Her cheeks burned. 'I'm not lying—'

'Are you saying you didn't want me earlier…?'

Beth drew herself up stiffly. 'You think you know everything, don't you, Nick? Think that every woman you meet has to fall down adoringly at your feet?' She gave an impatient shake of her head. 'Well, think again! I *didn't* want you earlier, and I don't want you now, either!'

Nick considered her accusations. 'One—no, I *don't* think I know everything. Two—I would prefer that any woman who did feel the need to fall down in front of me adoringly concentrated her attentions on another part of my anatomy entirely. And three…' his voice lowered huskily '…deny it all you want, Beth, but you *did* want me.'

Her eyes flashed like twin sapphires. 'You're a conceited, arrogant—'

Nick silenced her in the easiest and quickest way possible—by claiming her mouth with his own and so cutting off all further conversation.

She tasted as good, as headily erotic, as Nick had imagined she would, her lips soft and delectable against his as she gave a low groan of capitulation, her lips parting invitingly beneath his.

Beth's senses were assaulted with sensation. The heat of Nick's lips as they moved hungrily against hers. The hardness of his chest against her aroused breasts. And the heady pleasure of his hands as they moved restlessly down the length of her spine before he pulled her hard against him in crushing need.

His hair felt dark and silky as her fingers became entangled in its thickness at his nape, and his skin was hot to the touch as his lips continued their heady and hungry assault on hers, his teeth gently biting before the hard thrust of his tongue entered the hot cavern of her mouth.

She did want this man, Beth acknowledged achingly. She wanted Nick with a hot fierceness that totally shocked her. Knew that she had felt this physical awareness of him from the very first moment she had looked up two days ago and seen him through the rain and sleet after she had tumbled into the road in front of his car.

Her throat arched as Nick dragged his mouth from hers to move down the length of her throat and then slowly up again, and Beth quivered with pleasure as she felt the rasp of his tongue against her earlobe.

Nick felt Beth arch against him as his teeth gently bit on that sensitive flesh, feeling the hard-tipped thrust of those soft breasts against his chest, and unable to resist the temptation of moving his hands beneath her sweater.

His mouth captured Beth's again as her skin burned against the coolness of his hands, her back soft and silky, the skin firm over the curve of her ribcage, the thrust of her breasts bare as he cupped her there, the nipple firm as a berry as he ran the soft pad of his thumb rhythmically across it.

Beth groaned, her fingers tightening in his hair, and Nick felt the trembling of her body as she arched into those caresses in silent pleading.

Nick's body was one pleasurable ache—a hard, pulsing ache that couldn't be fully satisfied in the close confines of the front seats of his car.

He wrenched his mouth away from hers. 'Invite me in, Beth!'

'What...?' She moved back slightly to look up at him in a daze.

His eyes glittered down at her in the darkness. 'Invite me up to your apartment,' he prompted huskily.

She continued to stare at him wordlessly for several long seconds, the enormity of what he was saying, what he was asking, almost overwhelming her. She knew exactly what would happen if she invited Nick into her apartment. What they both wanted to happen next. Making a complete nonsense of their earlier conversation!

'I can't, Nick!' She wrenched herself out of his arms.

He reached for her. 'Beth—'

'I said no!' Beth fumbled as she opened the passenger door, the instant blast of icy cold wind from outside sobering her, bringing her to her senses as nothing else could have done. She climbed hastily out of the car before turning back to look at him. 'Please tell Bekka that I'm really sorry I can't join her for the bowling tomorrow, or her birthday on Christmas Day.' Beth didn't wait for Nick to answer before slamming the door closed and turning sharply on her heel to hurry inside her apartment building.

'Beth?' came the tersely impatient query down the telephone line as soon as she answered the call.

A terse voice that was all too familiar! 'Nick—Mr Steele...?' she corrected firmly even as her fingers tightened about her mobile.

It had been four cold and icy days since the two of them had parted so ignominiously. Four long and lonely days and nights for Beth. Days and nights of self-doubt and self-recrimination for the way she had responded to Nick so completely.

Days and nights when Beth hadn't been able to stop thinking of him. Of the way he had kissed her. Of the way she had wanted him to go on kissing her—and more!

'Nick will do,' he rasped. 'I'm really sorry to bother you, and I wouldn't have done so, except—I find myself in something of a dilemma.'

Nick was in a dilemma?

This man had turned Beth's whole calm and ordered world upside down four days ago when he'd kissed her. Had evoked a heated response in her that still made her tremble just to think about it. Just the sound of his voice over the telephone now was enough to make her hands shake and her heart pound…!

'What sort of dilemma?' she asked warily.

Nick stood in his study at home, staring sightlessly out of the window into the back garden. 'Bekka's had your cold for the last three days—'

'I'm really sorry about that, but *you* were the one who insisted I come out to dinner with the two of you,' Beth reminded him indignantly.

'Bekka's cold isn't the problem. Well…only indirectly.' Nick grimaced. 'My housekeeper was out shopping earlier today and slipped over on the ice. Luckily someone called an ambulance and she was taken to hospital. I received a call from there a few minutes ago. Apparently Mrs Bennett has broken her ankle pretty badly.'

'Yes…?'

His mouth tightened as he heard the increased wariness in Beth's tone. Rightly so, probably, after the strained way the two of them had parted on Friday evening.

He should never have kissed her. Certainly never have suggested she invite him up to her apartment when she was obviously so vulnerable, when he knew how dangerous that vulnerability was!

In the same way he knew he shouldn't have allowed his thoughts to dwell on her so often in the past four days...

His mouth hardened. 'It seems, because it's a bad break and Mrs Bennett is in her sixties, that they've decided it might be better to keep her in overnight.'

'Yes...?'

He grimaced his impatience at Beth's continued guarded response. 'Obviously I need to go in and see her, but once I had explained about Bekka's cold the hospital made it obvious they would prefer it if she didn't take her germs into the ward. Normally I could have asked my parents to come and sit with Bekka while I go to the hospital, but unfortunately they flew to the States a few days ago to spend Christmas with my sister and her family—'

'Surely there must be someone else you can ask to sit with Bekka?' There was a slight note of desperation in Beth's voice now as she realised the reason for Nick's call. 'An agency, perhaps?'

'It's only a few days before Christmas—not a good time to be hiring a nanny...' Nick replied.

'In other words, I'm your very last resort…?'

Nick scowled. 'If Bekka hadn't caught your damned cold I could have taken her with me.'

'You're being unfair now!' Beth cut in indignantly. She was sitting down in an armchair by this time—her knees were shaking so badly just from speaking to Nick again that she'd had to sit or risk falling down instead!

'I apologise if it sounded that way,' Nick muttered stiffly. 'It's just that all Mrs Bennett's close family live in Scotland, and— Oh, just forget it. I'll send her things over by taxi and just hope she'll understand why I couldn't go in and visit her personally!'

Beth relented slightly. 'All you want me to do is sit with Bekka for a couple of hours while you go to the hospital…?'

There was a brief, telling silence. 'What else *could* I want…?' Nick finally enquired.

It wasn't a question of what Nick wanted, it was a question of Beth's complete inability to resist him…!

Much as Beth hated to admit it, Nick had become a danger to the calm and uneventful life she had been leading since her move to London a year ago. She was very aware that since their first meeting her emotions had been seesawing all over the place. Feverish and out of her control whenever she was in his company.

Flat and uninteresting—boring, in fact—when she wasn't.

So much so that the quiet Christmas Beth had planned for herself now seemed utterly unappealing.

She looked down at the baggy thigh-length blue jumper she was wearing over faded denims and calf-high black boots. Did she have time to put on some make-up and change before she went to Nick's house—?

No!

If Nick wanted her help that badly, then he could take her as he found her. 'I'll get in a taxi now and be there in fifteen minutes,' she assured him abruptly.

'Are you sure...?'

No, of *course* Beth wasn't sure!

It was completely hazardous to her hard-won peace of mind to be anywhere near the disturbing Nick Steele...

'As I said, I'll try and be there in fifteen minutes,' she said stiffly.

'I'll reimburse you for the taxi fare when you get here.'

'I'm quite capable of paying my own taxi fare, thank you.'

'You're doing this as a favour to me—'

'I'm doing it for Mrs Bennett and Bekka,' she corrected him firmly.

'We'll argue that point later,' Nick dismissed briskly, before ringing off.

Beth didn't intend doing *anything* with him later!

Even if she *had* been wanting—aching!—to see him again, be with him again, for the past four days…

CHAPTER SIX

'I REALLY appreciate you doing this for me,' Nick said as he opened the front door before stepping back to invite Beth inside the house.

'I'm doing it for Mrs Bennett and Bekka, remember?' Not quite meeting his gaze, she turned away to slip off her duffle coat before handing it to him, knowing she would be warm enough in the centrally heated house.

She didn't need to look at Nick to know how devastatingly male he looked in another one of those tailored dark business suits. Or to see the dark sheen of his hair to know that it was silky soft. Or to look into the chiselled perfection of his face to be aware of how her pulse was racing just being near him again...

'Beth...?'

She stared at the perfectly knotted tie at his throat. 'Yes?'

Nick didn't at all like the way Beth was once again avoiding even looking at him. 'Damn it, despite my telling you not to, you've been wallowing in guilt for the past four days!'

Irritation was evident in those dark blue eyes as Beth's gaze flickered briefly up to his face and then away again. 'Don't flatter yourself, Nick,' she snapped scathingly.

Was he? Was Nick mistaken in thinking that he and the kiss the two of them had shared the other evening were the reasons for those dark circles under Beth's eyes and the paleness of her cheeks?

He frowned darkly. 'Do you still intend to spend Christmas Day on your own?'

'I don't see what that has to do with you...'

Neither did Nick. Except he hated the very idea of Beth—anyone—being alone during the holiday period. But especially Beth... 'What about your parents?'

'They were killed in the same car crash as Ben,' she said abruptly.

God...!

Nick had become cynical about love and relationships in general after his marriage to Janet had failed so abysmally. Learning that Janet had cancer, and had been diagnosed as terminal, had at least allowed the two of them time to heal their differences and say goodbye to each other before she died.

Not that Nick believed there had been any rifts between Beth and her husband before he died, or between her and her parents, but sudden death made no allowances for goodbyes, and Christmas was a time that must surely bring that home to her...

He grimaced. 'We'll talk again when I get back.'

Beth looked fully into his face for the first time. And then wished she hadn't as she saw the concern that darkened those grey eyes. Her smile was tight. 'The subject is at an end as far as I'm concerned.'

'But—'

'I thought I had already made it clear that I don't need or want your charity or your pity!' Her eyes flashed deeply blue.

His eyes narrowed glacially. 'Why do you have to be so prickly all the—?'

'I thought you had to get to the hospital?' Beth cut in pointedly, her brows raised in challenge.

Nick's mouth thinned. 'I do. But—'

'Will you just go, Nick?' she said impatiently. 'The sooner you go then hopefully the sooner you'll be back. I *do* have a life of my own, you know,' she added pointedly. 'One that doesn't revolve around Nick Steele's wants and needs!'

'And what would you be doing now if you weren't here?' he challenged impatiently.

'None of your business.'

Nick knew she was being deliberately awkward. He simply didn't have the time right now to argue with her. But when he returned later this evening he intended making sure he found the time...

'Fine,' he bit out tersely. 'Bekka is waiting for you on the sofa in the sitting room, wrapped up warm in front of the fire, with the three cats draped all over her. The dog is in the kitchen, so take care if you have to go in there to get Bekka some more medicine. There are plenty of drinks and food in the fridge—'

'I believe I'm intelligent enough to work all those things out for myself.'

But not, it seemed, intelligent enough to know when not to prod and poke at a sleeping tiger...!

Nick had found himself thinking of this woman far too much the past four days. Remembering how good Beth had felt when he'd held her in his arms. How responsive her lips had been against his. How aroused he had been by her. How badly he had wanted her!

How badly he *still* wanted her, Nick acknowledged.

How did this ultra-sensitive and consequently prickly woman still manage to look sexy, with her face bare of make-up, her auburn hair brushed back from her face and secured in a ponytail, and wearing a long and baggy jumper that appeared to be several sizes too big for her?

Nick had absolutely no idea, but somehow Beth Morgan managed to do it!

He nodded abruptly. 'I should only be a couple of hours.'

'I'm sure that Bekka and I will manage just fine without you,' Beth assured him.

Nick's eyes narrowed in warning. 'Just carry on the way you're going, Beth...'

She arched auburn brows. 'And what?'

His smile was feral. 'I'll let you know when I get back.'

She gave him a wry smile. 'And am I supposed to live in fear until then?'

Nick gave a slow, warning shake of his head. 'You're playing with fire, Beth.'

Beth felt a quiver of apprehension run down the length of her spine as she looked up into those narrowed grey eyes. Or could it be expectation...? She was deliberately baiting this man, she knew. Couldn't seem to help herself. Couldn't stop herself from forcing a response from him. *Any* response.

The promise of retribution she could read in those mocking grey eyes warned her that she wasn't going to like that response if she carried on deliberately baiting him.

Or that she might like it too much...!

She drew in a shaky breath. 'Just go to the hospital, Nick,' she advised heavily.

Nick continued to look down at her frowningly for several long seconds before giving an abrupt nod of his head. 'Plan on having dinner with Bekka and me later.'

She bristled. 'Isn't it usual to *ask* rather than assume?'

He gave a humourless smile. 'Where you're concerned? No.' He gave a shake of his head. 'On the assumption you're going to refuse to accept any payment for sitting with Bekka—'

'You assume correctly!' she snapped.

Nick nodded. 'The least I can do is offer you dinner.'

'Offer, yes. Assume, no. Besides,' Beth added, 'you already gave me dinner four nights ago. Unless...' She looked up at him suspiciously. 'When you said "plan on" having dinner with you and Bekka were you actually implying that I should cook it first?'

He chuckled throatily. 'Not much gets past you, does it, Beth?'

'You *do* want me to cook dinner!' she gasped incredulously.

'You know the old saying—"feed a cold, starve a fever".' Nick shrugged. 'And obviously Mrs Bennett isn't here to do it. Of course you could just leave Bekka to my less than proficient skills in the kitchen...'

'You— I—' Beth's eyes were now flashing a deep blue in disgust. 'Just go, Nick,' she advised again in carefully modulated tones.

'I'll be glad to, now I know the problem of dinner is settled,' he agreed brightly.

'Nothing is "settled", Nick,' she warned him firmly.

'Sure it is.' He gave her a triumphant grin before leaving.

Beth stood in the hallway fuming for several long minutes after Nick had gone.

He was the most arrogant, infuriating—

She had told herself all of this before! Several times, in fact. And yet here she was, back at Nick's house, taking care of Bekka, and with the added expectation on Nick's part that she would cook dinner for them all this evening...!

'I see that you're feeling better, Bekka,' Nick said thankfully when he returned early that evening and entered the kitchen in search of his young daughter and Beth, and found the two of them in there preparing dinner together, along with the huge cross-breed of a dog that Bekka had adopted six months ago. There was definitely some Irish Wolfhound in there, if Paddy's colouring and size was anything to go by—or perhaps it was just wolf!

'Daddy!' A happily grinning Bekka rushed over to give him a hug. 'How's Mrs Bennett?'

'Well enough to come home tomorrow,' Nick assured her as he returned the hug, at the same time giving the traitorous Paddy a censorious glare as the mutt completely ignored him to lean slavishly against Beth's leg, looking up at her adoringly. Nick usually had a fight as to whether or not the dog would even let him into his own house, and in the few short hours he had been gone Beth had managed to tame the beast.

The whole household seemed to be falling under this woman's spell!

'Dinner smells good,' Nick muttered, as Bekka returned to stirring something in a saucepan on top of the cooker.

'Let's hope it tastes the same way,' Beth drawled, telling Nick that she still hadn't completely forgiven him for emotionally blackmailing her into making dinner—primarily for Bekka's sake, but for the two of them, too.

In truth, Nick was no longer sure that it was a good idea, either, as he inwardly acknowledged that the highly domestic scene he had walked in on a few minutes ago was a little too cosy for his comfort. Although Beth didn't look any more relaxed than he did, Nick noted, as she deliberately turned her back on him to carry on peeling the potatoes in the sink.

'What is it?' he prompted curiously as he detected the delectable smell of garlic rising from the pan Bekka was stirring so diligently.

'It's something called Pork Tumbet.' Bekka turned to grin at him.

'It's just pork chops covered in seasonal vegetables and cooked in a tomato and garlic sauce. Then the whole thing is covered in sliced potatoes and baked in the oven,' Beth dismissed lightly, still without turning.

'Sounds good. It smells good, too,' Nick murmured appreciatively.

As expected, Beth had spent an enjoyable couple of hours keeping Bekka entertained. The two of them had played draughts and then a few easy card games, and she and the three cats and Paddy the dog had become firm friends. But for all of that time Beth had been aware that Nick would be returning home soon. And not quite sure how she should behave towards him when he did.

It was the thought of having to sit down and eat dinner with Nick that was making Beth feel so nervous. Of course once she had put the food into the oven there was absolutely no reason why she actually had to stay and eat it with them.

That was obviously her way out of this; she would finish preparing the tumbet and put it in the oven, advise Nick on how long to leave it there, and then she would organise another taxi to take her home.

Beth turned, with the intention of telling Nick exactly that, only to draw sharply back against the kitchen unit as she realised just how close he was to her.

So close Beth could smell the elusively expensive aftershave he favoured.

So close she could see the darker ring of grey that encircled the iris of his eyes as she looked up at him.

So close that, once she had quickly glanced away and down from that compelling gaze, she could see the pulse throbbing in his throat.

Could feel her own pulse beating to that same erratic rhythm...

CHAPTER SEVEN

BETH forced a calmly relaxed expression on her face as she looked up at Nick. 'I'm going to arrange for a taxi to come and take me home in fifteen minutes.'

'Why?' Nick frowned his displeasure.

'I—because there aren't any buses from this area to my apartment,' she stated lightly.

'Take it from me, Beks, it's a bad sign when the chef won't stay long enough to eat her own food,' Nick told his daughter teasingly.

'Not at all,' Beth answered. 'But, as I told you earlier, I do have a life of my own.'

Nick remembered everything this particular woman had ever said to him. And he was also becoming aware of the subtlety of all her moods—and her driving need at this particular moment was obviously to get as far away from him as possible...

He turned to his daughter. 'Beks, could you just go and check that I turned off the headlights on my car before I came in?'

'As long as you keep stirring the sauce while I'm gone,' his daughter warned sternly.

'I'll do my best,' Nick replied, his narrowed gaze returning to Beth's slightly flushed face once Bekka had gone out into the hallway. 'Okay, so what did I do now?' he asked wearily, once the two of them were alone.

'What makes you think you've done anything?'

'Possibly the fact that, even though you've cooked the dinner, you refuse to stay and share it with us?'

'Is it really necessary for me to eat it as well as cook it?'

Nick shrugged. 'It seems a pity for you to have to prepare something for yourself when you get home.'

She shrugged slender shoulders beneath that over-large sweater. 'The tumbet won't be ready for another hour or so.'

'And is spending another hour or so in my company such a problem?' he probed huskily.

'Of course not,' she said sharply. 'I just—I thought you promised Bekka that you would keep stirring the sauce?' she reminded with a frown.

'To hell with the sauce!' A nerve pulsed in Nick's tightly clenched jaw.

'The tumbet will be ruined if the sauce burns,' Beth pointed out ruefully.

'To hell with the tumbet too!' Nick took the

saucepan off the hob before taking a deliberate step closer to Beth, so that he now towered over her much slighter form. 'Tell me the real reason you're refusing to stay and have dinner with Bekka and me,' he demanded.

Beth feigned an uninterest she didn't feel as she gave another dismissive shrug. Feigned, because she was too aware of Nick, of his close proximity, to feel in the least uninterested!

'You're very pale, Beth. I think you need to eat...'

'What I need is to be allowed to leave here so that I can get on with my own life!' Beth knew by the way Nick's eyes narrowed on her speculatively that she had spoken more forcefully than she had intended. Than was prudent with a man as perceptive as Nick Steele.

But she couldn't be here with this man and his young daughter. Found this whole domesticated scenario too disturbing. Almost as disturbing as she found Nick himself...!

Beth pushed away from the kitchen unit to move abruptly away from him. Away from the sensual spell his proximity was once again weaving about her already heightened senses...

'It will take me another twenty minutes or so to get the tumbet in the oven, and then I'm going home,' she told him abruptly, before turning away with the intention of removing the roasted vegetables from the oven.

'Beth, what the—'

'Take your hand off me!' she gasped as he grasped her arm.

Nick looked down searchingly into that pale and delicately lovely face; Beth's eyes were huge and haunted, her cheeks paler than ever, her lips trembling slightly, her chin raised in the constant challenge this woman seemed to feel she had to show to the world. To him in particular…?

He gave a shake of his head. 'I want you to stay and have dinner with us, Beth.'

'Unfortunately those wants conflict with my own.' She held his gaze as she firmly, determinedly, moved out of his grasp.

Nick let her go, not wanting to bruise a single inch of that delicately pale skin. 'What *do* you want, Beth?'

She drew in a ragged breath. 'I want you to leave me alone, Nick. For you not to call me again. To stop involving me in your own and Bekka's lives.'

'Isn't that going to be a little hard to do when you're one of Bekka's teachers…?'

'I meant your personal lives,' Beth insisted.

'And by personal lives, you mean…?'

'I mean insisting I go out to dinner with the two of you,' she said impatiently. 'Inviting me to go bowling.

To spend Christmas Day with the two of you here—'
She broke off as her voice broke emotionally. 'To
looking after Bekka. To cooking dinner for the two
of you…'

'Beth—'

'Please don't touch me, Nick!' She backed away
from him, her cheeks chalky-white now. 'I—it was
hard for me when Ben and my parents—when they
all died. But somehow, little by little, I survived. I
survived, Nick!' she repeated shakily.

'I can see that,' Nick murmured distractedly, and
he thrust his hands into his trouser pockets—before
he gave in to the impulse he had to take this woman
in his arms and attempt to make all the pain she had
suffered go away!

Beth was so young, so delicate, too damned fragile to have suffered and survived the things she had
been through—the death of her parents and her
husband.

'I intend continuing to survive,' she added
firmly.

'By keeping yourself emotionally apart?' Nick
guessed.

Tears glistened on her lashes as she nodded. 'And
we both know how to do that, don't we?'

Nick had meant to pierce that prickly exterior Beth
presented to the world. To have her talk to him, tell

him things about herself, anything about herself, as long as she let him in.

And by doing so he had hurt her. Had brought all that pain and suffering back into stark relief.

'Your car lights are off, Daddy,' Bekka announced happily as she came back into the kitchen. 'And there are some carol singers at the door,' she added excitedly as she slipped her hand into his. 'Can we go and listen to them and then give them some money?'

Nick dragged his gaze away from Beth to smile down at his daughter. 'Sure we can.' He gave her hand a squeeze before glancing across the kitchen. 'Coming, Beth?'

'I—no,' Beth refused. 'I'm just going to finish up here and then call a taxi, but the two of you go ahead,' she urged lightly.

He frowned darkly. 'We haven't finished talking, Beth.'

'I think we've said all that needs to be said, don't you?' she dismissed.

Nick continued to look at her broodingly for several long seconds before he felt Bekka's renewed tugging on his hand and allowed his daughter to pull him out into the hallway.

Beth sat down on one of the kitchen chairs as soon as she had finished talking to the taxi company and put the tumbet in the oven, very aware of her need to get away from here. Away from the cloyingly domestic atmosphere of just being here with Bekka and Nick. And the maelstrom of emotions that created inside her.

She had loved Ben so much—been devastated when he died. Her only way of coping with his loss, and that of her parents, had been to remove herself from the place where she had spent so many happy years with all of them. To move to London, a place where she could be assured of anonymity. A place where she could live quietly and privately, separate and apart from all emotional involvement.

Being here like this with Nick and Bekka had given Beth a painful glimpse of a life that she had long ago decided could no longer ever be hers. A full and happy life. A life that included a husband and children of her own.

After Ben had died Beth had told herself that if she never loved again, never had any of those things, then she could never be hurt again, either. Would never again have to go through the pain of losing someone she loved.

She realised now how foolish she had been to believe herself capable of shutting out all emotion. How stupid, how utterly, utterly stupid that belief had been, when just being here again with Nick and Bekka told her it was already too late—that without meaning to she had already allowed herself to care again. Not just for Bekka, but for Nick too.

To more than care for him…?

Beth shied away from admitting even to herself to feeling any more than attracted to him. If she didn't acknowledge it, then perhaps it would just go away!

Just as Beth intended getting away from here, the moment her taxi arrived!

'I told the taxi driver to wait outside.'

She spun round guiltily to face Nick, his eyes hooded as he stood in the kitchen doorway looking across at her. 'Where's Bekka?' she prompted brightly.

'Still listening to the carol singers.'

Beth nodded abruptly as she gave Paddy an absentminded pat on the head before picking up her handbag. 'I'll say goodbye to her on my way out.'

Nick frowned as he remained unmoving in the doorway. 'We haven't finished our conversation yet, Beth.'

She swallowed hard. 'There's nothing else to say.'

Nick crossed the room to stand in front of her. 'Damn it, Beth, talk to me!'

'My taxi is waiting—'

'I instructed the driver to wait until you're ready to leave,' Nick told her.

Beth gave a pained frown. 'I've done what you

asked me to do and taken care of Bekka while you went to the hospital. I've even cooked dinner for both of you. I think the least you can do for me is to let me leave without fuss.'

His mouth firmed. 'Run away, you mean?'

Beth gasped as the barb struck home. 'That was uncalled-for, Nick!'

Yes, it had been, he acknowledged self-disgustedly. Uncalled-for and unnecessarily cruel. 'I don't want to hurt you, Beth, I just—I want to help you,' he encouraged gruffly as he reached out and grasped both her hands in his.

She drew in a ragged breath. 'You can't help me, Nick. No one can. Now, would you please just let me leave?' she pleaded emotionally.

Nick could see that she was going to cry. He had managed to make Beth cry when all he'd wanted was to—

What? What did he want from her?

More to the point, what did he possibly have to give a woman like Beth? A woman who had been so hurt by life, by the loss of the husband and parents that she'd loved, that she had decided never to allow emotion into her life again.

As cynical as Nick's own feelings were towards love, he knew he was the last person—the *very* last person—to give anyone advice on the subject!

Even so, it was hard to stand back and watch Beth

as she left. To know that he had helped cause those unshed tears that glistened on her long dark lashes as she walked away from him…

CHAPTER EIGHT

'NICK...?' Beth felt the colour drain from her face
as she answered the ringing of the doorbell to her
apartment the following afternoon and found him
standing outside in the hallway. 'What have you done
with Bekka?' she asked as she realised Nick was
alone.

'Bekka is at home with Mrs Bennett,' Nick supplied evenly, his grey gaze guarded.

'She's better?'

He nodded. 'And wondering what all the fuss was
about.'

'That's good.' Beth nodded, trying not to notice
how attractive Nick looked in a black cashmere
sweater and black denims, his hair brushed back
from the rugged handsomeness of his face. 'What
can I do for you?' she queried brightly.

'Inviting me in would be a good place to start...'

Beth gave a pained wince. She'd had plenty of time
since yesterday evening to realise how completely

she had let herself down during her last conversation with Nick. How much of herself, her vulnerability, she had revealed to him.

She gave a self-conscious grimace. 'I was feeling a little—emotional yesterday evening. Christmas is always a difficult time of year, isn't it?' She attempted a laugh that didn't quite come off. 'I hope I didn't embarrass you too much?'

'Not at all,' Nick dismissed smoothly.

'That's good.' Beth nodded. 'I don't know what came over me,' she added awkwardly as Nick continued to look down at her broodingly.

'Don't you…?'

'No,' she assured him sharply.

'I really think you should invite me in, Beth,' Nick added tensely.

'I— Why?' Her wariness deepened as the tension surrounding them increased.

Nick gave a derisive smile as he easily sensed that wariness. 'Because it's the polite thing to do?'

'I think it's a little late to worry about politeness between the two of us, don't you?' She hated to imagine what Miss Sheffield would say or do if she knew of the way Beth had spoken to the school's 'most influential parent' this last week!

Nick's decision to talk to Beth calmly, rationally, completely deserted him now that he was faced with the flesh and blood woman. Most of all the flesh!

She was wearing another overlarge jumper—red today—with fitted jeans, and Nick wanted nothing more than to take all her clothes off and explore the satiny flesh beneath

Beth's eyes widened in alarm as Nick strode past her into her apartment. 'I— But— You can't just come here like this and expect to—'

Obviously he *could* just come here like this and expect to be allowed in!

Beth almost had to run to keep up with him as he walked forcefully down the hallway into her sitting room, his grey gaze taking in at a glance the sun-yellow walls and terracotta-coloured sofa and chair, and the small decorated Christmas tree in the window, with its half a dozen presents beneath, before he turned those piercing silver eyes on her.

Beth squirmed at the sensual warmth she could see in them. 'You're coming here really isn't a good idea, Nick,' she muttered desperately.

'Tell me about it!' he muttered.

She gave a baffled frown. 'I don't understand why you've bothered if you already know that...'

'I'm here because I'm sick and tired of fighting my need to make love to you!' he snapped.

She gasped at the starkness of Nick's statement, even as she stared up searchingly into that sensually handsome face. 'I...' She moistened suddenly dry lips. 'You are...?'

'Oh, yes,' Nick breathed with feeling.

Beth swallowed hard. 'And is this how it works? You come here and tell me you need to make love to me, and just expect me to acquiesce?' Her voice rose indignantly.

'Well…no. Not quite,' Nick answered with slow mockery. 'I've always thought of lovemaking as a two-way thing, Beth, and as such I would like you to make love to me too. But I'm happy to offer you any guidance you might need in that area if you feel you're a little rusty,' he added dryly.

''You're happy to *offer me guidance*…' Beth repeated incredulously. 'I'm a biology teacher, Nick; I *do* know how a man's body works. Plus I was married for three years!'

Nick was only too aware that Beth had been married. To a man she had obviously loved very much. And who had no doubt loved her.

It was a hard act to follow, and not something that Nick particularly relished. He wouldn't even be contemplating it if he could have stayed away from her…

'I've been honest about what I want, Beth. How about you give me that same honesty?' he encouraged.

Beth moistened her lips with the tip of her tongue, very aware of the loud pounding of her heart, of the wild flutter of excitement she felt in her chest just being near Nick like this.

Being honest with Nick would mean admitting how being with him made her feel. How much Beth wanted to be with him. How much she wanted to have him touch her and be able to touch him in return.

Honesty to herself meant admitting all of those things—and something else. Something that even now Beth shied away from admitting even to herself.

She drew herself up determinedly. 'Will you just think about what you're saying, Nick?' she reasoned heavily. 'I'm your daughter's teacher. Even if I wanted to I can't just have an affair with the father of one of my pupils!'

'I'm only interested in whether or not it *is* what you want.'

Did she want to have a relationship with this ruggedly handsome and exciting man? An affair no doubt brief, but for the time it lasted also intensely passionate?

Nick reached out and held the tops of Beth's arms as he stared down at her intently. 'We're the only two that matter now, Beth,' he insisted persuasively.

Beth stared up at him, knowing by his tension, by the fierce glitter of those grey eyes, that Nick was perfectly serious. That at this moment he wanted her—in his life and in his bed.

Flattering as it was to realise the depth of his desire, it wasn't enough…

She gave a pained frown. 'For how long, Nick? A few days? A week? Perhaps even a month? Or do you think one night would be enough? That once you've made love to me you would lose all interest?'

His mouth tightened. 'Isn't that a risk all couples take when they first get together?'

'We aren't a couple, Nick, and we never will be,' Beth murmured regretfully.

He shook her slightly. 'Your responses tell me that you want me just as much as I want you…'

'I'm not denying it,' she said softly; how *could* she deny something that must be obvious every time Nick so much as touched her? 'It just isn't enough for me, Nick.'

He put her away from him to thrust his hands into his pockets. 'What more do you want from me, Beth? Hearts and flowers? Declarations of undying love? Promises of for ever?' He gave a rueful shake of his head. 'I've already told you that I'm not the man who can give you any of that.'

Beth had spent all of last night and most of today thinking about her earlier conversation with Nick, about what it was she wanted for her life.

It had been two years since Ben died. Two years. And without Beth even realising it she had begun to heal. To want more in her life than she had now.

Since leaving Nick yesterday Beth had realised exactly what she wanted for her future. She wanted what she'd had with Ben. Nothing less, and perhaps more.

She and Ben had grown up together, become young adults starting out on life together, and had intended growing old together. They had been best friends as well as husband and wife and lovers.

Anything less than that was unacceptable.

But meeting Nick this past week had shown Beth that she now wanted more than that. That she wanted excitement too. The pulse-racing and heady thrill of a certain man's presence. The pleasure of just looking at him. The tingling arousal to be felt in his touch.

All of the things she had found in just being with Nick...

Tears misted her vision as she reached up to lay her fingers gently against the rigid hardness of his cheek. 'I'm sorry I can't give you what you want, either, Nick.'

Nick didn't want her pity, damn it! 'You intend to just continue living the sterile and lonely life you have now?'

'No,' she answered huskily. 'I'm hoping... Yesterday, seeing what it was like to be part of a family again, was painful for me. Talking to you about those feelings even more so. But it also helped me to realise that the only reason it was so painful is because I want those things again!' Her eyes glowed deeply blue. 'I want to fall in love again. To have someone love me. To have a husband and a family of my own.'

Great, Nick thought. Being with him and Bekka had helped Beth to know what she wanted out of life—and it sure as hell wasn't him!

Accept it, Nick, and move on, he told himself.

That had always been Nick's way in the past when things hadn't gone as he'd wanted them to—in personal relationships and business. There had always been another woman, another business deal, to claim his interest. There would be this time, too.

In time…

He gave a disgusted shake of his head. 'You do know you're searching for an impossible dream?'

She eyed him ruefully. 'I found it once, so why not again?'

'Because you were twenty-one years old at the time and didn't know any better!' he reasoned in frustration.

Beth smiled. 'I'm twenty-six years old now—and I'm glad I still don't know any better!' She laughed softly at his disgusted expression. 'You're a good man, Nick. I hope that one day—'

'Please don't wish love on me!' He scowled darkly.

Her eyes glowed teasingly. ''Tis the season…'

'Love is a myth, Beth!' Nick rasped.

She gave a shake of her head. 'That isn't true. And, knowing that, I have to be true to myself rather than settle for less than I deserve.'

Less than she deserved...

Was that really how Beth saw him? As offering her less than she deserved?

If so, then she was right to turn him down!

Nick grimaced. 'This is goodbye, then...?'

'We'll probably see each other at school occasionally...'

But not like this, Nick realised heavily. Beth would never allow them to be together like this again.

He sighed. 'I hope you realise that our dopey dog is so besotted with you that he's been moping around the house looking for you ever since you left yesterday?'

Beth laughed softly. 'Paddy is a darling!'

'With anyone else but you and Bekka he's vicious and bad-tempered! Since Bekka adopted him I've had a fight at the door every night just to get into my own house!'

She smiled as she shook her head. 'Paddy just needs you to understand him. To show him that he's wanted and loved.'

Nick's expression sharpened. 'Beth, this elusive emotion called love isn't the answer to everything!'

Her grimace was rueful. 'Of course it isn't,' she

accepted lightly. 'I just know that I'm totally incapable of settling for anything less.'

Beth wanted the sort of love that Nick, even though he had been married to Janet for over seven years, had never felt for any woman...

That he wasn't capable of feeling?

He frowned as he considered that was a distinct possibility. A possibility that meant Beth was leaving his life for good. 'I truly wish you a Merry Christmas and a Happy New Year, Beth.' He gave a weary sigh. 'I hope it brings you everything you wish for.'

'You too,' she said quietly.

Nick gave her one last, long, lingering glance before taking his leave.

Beth managed to maintain her composure for as long as it took Nick to quietly close the door behind him. Before the tears began to fall hotly down her cheeks.

Before she at last acknowledged—to herself, at least—that 'something else' she had realised since parting from Nick yesterday.

Not only was Nick the man who gave her a pulse-racing and heady thrill just being in his presence, who gave her pleasure just in looking at him, who filled her with tingling arousal just at a touch, but he was also the man she wanted as her best friend, her lover, and her husband.

Because she loved him.

And she knew there was no hope of Nick ever returning that love...

CHAPTER NINE

'YOU may as well stop looking at me in that accusing way, Bekka; I've already told you—I can't force Mrs Morgan into spending Christmas Day with us tomorrow!' Nick said with impatience as he and his daughter sat at a small table playing a board game together, late the following afternoon.

As it was Christmas Eve, Nick had taken the day off, intending to spend the time with Bekka completing last-minute Christmas present-wrapping and generally having fun.

It hadn't turned out that way. Far from it. Bekka's cold was almost gone, but she had been tearful and upset since he had told her that Beth had decided not to join them for her birthday tomorrow.

'I don't want to play any more.' Bekka pushed the board game away and stood up, tears glistening in her eyes as she looked at Nick. 'I don't know how you can even *think* of letting Mrs Morgan spend Christmas Day on her own!'

The problem was that Nick had thought of Beth far too much during the seventeen hours—and nine minutes!—since they had parted so finally the night before.

Thought of her. Ached for her. Ached for them both.

Because he couldn't give her what she wanted.

What she deserved.

Beth Morgan was the most stubborn, maddening, frustrating, beautiful woman—inside as well as out—that Nick had ever met.

Or was ever likely to meet.

Janet had been more beautiful. Exceptionally so. That beauty had allowed her to be one of the highest paid models in the world, making Nick the envy of all his friends when she'd agreed to marry him. That envy had continued after they'd become the 'perfect couple'. The arrival of Bekka only a year after they were married had completed the perfect family picture.

Unfortunately that outward perfection had hidden deep flaws in their private relationship. The main one being that they hadn't been in love with each other. They had looked good together, and Janet had been the perfect social hostess for Nick the successful businessman, but once the two of them were alone they'd had nothing in common—nothing to talk about except their glamorous and artificial life.

There had certainly been none of those deep and emotionally searching conversations between himself and Janet that he'd had with Beth Morgan in just the week he'd known her!

Bekka had asked him how he could think of letting Beth spend Christmas Day on her own, but despite being with Bekka Nick also felt alone.

Everything in his life was exactly as it had been before he'd met Beth. He had Bekka. His business. This house and its menagerie of pets—even the dopey dog had reverted back to type, growling at Nick this morning as soon as he came out of his bedroom!

Yes, everything was the same. And yet inside, where it mattered, Nick knew that *he* wasn't. That he had never felt so alone.

Because he wanted Beth.

'I wanted her here with us as much as you did, pumpkin,' he assured Bekka huskily.

'And?'

Nick frowned. 'And what?'

'If you really wanted Mrs Morgan here then she would *be* here,' Bekka reasoned.

Nice to know that one of the women in his life thought he was omnipotent!

One of the women in his life…?

Beth wasn't in his life.

And she should be!

What was he doing, sitting here playing board games, when he could be with Beth? When she could be here with the two of them? When he and Bekka could be the family Beth had said she wanted…?

He stood up abruptly. 'I have to go out, Bekka.'

His daughter's eyes widened expectantly. 'To see Mrs Morgan?'

Nick gave a grimace as he ruffled Bekka's hair playfully. 'We'll see. Didn't Mrs Bennett mention something earlier about feeling well enough to supervise you making gingerbread angels to put on the tree?'

'We… Yes…' Bekka gave a frown. 'Will you be back in time for dinner?'

'Let's hope so,' Nick answered.

There was always the possibility, after the mess he had made of things the previous evening, that Nick might have to camp outside Beth's apartment door until she agreed to let him in. Whatever the outcome, Nick knew that he couldn't sit here any longer thinking what if…?

'What on earth—?' Beth froze in the doorway of her apartment as the largest bouquet of red roses she had ever seen in her life was slowly lowered to reveal Nick as the person carrying the beautiful blooms.

It was almost six o'clock on Christmas Eve—a

time when Beth had imagined Nick as being at home with Bekka—and yet here he was, standing on her doorstep.

And carrying that enormous bouquet of red roses…

Her heart began to pound loudly in her chest. To hope. 'You're a little early for First Footing, and I believe the traditional gift is coal,' she said with a wry smile.

The expression in Nick's eyes was guarded. 'I've decided it's time to start some traditions of my own.'

What sort of traditions…?

Beth swallowed hard as she stepped aside. 'Would you like to come in?'

'Yes.' His eyes gleamed a pale, intense silver. 'But first I would like you to take these flowers from me so that I can give you your other presents.'

Beth gathered the roses into her arms, their heady perfume adding to her light-headedness. To the hope steadily building inside her…

'My other presents?' she prompted shyly as Nick strode past her into her apartment, carrying a large gold foil carrier bag.

It hadn't even occurred to her to buy anything to give Nick for Christmas; how could it, when Beth hadn't thought she would ever see Nick again except as the parent of one of her students?

'It isn't Christmas yet, you know,' she added teasingly as she followed him through to the sitting room.

As usual he looked wonderful, in a black long-sleeved polo-shirt over faded denims. Although the darkness of his hair was slightly windblown, and his jawline was shadowed—as if he were in need of a shave. As if he had left home in a hurry…?

'New traditions, remember?' Nick said huskily, his gaze hungry as he took in Beth's appearance in a seasonal figure-hugging red sweater and jeans. 'I've tried to remember everything.' He placed the bag down on the coffee table. 'The flowers you have. This was the best I could do as the 'heart'.' He produced a heart-shaped box of chocolates from inside the bag and held it out to her.

Beth slowly put the flowers down on the table so that she could take the box of chocolates. 'Nick, what's going on…?'

Good question, Nick acknowledged.

He was risking everything—that was what was going on. Discarding everything that he had been. Everything that he now was. In the hope of replacing it with everything that he could be. Everything that he wanted to be!

He winced. 'Could you just let me do this first, Beth, and then we can talk afterwards?'

She looked slightly bewildered. 'If that's what you would prefer…'

'It is,' he assured her with a self-conscious smile. 'Next on the list, I believe, were declarations of undying love—'

Beth gasped. 'Nick…?'

'Beth, please!' A nerve pulsed in his tightly clenched jaw as he glowered at her. 'You can throw all my gifts back in my face afterwards, okay? At least let me give you the satisfaction of making a *complete* idiot of myself first!'

She gave a sharp shake of her head. 'But I don't want—'

'This isn't just about what *you* want any more, Beth,' Nick rasped forcefully. 'I have some wants of my own now too. The first one being that you allow me to finish telling you how I feel—okay?'

Her throat was dry as she swallowed. 'Okay…'

Nick drew in a ragged breath. 'My first marriage wasn't as happy as yours obviously was. How could it be when Janet and I weren't in love with each other? I think we respected each other at first, appreciated what each of us could bring to a marriage. Janet had the self-confidence and beauty to be a businessman's perfect wife, and I had the successful business that brought in the money to keep us both in the life we enjoyed.' He frowned darkly. 'Not, I realise now, ideal reasons for marrying each other.'

'You had Bekka together, and both obviously loved her, which is why she's such an adorable little girl. That has to count for something,' Beth put in softly.

'For something, yes,' Nick said gruffly. 'But it obviously wasn't enough to keep the marriage together. What I'm really trying to tell you, Beth, is that I've never been in love. That I didn't know how to love.'

'Nick, you really don't have to tell me these things if it's painful for you,' Beth assured him quickly.

'Oh, I really do, Beth. Now, this next present you don't have to accept right now.' He hesitated before taking the gift from inside the bag. 'Obviously I have no idea what sort of engagement ring Ben bought for you…'

'We were students, Nick; a small—very small— diamond was the most we could afford!' Beth recalled affectionately.

He nodded. 'And I'm sure that to you it was the most beautiful ring in the world.'

'Yes.'

'As I said, you don't have to accept this now.' He took a small, expensive-looking jeweller's bag from inside the larger one. 'Or you could accept it and just wear it on your right hand.' He held the little bag out to her by the strings. 'Of course the declaration of undying love goes along with it, but—'

Beth made no effort to take the bag. 'Nick…?'

He quirked dark brows. 'Beth?'

Beth had been stunned when she'd found Nick standing outside her apartment carrying that huge bouquet of roses. Her heart had ached for Nick and Janet as he'd talked of a marriage based on mutual needs rather than love. But surely this—giving Beth a ring—had to mean—

She took the jeweller's bag and put it down on the coffee table without so much as looking inside it. 'Nick, are you saying—? Are all these things your way of telling me that you're in love with me...?' she said slowly.

His mouth twisted. 'I was hoping you could tell *me* that!' He grimaced. 'I think about you every minute of the day and night. I can't eat because my stomach is churned up in knots all the time. I can't sleep because every time I close my eyes I see your face.' He drew in a harsh breath. 'Worst of all, I feel so damned cold and lonely inside when I'm not with you. Deep down inside. Like I'm never going to feel warm again. Is that love?'

Beth's breath caught on a choked laugh at the self-disgust she could clearly see in Nick's expression. 'Those things are part of it, yes—'

'The worst part I hope.' He sighed heavily as he ran a distracted hand through the dark thickness of his hair. 'I've never felt so miserable in my life!'

Beth's eyes misted over with tears as she slowly

walked towards him. 'That's because you don't know yet whether you're loved in return. Once you do—oh, Nick, it's the most wonderful feeling in the world!' she told him happily as she came to a halt in front of him.

Nick looked down at her intensely. 'I so much want to be all those things you said you want for your future, Beth. The things I know you deserve,' he said fiercely. 'I want that so badly, Beth!'

'You already *are* those things, Nick,' Beth assured him as she gazed lovingly into his ruggedly handsome face. 'I'm in love with you too, Nick. I *love* you! So very much,' she breathed softly, and she reached up a tentative hand to touch his rigidly clenched jaw.

'You love me...?' Nick looked stunned. 'But last night you said—you told me I couldn't be a part of your life—'

'Because I already knew I had fallen in love with you,' she explained. 'Because I couldn't be with you, have any sort of relationship with you, knowing you didn't feel that same love for me. Nick, I love you in a way I've never loved anyone before!'

He looked down at her uncertainly. 'Never...?'

'Never.' She nodded emotionally. 'The way I loved Ben was so completely different to what I feel for you, Nick. I realise now that we were friends who grew to love each other and then got married. You—' She drew in a shuddering breath. 'You I love with every beat of my heart, every breath I take, with every single part of me!'

Nick felt it then. Felt the wonder that Beth had described. Felt that loneliness inside him evaporate as if it had never been. And that hole in his heart, that he hadn't even realised was there until Beth walked out of his life, became filled to bursting with the love he felt for this woman. Every last vestige of unhappiness, uncertainty, fled in the face of the love he could see shining in Beth's beautiful blue eyes. For *him*. Only for him.

'How could I have been so stupid?' he groaned achingly. 'How could I have dismissed love as a myth all these years? Why didn't I realise before how much I love you?'

He finally took her into his arms, crushing her against him as he buried his face in the glorious auburn of her hair. Holding her to him as if to make her a part of him. As if to take her deep inside him where he would never have to let her go again.

'Oh, God, Beth—I don't think I could have stood another day, an hour, even another minute, without telling you how very much I love you!' he admitted shakily.

Beth laughed huskily, happily, as she gave herself up to the absolute pleasure of loving Nick and knowing herself loved as deeply in return.

Nick held Beth securely in his arms as he reached over and took the ring box from inside the jeweller's bag. 'Will you marry me, Beth?' He flicked the box open to reveal the ring inside—a huge sapphire that was the exact colour of Beth's eyes, surrounded by half a dozen smaller diamonds.

'Oh, yes, Nick, I'll marry you,' she accepted wholeheartedly, without even glancing at the ring.

He took the ring out of the box, but didn't put in on her finger. 'You realise by saying yes that you'll not only be marrying me, but Bekka too? Along with three spoilt cats, a schizophrenic dog, a hamster and, believe it or not, a rat?'

'Oh, I think I'll cope.' Beth grinned. 'As long as I can be with you, Nick, loving you, knowing you love me, everything else will fall into place.'

Nick took her left hand in his. 'I promise that I will love you for ever, Beth. That I will do my very best to make you happy for the rest of our lives together,' he vowed as he slipped the sapphire and diamond ring onto her finger.

'I'd like more children, Nick,' she said uncertainly, not sure how he felt about adding to his already con-siderable household.

He gave a teasing glance at his wristwatch. 'This minute? Or can it wait a while?' His arms tightened about her. 'Beth, I want nothing more than to make love to and with you,' he assured her gruffly. 'In fact,

I've fantasised about it many times! But when it happens I would like us to have time—a lot of time!—to fully explore and enjoy each other.'

'Bekka?' Beth guessed softly.

Nick nodded. 'I promised her I would be back this evening.'

'Then let's go home, Nick.' Beth glowed up at him. 'Let's go home and spend Christmas with Bekka!'

And what a Christmas it was, as the three of them celebrated not only Christmas but Bekka's birthday too, with the little girl declaring that knowing Beth was soon going to be her mother was the best birthday present she had ever had.

Which in no way lessened her enthusiasm for opening her Christmas and birthday presents the following morning!

Beth's eyes glowed as she and Nick stood together, watching the little girl open her gifts.

Nick's arms circled about her waist from behind as he pulled her back against him, his breath a warm caress against her neck. 'I love you so much, Beth!'

She turned her head slightly to receive his lingering kiss. 'I love you too, Nick,' she replied, her hands resting lightly on his arms as she hugged him to her, the diamond and sapphire ring glittering on her left hand. 'So very, very much.'

She was part of a family again, Beth realised emotionally as she turned back in time to laugh as Paddy and the three cats vied for Bekka's attention amongst the rising mound of Christmas wrapping paper.

Her family.

And most of all she had Nick.

The man she loved with all her heart.

One Christmas Night in Venice

Jane
PORTER

Jane Porter grew up on a diet of Mills & Boon® romances, reading late at night under the covers so her mother wouldn't see! She wrote her first book at age eight and spent many of her school and college years living abroad, immersing herself in other cultures and continuing to read voraciously. Now Jane has settled down in rugged Seattle, Washington, with her gorgeous husband and two sons. Jane loves to hear from her readers. You can write to her at PO Box 524, Bellevue, WA 98009, USA. Or visit her website at www.janeporter.com

Dear Reader,

There are few spots more magical in my mind than Venice and no place more perfect for a Christmas story than this romantic city built on water and lagoons. Most people know the summer Venice when it's overrun by tourists, heat and noise. However, my favourite Venice is the one that's periodically flooded in winter and, even more spectacularly, powdered by snow.

One Christmas Night in Venice came to me after I saw photos of a Carnival masquerade ball held at one of Venice's great palazzos. I was enthralled by the glamour, beauty and mystery of the costumes, the masks and the palazzo's grand architecture. Almost immediately the story came to me—a young couple torn apart by a tragic accident and then miraculously brought together one Christmas night in a city as magical as love itself.

I hope you'll enjoy Diane Mayer and Count Domenico Coducci's story. It's a story about Christmas, the magic of Venice and the miracle of love.

Yours,

Jane

CHAPTER ONE

WHAT was she doing here? How could she possibly have thought this was a good idea? Getting resolution was one thing, but this was madness.

Diane Mayer hovered inside the opulent ballroom of fifteenth century Ca' Coducci, one of Venice's beloved jewels on the Grand Canal, realizing she'd made a huge mistake coming to the masquerade ball hosted by the noble Coducci family in their *palazzo* tonight. Tickets were costly for the gala fundraiser, but a friend had passed his on to her and, since she was already in Italy for business, she had impulsively decided to come.

Fool that she was. Closure? How did she expect to get closure coming here? What kind of resolution did she think she'd have?

For God's sake, she'd honeymooned here in Venice. Ca' Coducci had been her husband's home. The noble Coduccis were her husband's family. But five years ago she'd lost it all in the blink of an eye.

That was all it had been. The blink of an eye. Domenico had taken his eyes off the road for a moment, just long enough to turn, look at her, smile, and then they'd been blinded by light before that horrific bone-shattering impact that had crushed their car to bits.

Sucking in a nervous breath, wishing she was back at her hotel instead of at the party, Diane adjusted her white shepherdess mask as costumed guests swirled past.

Goddesses and nymphs, satyrs and maidens, unicorns, angels, and even fairytale characters laughed and danced through the doorway into the vast ballroom, a room lit entirely by candlelight. Fat ivory candles glowed in sconces, with smaller candles in glass votives on the floor, while the ballroom's gold ceiling, distinguished by three enormous glass chandeliers, glittered and shone, casting golden light on the fantastical masks and costumes below.

And no couple was more fantastic than the winged lion and golden Venus slowly circling the room

Diane, who rarely noticed people, who loved art and architecture more than society, stared, fascinated. Enthralled. How beautiful the two of them were together.

They were a stunning pair, perfectly matched, gilded by the candlelight.

Venus' mask barely concealed her exquisite face,

but it was he, the winged lion, symbol of St. Mark, Venice's patron saint, who captivated her.

He was a work of art, in the softest golden leather pants which had been fitted to powerful legs. A red and gold robe fell from his broad shoulders, leaving his muscular chest and hard, flat carved torso tantalizingly bare. His arms were thickly muscled and bare, too, while his face was hidden by a gold lion mask that nearly covered his face completely, beginning at the brow, extending over his nose, skirting his upper lip and then dipping low to follow his jaw. A thick gold mane covered his hair and wings— enormous gold wings—sprang from his back as if he were an archangel about to take flight.

It was more than a costume. It was a fantasy. He was man and beast. Fierce. Regal. Seductive. Lethal.

Diane's throat closed and her heart ached. For a heartbreaking moment she thought of Domenico, even as the candlelight illuminated him, shadowing his face and outlining his size.

He was tall, even taller than Domenico, and broader through the shoulders, and yet he made her long for the life she'd lost. Love, pleasure, possession.

Sex. Seduction.

God, it had been years since she'd been with anyone—years since she'd been touched, loved, held. She hadn't wanted to be touched, held, but this beautiful, impossible fantasy made her crave and hunger and dream.

Dream.

Maybe someday. Maybe one day. If she was lucky.

And then the mythic winged lion turned his head, thick gold mane brushing his shoulders, to look her way, to look at *her*, and her heart skittered to a stop.

So like Dom. Those eyes. That expression.

Her heart squeezed even tighter and her head spun. She leaned on her shepherdess staff, her bad leg about to collapse. So much of him reminded her of Domenico. The height, the shape of his broad chest, the muscular, tapering torso, the narrow hips above long strong legs. It was almost as if the Coducci *palazzo* was playing tricks on her imagination. Ghost, angel, beast.

It's not Dom, she told herself. Can't be. Domenico's dead.

And yet this beautiful winged lion, this symbol of the city, looked at her as if he could see beneath her mask, beneath her costume. He looked as if he could see straight through her. Right to her heart.

Just like Dom had.

Her hand trembled violently on the staff. The winged lion was approaching.

"Ti senti bene? Are you all right?" Conte

Domenico Coducci asked the tiny shepherdess in the white tulle gown, having watched her for the better part of an hour. She'd arrived alone and had remained alone, and he'd noticed how her hand shook on her shepherdess staff.

She took a nervous step back, eyes wide behind the sleek white mask molded to her face. The mask hid everything but her eyes, and her blue-green gaze stared up at him transfixed. He'd never seen any eyes quite so sad, and for a moment her sorrow touched him. Strange, because nothing touched him. Nothing could. On the inside he was dead, and yet…and yet… something stirred inside him now. A fragment of memory. A whisper of hunger followed by a slash of pain.

But, no, it couldn't be, and just like that he steeled himself against the memory and the emotion. "Can I get you something to drink?" he added, putting a hand out to her elbow as she swayed on her feet.

"No. I'm fine. *Sto bene*." She stumbled back another step and tears shimmered in her eyes.

The tears cracked the armor around his heart. Don't cry, he wanted to tell her, don't be so sad. Which was even more perplexing as he wasn't a tender man. Didn't comfort. Didn't love.

He shouldn't even be here. There was no point. She wasn't his responsibility. He had a houseful of wealthy, influential guests. A Christmas gala to host.

And a beautiful fiancée waiting for him across the room. But this little shepherdess… She reminded him of someone he'd desperately loved and lost. Not that he wanted to remember. He was done remembering, done living in the past.

He drew a swift, rough breath. There was no past. Only the future. And his future was with Valeria. Valeria and his son. "If you're sure you're fine," he said coolly, moving back a step, determined to put space between them. Mistakes were made when one let emotions cloud reality.

She nodded once, and that was all he needed. He'd done his duty. Displayed proper hospitality for a guest in his home. With a curt goodnight he walked swiftly away, his sumptuous robe swinging from his shoulders, powerful hands clenched at his side.

The past, he reminded himself harshly, was dead.

Diane shuddered as he walked away.

His voice. Dom's voice. He'd sounded just like Dom. Spoken like Dom. Touched her like Dom.

But Domenico was dead. *Dead*. Gone. Buried in the family vault. And this, the beautifully restored *palazzo*, belonged to Dom's sister, who had graciously donated the use of the waterfront palace to the charity Foundation for their fundraiser.

She knew this. Knew the facts. But facts right now

didn't explain anything. The facts somehow were wrong.

Diane watched the tall winged lion join the magnificent Venus. Their heads tipped together and Diane's heart ached. Jealous. *Jealous.* Crazy as it was, she felt as if she was watching her beloved with another woman.

It made her ill. Her stomach heaved. Time to leave, she told herself. You're losing your mind. Confusing reality and fantasy. Letting the costumes and masks distort your mind and cloud your memory.

In the antechamber a uniformed maid emerged with Diane's dark wool cloak. Pietra, Diane thought, recognizing the maid who'd just started working for the Coduccis when she and Dom had honeymooned here seven years ago. "Thank you, Pietra," Diane said softly from behind her mask.

The maid smiled. "You know me?"

"Of course." Feeling lost, and needing to connect, Diane lifted her mask, revealing her face. "It's Diane. Diane Mayer-Coducci—"

The rest of Diane's words were drowned out by Pietra's shriek. *"Madre Maria, protegger mi dal fantasma!"*

Diane, fluent in Italian, had no problem translating the maid's strangled cry. *Mother Mary, protect me from the ghost!*

"Pietra," Diane choked, embarrassed by Pietra's theatrics. "It's me. Diane. Domenico's wife—"

Pietra screamed again, louder than before.

Diane's flagging confidence deserted her and, clutching her cloak to her breast, she limped out as quickly as her bad leg would allow her.

Such a mistake coming tonight. How could she have thought that it would invite anything other than more pain and suffering? So stupid to want a peek at the life she'd lost.

Shivering, Diane struggled with her cloak and mask and shepherdess staff. It was freezing cold and the Venetian fog had settled in, veiling the Grand Canal, making the gondolas at the water's edge appear to float in the air. Just go home, she told herself, get out of here and go home.

Diane was but steps from the bobbing gondolas when a firm hand descended on her shoulder, stopping her.

"What game is this?" The deep, rough male voice gritted, even as a warm palm bore down on her thin bare shoulder, forcibly turning her around.

A shiver raced through her. That voice again. A voice she'd thought she'd never hear again. Could it be?

Was it possible?

With her mask dangling in her fingers, she turned toward him, lifting her face to the light.

He hissed a breath as his gaze searched her face.

"What?" she whispered, her mouth drying.

Fury darkened his eyes. "My lady, you've taken the masquerade too far."

"I don't know what you mean."

"You do."

She shook her head, denying his accusation. "Take off your mask." Her voice was raspy, her mouth dry as sand. "Please."

"Who are you?" he demanded, his voice as sharp as cut glass.

"Let me see you," she begged.

He looked at her for the longest moment before reaching up to lift the lion's mask from his face.

The impressions hit her fast, furious—the forehead, the eyes, the cheekbones, the strong patrician nose.

Domenico.

Diane bit ruthlessly into her lip, biting back the pain.

Trickery—the moon, the light, the December night.

Trickery—this Venetian fog.

How cruel the night to conjure beautiful, dark, sensual Domenico.

Her heart ached. Her body grew feverishly warm. He looked so much like her Domenico that desire licked her veins.

Cruel night.

Cruel city of masks and balls and dreams.

Cruel city floating on pillars in the sea.

"Domenico?" she breathed, heart thumping wildly.

"Who are you?" he demanded.

Her bewildered gaze held his. Was it him? Could it be? "Diane."

He groaned deep in his chest and took a menacing step toward her. "Do not speak her name. You have no right."

It was him.

But it couldn't be.

Dom had died. Dom and the baby had died. Only she had survived the accident outside Rome. Only she, and barely at that.

In agony, Diane dropped her mask. It cracked as it hit the stone pavers, and even as it shattered Diane reached out a trembling hand to lightly touch his bare chest. His chest was hard, taut with sinewy muscle, the skin warm, firm.

"Domenico."

He took a step closer, looming over her. The lamp flickered yellow light over his profile and it was him. Beautiful. So beautiful. Tears scalded her eyes. "It is you," she whispered.

He took her hand from his chest, bent his head to reject her.

The light flickered again, and it was no longer his beautiful face but the face of a stranger. Scarred. Burned. Changed.

Not Domenico at all.

Diane's weak leg gave out and she collapsed, tumbling at his feet.

CHAPTER TWO

DOMENICO caught the fragile shepherdess just before her head slammed against the stone. Her heavy staff clattered to the ground instead, joining her broken mask.

She was small, light—lighter than Diane. Because this wasn't his Diane. No matter what this woman said. No matter the game she played.

But he couldn't leave her here. The night was cold and her cloak was nearly as thin as her sheer costume. Effortlessly he swung her up, lifting her high against his chest. It angered him that she felt more like an angel than a woman. So frail. Too frail.

His robe swirled around his legs as he carried her back to the *palazzo*, and he tried to concentrate on the cold and the fog instead of the woman in his arms.

When she'd touched him he'd burned. That brush of her fingers across his chest had hurt. Not tingled. *Burned*.

Just like the fire that had consumed the car the night of the accident.

His gaze dropped to the top of her head with its elaborate white wig. How strange that he felt nothing when Valeria touched him, and yet he felt everything when this little impostor touched him.

Jaw hardening, he resolved to get to the bottom of this charade—but it would be in private, away from the guests and the revelry.

A wide-eyed Pietra held the door open for him and, entering the *palazzo*, he walked past the grand staircase to the back of the house, where another staircase ran upstairs to the family's personal rooms.

He climbed the stairs in twos to his private suite on the third floor and placed the now silent shepherdess on the sitting room's antique sofa.

"Well?" he said brusquely, stepping back to have a hard look at her. She was beautiful. Ethereal. Impossibly fragile. "What is this about? Has someone put you up to this? Are you in need of money?"

The shepherdess tilted her head back, white ringlets cascading over her slender shoulders as she stared up at him, her eyes a stunning blue-green, overly brilliant in her pale face. *"No."* Her voice shook and he wanted to shake her.

Those eyes…that voice…so like Diane it almost fooled him. Almost, but not quite. Yet the damage was done. He was thinking of her again. Feeling what he'd once felt. Love. Loss. Grief.

Rage.

And the rage hit him anew, fresh fury washing over him, through him, stealing his calm, darkening his mind. He already blamed himself for Diane's death—he had been at the wheel, after all—but how dared this woman? How dared she mock him? How dared she impersonate his beloved wife?

Domenico stepped closer and lowered himself to his haunches, crouching before her so their eyes were level. "I warn you," he said softly, dangerously. "I am not a patient man. I will not tolerate this. Tell me why you're here and what you want or—" He broke off, his hands squeezing, knotting, kneading. He'd break her. Destroy her. Because, God help him, what kind of woman would do this?

He'd never loved anyone as he'd loved Diane. Diane had been his heart. His life. He'd defied everyone to marry her. He'd lost everything to have her. And he hadn't cared. He'd loved her so completely. With every inch of his heart.

She'd never believed him. Never trusted him. Unable to accept that he'd rather lose his inheritance, his family, than lose her. It hadn't been just rash promises, either. He'd given it all up on the day he'd married her. His mother, enraged that he'd marry a commoner, and an American at that, had stripped it all from him, though she could never take his title. It was his father who had allowed them to stay at Ca' Coducci for their honeymoon, but that had been their one and only visit here together.

He hadn't cared, though. He'd had his own business in Rome, and an apartment, and a beautiful wife he'd adored.

It was all he'd needed. Work, love, life.

But then Diane had died, and miraculously he'd been returned to the family bosom. Restored just like the prodigal son.

Only he hadn't wanted to be returned to the family bosom. He'd wanted Diane.

And this woman, this shepherdess, presumed to be his love, his life.

God help her, she was in trouble now.

"Or what? What would you do?" she flashed, eyes blazing back at him, expression defiant. "Throttle me? Hit me? What would you do that could create greater pain than has already been given to me?"

He was close enough to see the flecks of turquoise in her irises, and the faintest of lines at the edge of her eyes. A small dimple—no, a scar—winked at her throat.

Trachea, he thought, heart slowing, stomach cramping. A tracheotomy scar.

Someone had cut her trachea, opening her air tube so she could breathe. Throat squeezing closed, ice water filling his veins, he staggered to his feet, moved blindly away, his robe swirling.

Impossible.

Couldn't be.

Diane was dead. *Dead.* And the dead did not come back to life. Not even in magical Venice. Yes, in the first year after the accident he'd dreamed of her night after night—dreamed she was still alive, dreamed they were together still—but he hadn't dreamed of her in over a year now, and finally he was free to move on. Knew he *had* to move on, whether or not his heart was ready. Because his son needed him to move on. His son needed a mother, a family.

But this woman…so very much like Diane.

He turned his head slowly, slowly, and she was still there, sitting still, regal, *defiant* on his sofa.

"Do you abuse women now, Dom?" she choked, her cheeks suffused with color. "Is that what death has done to you?"

Diane would have never spoken to him this way.

Domenico ground his teeth together to keep from shouting. He didn't shout. He didn't care. He didn't feel. But right now he was wild on the inside. Wild, bewildered, stunned.

He'd died when they'd told him Diane was gone. He'd gone into cardiac arrest. And he'd been glad he was dying, had known he was dying. Wanted it.

But they'd brought him back after three minutes.

Brought him back to the living. Only he wasn't the same. Part of him was gone forever.

Even now, thinking maybe, maybe, it was her, he couldn't feel. Couldn't hope. Couldn't dream.

He'd loved her too much. And losing her had almost killed him. He would never love anyone—not even his Diane—again.

"I do not hurt women," he said, drawing a slow, deep breath. "And I would never hurt you." He paused. "If it is you."

"It is me. And you know it's me. Ask me anything."

"What was the painting I was standing in front of that day we met at the university library?"

The smallest of smiles played at her mouth. "Jacopo Tintoretto's *The Finding of the Body of St. Mark*. It was on loan from Brera in Milan." The smile disappeared. "We talked about your Venetian family, and how St. Mark was your favorite apostle." She looked up at him, her head shaking in disbelief. "How, Dom? How is it possible? You're supposed to be dead."

And I am, he thought, gazing down at her, even as it struck him that his wedding was exactly three weeks from tonight.

Dio buono. Good God.

Valeria.

He glanced at the door, thinking Valeria should

be here. Knowing that Valeria, his future wife, was not going to react well to hearing that his wife was still alive.

Eyes narrowed, he stared at Diane's oval face, with its bright pink spots of color, and remembered the way her hand had felt against his bare chest.

Warm, so warm. It had cut right to the heart of him. It had been both pleasure and pain—maybe even more pain than pleasure. And it hit him like a thunderbolt—Diane, only his Diane, would make him hurt like that. Only his Diane could make him feel so much. Only Diane...

As if on cue, the future Countess Coducci entered the sitting room, her tall, statuesque body nearly naked and gleaming in gold. She lifted off her mask as she moved toward him, freeing her long blond hair and sending it tumbling down her back.

Valeria was one of Italy's greatest beauties. Educated, elegant, refined. She understood him, too, accepting Domenico as he was instead of insisting on more. So many women wanted more. They didn't understand there wasn't more. Could never be more.

Valeria's honey-hued eyes glanced quizzically at Diane before looking back to him. "I heard a guest was ill," she said, coming to his side and laying a light hand on his arm. "And that you were seeing to her personally."

He heard the way she emphasized *personally*.

Valeria was not happy, didn't approve, but she wouldn't criticize him in front of others. She didn't just understand him, she understood the dynamics of their relationship.

He glanced down now, at the long, tight gold glove encasing her forearm. The glove artfully left the back of her palm and her elegant fingers bare. The gold glove was erotic. *She* was erotic. But she, like every other woman, left him cold.

"She looks fine," Valeria added, examining Diane from beneath her gold-tipped false eyelashes. "What was the problem?"

Dom didn't even try to soften the blow. "The problem is this is Diane."

One of Valeria's winged brows lifted higher. "Diane?"

"My…late…wife."

Valeria regarded him calmly. "But doesn't *late* imply she's dead?"

"It would, yes. But as you can see she's not."

"I don't understand."

"Neither do I." And then he took Valeria by the arm and led her to the hall outside the sitting room, where they could have a modicum of privacy.

Diane watched them walk out of the room together. They were perfectly matched. And she—she was the outsider.

Hands balled in her lap, Diane tried to stay calm,

but her mind felt unhinged. This was a dream within a dream. It was all too surreal. What was Domenico? Winged lion, golden symbol or archangel? And who was his Venus? His wife? His lover? His children's mother?

But the very idea of him fathering another woman's children sent pain shrieking through her. He was the father of *her* child, the child she'd lost in the accident.

She squeezed her eyes closed, trying to empty her mind and clear her vision. But when she opened her eyes again all she saw was Dom, and all she heard was his conversation with his golden Venus.

It was easy to hear every word. They hadn't bothered to close the doors. Maybe they didn't think she could hear them, or maybe they didn't care. And even though they were speaking Italian Diane had no problem following the rapid, emotional exchange.

"So she was a guest at the party?" Venus asked.

"Yes."

"It's too incredible. Her showing up here. Now." The gilded woman drew a short, sharp breath. "Are you sure it's her?"

"Yes." Domenico's answer was hard. Decisive. "There is only one Diane."

In her seat on the couch Diane doubled over, her chest constricting, air bottled in her lungs. Dreams didn't usually hurt, did they? But she hurt now. *There is only one Diane.*

That was something only her beloved Domenico would say.

He the great romantic. He who had sacrificed everything for her…his family, his wealth, his history… to start fresh with her. They'd been so young, and brave. Had thought they could do anything if they were together…

It had been a beautiful thought. And apparently very naïve.

"What is she doing here?" Venus persisted.

"I don't know."

"The timing of her appearance seems a little too good to be true. A week before Christmas and three weeks before our—" She broke off, and turned to march into the sitting room to cast Diane a withering glance. "Why did you sneak into the party?"

"I did not sneak!" Diane flashed, sitting tall, her back ramrod-straight. "I had a ticket just like everyone else."

"A ticket to see Domenico?" Valeria scoffed. "If you wanted to see him why not just come to the door?"

"It was a ticket to a ball, a fundraiser, not a ticket to see Domenico. And I came because I wanted to see the palace. I was curious. And foolishly I thought perhaps coming here tonight I'd finally have closure—"

"I don't believe you," Valeria interrupted.

Color stormed Diane's cheeks and she longed to be on her feet. She needed power and strength, and sitting on this damn sofa gave her neither, but she couldn't get up without her cane. Couldn't do anything but sit there and cling to what was left of her dignity. "Frankly, I don't care what you believe. I don't have to answer to you. This is between my husband and me."

"*Your* husband? He's *my* fiancé. Soon to be *my* husband—"

"Valeria!" Dom interrupted.

Venus faced him, expression pleading. "Domenico, this can't be. She's dead. I know you were still in the hospital, in Intensive Care, but your mother went to the funeral. She brought you back the order of service. You keep her ashes in the chapel—"

"But it was Dom who died," Diane broke in furiously. "Dom and the baby died. *I* was the only one who survived. At least that's what his mother said."

Diane felt rather than heard Dom's sharp inhalation.

And then it hit her—brutally hard. *His mother said...*

His mother...

His mother had lied.

Hadn't she?

The realization must have hit Domenico at the same time. "Valeria, if you'd excuse us?" he said, his gaze fixed on Diane's face.

Valeria opened her mouth to protest, but thought better of it and with her head high walked out of the room.

Diane watched Valeria leave and listened to the door click closed before glancing up at Domenico, who hadn't moved from his position at the end of the blue brocade sofa.

Dom's dark eyes bored into hers, his expression intense. He was a strong man, a passionate man, and fierce emotion tightened his features now. "My mother told you I'd died?" he repeated, his cool, empty voice contrasting sharply with the emotion burning in his eyes.

Diane nodded with difficulty.

"When?" he asked.

"When she came to see me."

"Where was that?"

"New York."

"New York?" he echoed, still studying her with that penetrating, troubling gaze. "Is that—?" He broke off, hesitated, and when he spoke again, his voice was deeper, harsher. "Is that where you were?"

She nodded again. "After the accident. Your

mother made arrangements to have me flown there once I was stabilized. I spent months at the hospital for reconstructive surgeries, and then another year at the hospital's sister facility for rehab."

"You said my mother made the arrangements?"

His voice continued to grow harsher, and she swallowed with difficulty, unnerved by this new harsh Domenico. "Apparently. To be honest, I don't remember the flight or the first surgeries," she answered, forcing a note of calm into her voice. "Or much of the rehab. It's all a blur."

"Apparently," he mocked.

Tears scalded the backs of her eyes and she had to look away, concentrate very hard on the enormous gold-framed oil painting on the far wall. *This* Domenico harbored a beast.

"Perhaps you misunderstood her," he added bitterly.

Her head snapped around to face him. "You think I'd imagine my mother-in-law telling me that my husband and child were dead? You think I'd create grief for the pleasure of it?"

Her voice rose, and she wanted to rise, too. Wanted to march across the room to hit him. Slap him. Shake him. Love him. But her cane was missing, and she wasn't strong enough to get to her feet from the low sofa without it.

"No. But perhaps in translation her explanation, your interpretation..."

His voice drifted off and she hated him then. Hated him and his dark, haunted eyes and his scarred noble face and his wealth and privilege. Because he hadn't died. And he wasn't alone. He'd lived, and he'd been here in the bosom of his beloved family while she'd struggled on her own. But of course they'd taken him back. He wasn't the problem. She was. And she was gone.

Her chin lifted a notch. "I'm fluent in Italian and your mother was fairly fluent in English. I can't imagine how we could misunderstand each other so completely. She did, after all, come and see me. You, on the other hand, did not."

Domenico's expression darkened. "My mother was afraid to fly."

"But not enough to stop her bringing me my settlement." Her lips curved faintly, mockingly, pain making her heart pound and her pulse race. "According to your mother you were in debt at the time you died and unable to leave me anything. Your mother, however, scraped together twenty thousand dollars to help me start my new life, perhaps put a down payment on a condo somewhere. She also promised to pay the bulk of my medical bills. It was the least she could do, she said. It was in your memory. She said you'd want her to do it."

He stared at her, his dark eyes shuttered, his expression inscrutable.

"I don't have my cane, so I'll need my costume staff," she added, with as much dignity as she could muster.

His dark head inclined. "I'll send for it."

"Thank you."

He crossed to the table behind her and pressed a hidden button. Moments later the butler appeared. Domenico relayed his request but the butler had already retrieved it. "I have it here," he said, reaching for the wooden staff propped outside the door. He carried it into the room and presented it to Diane with a bow. "For the Contessa."

The Contessa.

Diane's lower lip trembled. And just like that she was the Contessa again.

Impossible. Improbable. The dead did not come to life. Tragedies did not reverse themselves. Nightmares do not have happy-ever-afters.

Hand shaking, she reached for the staff. "Thank you, Signor d'Franco." Her voice came out low, hoarse.

"You remembered!" the butler exclaimed.

"I remember everything," she said thickly, and the tears she'd been fighting returned. And when the tears wouldn't be held off she covered her face rather than have either man see her cry.

CHAPTER THREE

DOMENICO knew Diane was crying, and he wanted to go to her, comfort her, but he had no words of comfort to give. Couldn't even imagine what would soothe her given the circumstances.

His mother had lied.

It'd been *his* mother who'd done this to them. Lied to both of them. Incredible to think that she'd tell both of them the other had died.

Diane's gone, Domenico. You have to face the facts, understand her injuries were too serious. She won't be coming back.

Only his mother hadn't understood that her news had shattered him. He would have rather died a hundred times over than hurt a hair on Diane's head.

He hadn't wanted to live without her.

And it was his mistake that had killed her. His carelessness, his lack of control.

He'd internalized that lesson all too well. Control

was everything. Life and death. Black and white. Even the briefest loss of control could be fatal.

Now his mother's despicable actions compounded his own.

"I am sorry," he said harshly, not so much angry with her as he was with his mother and himself. They'd hurt Diane terribly. And her pain wasn't over yet. She still didn't know the whole truth.

Didn't know her baby wasn't dead.

Didn't know her baby had survived and been raised by him and members of his family these past five years.

Domenico drew a deep breath, and then another as he imagined breaking the stunning news. Because it would floor her. Crush her. She'd missed the first five years of her son's life, and if she hadn't shown up tonight she might have missed the rest of his life.

Diane should hate him.

He already hated himself.

And helplessly he watched her cry, her small shoulders shaking with silent sobs. His fingers bunched into fists and his stomach rolled. To have her back only to cause her more pain. How was it fair? How could he ever be forgiven?

"I *am* sorry," he repeated. "I've no excuse. And my mother isn't even here to be held accountable for her actions. She died two years ago from cancer."

"How convenient," Diane choked, lifting her i.
to stare up at him. "And cruel."

But his mother hadn't just been cruel. She'd been
diabolical. She'd known she was dying and yet she'd
taken her secret to the grave with her. That made her
sins even worse. She'd never liked Diane, never ap-
proved of her as his wife—not when there were aristocratic Italian women far more suitable—but to tear
them apart when they were the most vulnerable...

Unthinkable.

Unforgivable.

"We need to talk," he said, battling with the black
emotions filling him, darkening his mind. "Allow me
to send for your things so we can change out of these
ridiculous costumes."

"I don't need to change," she answered dully. "I
just want to go. If Signor d'Franco could call a water
taxi for me?"

"You can't leave."

"I won't stay." Her chin jerked up and her eyes,
liquid with tears, blazed up at him. "I'm on a morning flight back to the United States and I need to be
on the plane. I *will* be on that plane."

She'd never been more beautiful, he thought, than
now. Her high, prominent cheekbones. The heart-
shaped face. Those eyes... "We're not finished here,
Diane. There's more I have to tell you—"

"Well, I don't want to hear it. I've heard enough.

You've clearly moved on. I wish you and Valeria—I think that is her name—a long, happy marriage since it was denied us." Determinedly she pushed herself to her feet with the aid of the staff and headed for the door.

Domenico intercepted her before she'd traveled halfway across the room, blocking her path with his powerful body. "It's not that simple, my love. You can't just walk in and walk out and expect everything to be the same. Nothing's the same. You are here. And you are alive. And you are my wife."

"*Was* your wife," she answered fiercely, head tipped back to look at him. "*Was*, as in past tense. Because if you recall there was a funeral. According to Valeria, my ashes are somewhere in your chapel. I'm dead to you and I'd prefer to remain that way."

"I can't let you."

"Why?" she practically shouted. "You've done just fine without me. You're in love and engaged and ready to make another woman your wife—"

His hands clamped down on her shoulders as he dragged her up against him. "You're wrong," he retorted, his deep voice thundering in her head. "I didn't do fine without you. I couldn't live without you." The words were torn from him, and they weren't gentle. They were rough, tortured, like glass scratching metal, because his heart was made of metal. His heart was worth nothing at all. "And maybe I'm not who I was, but there's no way in hell I'm going to let you walk out that door."

Her eyes, still that arresting blue-green, shimmered with liquid. She'd always had the most beautiful eyes. The most beautiful heart. Tender. Loyal. Loving. "You don't have a choice," she whispered, the first tear falling. "Now, let me go."

He stared into her beautiful face, studying the new faint lines at her mesmerizing eyes, the set of her full mouth, wanting to take her in, memorize every detail. He'd never known anyone like Diane when they'd met at the university in Florence. She'd been pursuing an advanced degree in Italian Renaissance Art. He'd been touring the recently restored university library—a restoration made possible through the generosity of the Coducci family, *his* family.

She'd been one of the two docents conducting the tour, and he'd been enchanted by her eyes, the shape of her face, her accent, her passion for Renaissance art. She'd been so real, so fresh, so expressive. He'd never enjoyed a tour quite as much as that one, and had watched her as she'd talked rather than look at the friezes, the arches, the canvases covering the enormous walls. He'd grown up in a palace, surrounded by relics and ruins, and his tastes ran to the modern. New. Bold. Controversial.

Like his apartment in Rome.

Like his choice of her for his bride.

The Coduccis were a rich, ancient, noble line, and Domenico was to have selected a wife from a suitably rich, ancient, noble line. But instead he'd chosen Diane. Diane from Chicago. Diane from a working-class family.

He'd always suspected that his mother would have overlooked Diane's lack of ancestry if she'd been rich. But Diane's sin had been that she was poor.

And thus he'd been cast off, isolated from his family. But Dom hadn't cared. It was his life. His choice.

And now the past was back.

"I can't," he answered, trying to ignore the grief in her eyes and how her knuckles shone whitely where she gripped the staff.

"Why not?"

"The baby—" He broke off, took a deep raw breath. "He didn't die." Domenico's eyes searched hers waiting for the news to register. "He lived. He's alive. He's here—with me."

He'd expected a scream, a cry—something. But she stood utterly still, her enormous eyes locked on his.

"Diane, you're a mother," he pressed on, not understanding why she didn't respond. "The baby didn't die. You have a son."

And then she did the strangest thing.

She laughed.

Laughed. Even as her eyes welled with fresh tears.

But her laugh wasn't a happy laugh. No, it reminded him of ice cracking. Cold. Brittle. Fragile. "I don't believe you. You lie."

Diane tipped her head back and looked into the face of the man she'd loved with all her heart and mind and soul. The man who'd had everything. She'd never understood why he'd wanted her. Needed her. But he'd said he did.

He'd said.

And now he said their baby hadn't died. Their baby was here. Alive.

Alive.

She shivered, shuddered, her blood freezing in her veins. There was no child. Her child had died. Her baby hadn't survived. Domenico's mother couldn't have been so cruel. "I don't want any part of this… deception…play…masquerade…whatever it is. Let me go. I must go."

"Don't be scared. It's going to be okay. We'll make it okay—"

She silenced him with a furious slap across his face, hitting him hard, as hard as she could. She could hear the slap echo shockingly loud in the chamber. Worse, the blow stung her hand, making her palm ache.

Even so she moved to slap him again, but he caught

her hand, trapping it in mid-air so she couldn't. His grip was like iron around the slight bones of her wrist but he didn't hurt her, just held her hand immobile, frustrating her further.

"I hate you." She spat the words at him, unleashing the full weight of her rage and sorrow. "And if what you say is true, I will never, *ever*, forgive you."

For a moment all was silent, his hand still clasped around hers, his eyes boring into her.

She thought she already hated him. He had entered her life in a blaze of glory and then he'd left it just as abruptly, in a blaze of fire. And yet all this time he'd been alive. All this time he'd had their son...

How could she forgive him?

And, more to the point, how could she forgive herself for loving someone who had such power to hurt her? Break her? Because he had. He had five years ago and he'd do it again if she let him.

"Then you will never forgive me," he countered, his fingers sliding down her wrist, making her skin tingle and burn even when his head dropped, blocking the light, and his mouth captured hers.

Diane jerked at the touch of his mouth, her senses splintering as he pulled her body against his. He was warm—so warm and strong. She shouldn't be surprised. His costume had revealed layer upon layer of dense carved muscle but, pressed to the length of him, his power overwhelmed her. He wasn't merely male and virile. He was male and physical, and impossibly sexual.

She stiffened at the pressure of his lips on hers. It wasn't a gentle kiss, nor tender, was punishing more than anything. The barely leashed tension in his body made her aware of just how far things had gone.

He was suffering. Suffering as much as she was. Maybe even more. Ignoring her whimper of protest, he deepened the kiss and then parted her lips, allowing his tongue to ruthlessly claim her mouth. He was, she thought dizzily, possessing her, taking her mouth the way he'd once taken her body.

Fiercely. Thoroughly. Passionately.

And that was when she felt the change in him. The kiss was no longer angry. It was still hot, perhaps even hotter, but it had exploded into something else. Something far more dangerous.

Something like hunger.

Like desire.

Like love.

But, no, he didn't love her anymore, and she didn't love him, but it didn't seem to matter. Not when she shivered in his arms, body aching, humming, throbbing. Yes, he was a beast, this new Domenico, this man with the savaged face, but his lips, his skin, his body stirred her, tormented her, making her want—him, skin, satisfaction.

There'd been no one else since the accident. No

other man in the past five years. No one for her but Domenico. She'd only ever loved Domenico. But he'd moved on...he'd—

She dragged her head back, breaking the kiss. "Take your hands off me," she gritted, heart pounding, blood drumming in her head. *"Now."*

For a long moment he stared down into her eyes, and then took a slow, measured step back. "You might hate me, Diane, but you still want me."

She did want him. She would probably always want him. He was a monster, inside and out, his interior perhaps even more scarred than his exterior. But the warmth of his lips and the touch of his tongue to her sensitive inner lower lip had made her burn, made her inner thighs, that place between her legs, ache.

"Where is my son?"

"He is not here right now—"

"Of course not."

"But he's returning in two days. You'll be reunited with him the moment he's back in Venice."

Her heart still raced, and blood still pounded in her ears. "How can I possibly trust you now?"

"You can trust me. I'm not my mother, not my family. I would never keep your son away from you. Stay. Wait—"

"How?" she cried, thinking that he might have

suffered but he'd had their child, he'd had his family, he'd had their support while she'd had no one. And the loneliness had been crushing. To go from Domenico's arms to the stillness of her new life. It had been such a quiet, hollow life. "How can we do this?"

"How can we not? You're his mother. You're the one he's missed his whole life. You're the one he desperately needs."

She was the one the child desperately needed? She was the one? And yet Domenico had been set to marry Valeria.

Diane drew an unsteady breath, her emotions chaotic, thoughts whirling in a dozen different directions. She put a hand to her temple, where the white wig dug into her forehead.

She'd never met her own child and she would have to wait another two days still. Two days wasn't that long in the big picture, but at the moment it felt like forever.

"Can you not send for him? Two days is too long to have me wait now. There's so much I want to know. So many years I've missed out on. It doesn't seem fair."

"It's not," he agreed bluntly, his expression almost sympathetic. "You should have been there these past five years. He needed you. He needs a mother."

Diane's heart suddenly felt as though it was

being ripped apart. Her son needed a mother. Was Valeria to have been that mother? "I'll stay. Until my son arrives. Then, and only then, we'll discuss the future."

CHAPTER FOUR

SHE stayed. How could she not? More than anything in the world she wanted to see this boy, this child of hers. The child she'd thought she'd lost.

Domenico sent for her things from her small hotel near St. Mark's Square, and then showed her to a suite of rooms which would be hers. Like the rest of the *palazzo*, her suite on the fourth floor had been renovated, and yet here the rooms hadn't simply been redone, but intelligently and sensitively updated. Walls must have come down and smaller rooms joined to create a large, spacious suite. The design was clean, classic, and aesthetically pleasing.

Like the finest, most luxurious five-star hotel room one could imagine. The softest of linens, fat and fluffy feather comforter and pillows, ambiance lighting.

The bathroom was even more opulent. It sparkled and gleamed from the creamy vanilla stone on the floor and the shower enclosure to the custom

cabinetry stained a dark, rich bittersweet chocolate
shade. The massive sunken tub was surrounded by
endless Italian marble. The silver fixtures shone. A
Murano crystal chandelier hung from the high ceiling, and matching glass sconces were set into the
stone of the wall.

It was, in short, simply gorgeous.

Domenico had been watching her face throughout
the tour of the suite. He'd opened doors, turned on
lights, pointed out the switch for a reading light at the
bedside table without a single comment or change of
expression.

But then at last, in the chocolate and cream marble
bathroom, she'd caved, her eyes widening, a hint of
rose in her cheeks as her lips curved in awe and delight. For a moment she was the Diane of old—eyes
bright, expression open. She loved the bathroom, appreciated its beauty, and she turned to him.

"It's—" she started to say, and even her voice was
lighter, buoyant. But then she looked at him, saw him,
took in his scar and his ruined face and she disappeared again. It was like a door being slammed. Her
mobile features froze. Her expression turned blank.
Her eyes shuttered.

Domenico's chest grew tight. His lungs ached and
he realized he was holding his breath, hanging on to
his emotions by a thread.

He'd been wrong. She wasn't an angel. She was a

ghost. A ghost of the woman she once was. And he'd done that to her. Done this to all of them.

"If there's nothing else, I'll leave you here," he said, his voice pitched so low it grated on his own ears. "There's a robe and slippers in the closet. A cashmere throw on the armchair. Make yourself at home. Your things should be arriving in the next half hour."

And then, without waiting for a response, he left her in the bathroom, with its decadent swirl of hot chocolate, marshmallow and cream.

"And your wedding?" Diane demanded thickly, her husky voice following him to the door. "Aren't you getting married soon?"

He stopped in the doorway, turned slowly around. "How can I marry again when I'm still married to you?"

"But you can't be. Your mother—"

"Probably pulled strings to get the death certificate issued. But you're not dead—which means we're still married, because there was no divorce. No annulment. It's something I'd never consider."

"So Valeria—"

"Is my concern." He cut her off before walking out the door.

With her bags and her cane transferred from her hotel to her suite at Ca' Coducci, Diane finally stripped out of her white tulle costume with its snug corset. She peeled off the white hose and the white beaded shoes and, wrapped in the plush robe from the closet, headed into the bathroom to soak in the tub.

She'd told herself she wasn't going to indulge in any of the little extravagances provided in the bathroom—no sea salts or scrubs, no candles, no soft lighting. But just soaking in the tub was luxurious, especially as she so rarely pampered herself.

But then she wasn't here at Ca' Coducci for pleasure, she wearily reminded herself. She wasn't here for Domenico, or to rekindle their relationship. She was here for one reason and one reason only: her child.

Her *son*.

Leaving the bath, Diane changed into pajamas, then wandered up and down the fine Persian carpet covering the marble floor before the pain of walking forced her to take a seat on the edge of her mattress. Sitting on the bed, Diane massaged her throbbing hip, hoping to ease the pain. Her pelvis and hip had been crushed in the accident, and even though the surgeons had rebuilt the hip socket with plates and screws there was still discomfort, and Venice's cold dampness just made it worse.

Still rubbing her hip, she let her thoughts scatter in every direction. The fantastical costumes at the masquerade ball. The candlelit ballroom with its golden shimmering ceiling. The winged lion that was Domenico.

So impossible. So incredible.

And then all the lies.

Domenico had never died. The baby had survived his premature birth. The late Contessa had deliberately kept them apart...

A picture of a small boy flashed before Diane just at thinking of the injustice of it all. A child with dark hair and dark eyes like Dom.

Their baby—their boy—would be almost five. And it hit her suddenly, violently, that she didn't even know her son's name.

Even as she was struggling to digest this newest realization she heard the sound of raised voices from down the hall. It was Valeria and Dom. Only Dom wasn't yelling. His voice was pitched too low to be heard through the door, but Valeria was definitely angry. Very angry. She was shouting at Dom, and then there was a thud and a crash as something fragile smashed into the wall and shattered into pieces.

Diane tensed, waiting for more, but nothing else happened. No sound, no voices, no footsteps. But a few minutes later a knock sounded on her door, and then the door opened.

"I'm sorry you had to hear that," Domenico said. He too had showered and changed from his costume into street clothes. He wore dark pants and a dark shirt, and with his thick hair the color of wet onyx combed back from his face he looked impossibly elegant. Until he turned his head, revealing the scar. The thickened skin puckered across his right cheekbone. Once Domenico's beauty had left her speechless, breathless, aroused. But this Domenico wasn't that man. This one had a face savaged by tragedy. An accident. A fire. A terrible burn.

And just like that she felt the impact of the accident all over again. One moment she was gloriously pregnant and vivaciously alive, riding in Dom's sports car on the way to a New Year's Eve party, and the next she was being airlifted to a hospital in New York.

There had been no goodbyes.

No funerals.

No closure.

It had taken her years to shut the door on him—*them*—and when she had it had nearly broken her. It had been the worst, hardest, most terrible thing she'd ever done.

And so she studied his scarred face, struggling to be as dispassionate as possible. It was an ugly scar. He'd always have it.

"I actually didn't hear much," she confessed. "Just some shouting."

"And the broken figurine?"

Diane grimaced. "Yes, and that. Was it valuable?"

"Of course," he answered dryly.

Her lips quivered and she nearly smiled. His tone had been so droll. A little amused, a little mocking. So much like the old Domenico.

"She's gone," he added. "Permanently. She won't be back."

So he had ended their engagement. Diane shuddered a little, unable to help feeling sorry for Valeria. Valeria had begun the evening as Domenico's fiancée and ended it being cast out on the doorstep.

"Did you love her?" Diane asked.

Domenico looked down at her, dark eyes narrowed, expression unflinching. "No."

"But you were going to marry her."

"It was a practical arrangement, not a love match. She knew it, and she accepted it. And don't look so appalled. Valeria was quite happy with the arrangement. She likes fine things and she enjoyed what my title and success provides."

Diane shivered. "That's so cold."

He shrugged and walked toward the bed. "It's what it is. I am what I am."

Diane tipped her head back to better see his face. "And what is that?"

Standing next to the bed, he reached out and lightly, intently, traced her profile with his fingertip.

His touch was warm, sensual as it caressed down from her brow over her small straight nose, across her lips, to rest at her square chin. "Ruthless."

Air caught in her throat even as fire licked her limbs. Her body clearly remembered him. Her body still wanted him. "You were never ruthless before. You were compassionate. Generous—"

"No."

"Yes. And loving. I'd never met a more loving man in my life."

He flinched as though she'd struck him. "Is there anything else you need tonight? Something to drink? A snack from the kitchen? Just let me know and I'll have it done."

She was going to refuse, and then thought it silly to let pride get in the way. "Do you have any aspirin?"

"Your head hurts?"

"No. It's my leg and hip. They're both really achy tonight. The cold makes the pain worse."

He gazed down at her, expression brooding. "Surgery hasn't helped?"

"I've had so many. But there was so much damage done I'm lucky that I can walk at all."

His jaw hardened as she spoke, his features growing increasingly harsh. "I did this to you."

"No, Domenico, it was an accident—"

"I was careless."

"You looked away from the road only a moment—"

"And it only took a moment, didn't it? I should never have looked away."

"You're human. People make mistakes. I never once blamed you, so you can't blame yourself—" She broke off when she saw that he wasn't even listening. He was waging a war inside his head.

"Dom…" She whispered his name but he didn't appear to hear her, too lost in the dark places of his mind.

Scooting forward on the bed, Diane reached for his hand, captured it in hers. "Domenico. Look at me."

It seemed like forever before he turned his head toward her, but still he wasn't seeing her. He was living and reliving some private hell.

"Dom," she said roughly, pressing his hand to her cheek without even realizing she'd done so. "I don't blame you. I never have. Not once. Not ever. Please. *Please*. Don't do this to yourself. Especially not now—not when you can see I'm here and safe—"

"And injured." His dark eyes bored into hers. "You have pain every day, don't you?"

"I've learned to live with it, and it doesn't hold me back. I've a new job as an art curator. I travel when I can. I have a good life. I'm not complaining. I refuse to. Life's too short. We both know it."

He gave her a jerky nod and carefully extracted his hand from hers. "I'll get you the pain medicine now." And he left quickly, closing the door behind him without a sound.

Domenico went to his own room, stepping over the shattered sixteenth-century marble figurine of St. Mark, the patron saint of Venice, still lying in the hallway. The figure was the one Valeria had thrown not even a half hour ago. It had been his mother's favorite. Ironic that it was the one Valeria should choose to toss at his head.

Not that he didn't deserve it. He hadn't been exactly gentle when he'd ended their engagement tonight.

Summoning one of the maids, he had her take the medicine to Diane. He couldn't do it himself—couldn't look into Diane's eyes and her lovely face… not when it hurt so much.

She was far more beautiful now, in her early thirties, than she'd been at twenty-five when they'd first met. He didn't know if it was age or suffering, but her face had matured, the sweetheart-shape transformed by new curves and planes, hollows and edges. And tonight he'd found himself wanting to explore her face with his fingertips and mouth, wanting to memorize her, know her, possess her again.

But it was too soon. She was afraid of him. He

saw it in her eyes every time she looked at his disfigured face.

He'd have to give her time to accept him the way he was now. Scarred. Ugly.

And yet tonight she'd taken his hand, pressed it to her cheek.

She'd said she didn't blame him. She'd said she'd never blamed him. Not once. Not ever. But how could she not? How could she not look at their ruined lives and blame him? Hate him? He certainly did.

A knock sounded at his door and he opened it to find Diane outside in her pajamas. Her hair had been scraped back into a ponytail, highlighting her strong jaw, wide mouth and square chin. A determined chin.

His mother had once said Diane had a weak face, but his mother had been wrong. There was nothing weak about Diane. She'd been through so much in her life—the death of her mother and brother—and yet she'd never given up. Had never been anything but loving.

"Did you not get the medicine I had sent to you?" he asked, forcing his attention from her mouth to her eyes.

"I did. Thank you." She seemed to be leaning more heavily on her cane now than she had earlier, and faint lines bracketed her mouth, yet her eyes were bright, blazing with emotion and intelligence. "Do you have a photo of him?" she asked. "I have to see him. I can't wait."

Of course she'd want to know more about Adriano. It was only natural she'd be curious…have questions… "I don't. Not here. I wish I did. Unfortunately they're all back at the villa in Rome."

"You don't live here?"

He shook his head. "I haven't been here in years. Not since our honeymoon."

"That long?"

"The *palazzo* has been uninhabitable. The restoration took a full five years. As you're aware, it's only just been reopened."

"And you really can't send for him? Bring him home now?"

"He's happy with his cousins. Adriano loves his cousins—"

"Is that what you named him? Adriano?"

His dark gleaming head inclined. "Yes. After your brother Adrian. It's what we agreed to do."

Diane looked away, bit hard into her lower lip to keep it from quivering. Domenico had honored her wishes. He'd kept his promise even though he hadn't needed to. "Thank you," she said huskily.

"I know how much Adrian meant to you."

She closed her eyes, holding back the emotion. Adrian, her only sibling and the last surviving member of her family, had died at sixteen in a tragic bicycle accident. A car had run a red light, slammed into Adrian as he rode his bike to high school, and that had been the end of him. He'd already been gone by the time officials had notified her of the accident. A school dean had pulled her out of class at the University of Illinois to break the news. Diane had been twenty, and the guardian of her brother for only a year, after their mother had died the year before, due to complications from what was to have been routine outpatient surgery.

It had only ever been the three of them—Diane, Adrian and their mother—and Diane had promised her mother she'd always take care of Adrian.

But she'd failed.

She hadn't taken care of him, hadn't been there when he was hurt, hadn't been there when he died. She'd failed in every way possible.

For a year she'd barely functioned. She'd attended class, studied when she could focus, and completed her undergraduate degree in Renaissance Art. It hadn't been until she'd spent the summer following her graduation in Italy that she'd begun to find herself again.

Italy had slowly healed her, and she in turn had fallen in love with Italy. Deeply. Passionately. She'd loved it all—the language, the history, the architecture, the art, the people themselves. After a year of working in Italy and polishing her Italian she'd applied to graduate school in Florence and had been accepted into the rigorous two-year studies. It had been in the final semester of her final year that she'd met Domenico. And he, of course, had turned her world inside out all over again.

If Adrian hadn't died Diane would have never gone to Italy or met Domenico.

If she hadn't come to the masquerade at Ca' Coducci tonight she would have never known Domenico or her baby existed.

Strange. Fate.

Diane drew a deep breath and forced a tremulous smile. "You don't know how happy you've just made me. Or how grateful I am—"

"Grateful?" Domenico interrupted harshly, forehead furrowing. "Adriano's always been your son— our son. I was never meant to raise him without you. I was never meant to raise him alone. We made him because we wanted to be a family. We wanted to create a family. I hate that he's grown up without you."

He meant it, too, she realized. "And Adriano? He's healthy?" she persisted.

"Beautiful."

Beautiful. Their son was healthy and beautiful.

Thank God.

CHAPTER FIVE

BACK in her room, Diane opened one of her windows overlooking the Grand Canal. The masquerade ball had finally ended and the last of the guests had gone home. It was late, very late now, and the white moon, three-quarters full, gleamed brightly off the water and cast silvery ghost-like reflections of the grand *palazzos* lining the canal on the lagoon's still surface.

Leaning on the thick stone windowsill, Diane watched a lone gondola glide past down below. The night was silent and still except for the soft splash of water and the creak of the gondolier's pole.

How different Venice was in winter. Much of the city was closed. The majority of the *palazzos* were shuttered until Carnival. And yet she preferred this moody, mysterious city to the city that groaned with tourists in summer.

'*La Serenissima Repubblica di Venezia*. The Most Serene Republic of Venice,' she whispered to herself, shivering at the sudden gust of cold air but reluctant to leave her spot. She'd always heard that Venice was known for two things—for being beautiful and for being impossible. And it hadn't been until she'd come with Domenico on her honeymoon that she'd understood what everyone meant. Venice *was* impossibly beautiful.

And tonight, in Venice, she'd entered a fairytale. Like Cinderella, tonight she'd gone to a ball and found her Prince Charming, and everything should end happily ever after at this point.

Only Prince Charming was also fierce and brooding and very intimidating.

Very, she thought, shivering again and finally conceding it was time to close the window and go to bed.

Diane slid beneath the covers, pulled the soft down duvet up to her chin and prayed she'd sleep.

And surprisingly she did. But her sleep was troubled, broken by dark, disturbing dreams.

She dreamed of blinding lights and shattering glass. Dreamed of more lights—red and blue—and of sirens shrieking in the night. She dreamed of antiseptic and sterile rooms. Dreamed of pain. Endless pain. And endless nights alone.

Diane lurched up into a sitting position, heart hammering sickeningly fast.

It was the old dream—the dream where she lost Dom and the baby.

But they weren't gone. Weren't dead. They'd just been stolen. Hidden away…

And, turning on the bedside lamp, she stared across the room to the fire which had nearly burned out, leaving just a few hot coals.

The Contessa had stolen five years of her life. She'd taken Domenico—Diane's only family—from her. She'd exiled Diane, sent her far from Italy and all that Diane had loved.

Why?

Tears stung her eyes and she pressed a knuckle to her mouth, pushing hard against her soft lip until it bruised against her teeth.

How could the late Contessa have knowingly, willingly inflicted so much pain on all of them? Diane knew the Contessa had never felt she was good enough for her son. But the Contessa's actions hadn't just hurt Diane. She'd devastated her own son too—and her grandson.

Why would a mother do it? How could a mother do it? To what end? Diane couldn't imagine ever hurting anyone that way, much less her own son. Not when every maternal instinct longed to cherish. Protect. Because wasn't that what mothers did? Protect?

And then it came to her in a whisper.

The Contessa had been protecting Domenico.

Surely that was what she must have thought she'd been doing? After all, Diane had been very damaged. Diane's doctors hadn't expected her to make a full recovery. They'd predicted she'd never be able to be independent again, would need round-the-clock care, always need assistance.

Perhaps the Contessa had decided she needed to protect Domenico from such a bleak future. From a wife who would be an invalid.

Or perhaps the Contessa had been overwhelmed at the idea of caring for them all. After all, Diane had been in a coma for weeks, and Domenico had been in a burns unit, and the baby... The baby would have been fighting for his life...

So the Contessa had made choices, and she'd chosen her son and his child.

And strangely, though her actions were misguided and hard to forgive, Diane could almost—*almost*— understand. Because if faced with a difficult deci- sion she, too, would want to protect her child. It was instinct.

Beneath the covers Diane lightly touched the Cesarean scar on her belly. She'd always been told that they'd cut her open in the emergency room to save the baby but it had been too late.

Only that was false. The surgeons had saved her son. He'd lived. And, yes, she'd missed his entire life, but he *had* life, and that was the important thing.

Having lost her mother and brother it was such a joy—and relief—to know her son was safe. Her son lived. And she was going to be part of his life.

One way or another, she vowed, turning the light out, she would be part of his life.

And she would protect him. She owed it to him.

Diane was already awake and dressed the next morning when Domenico sent word to her that he'd like her to join him in the morning room for breakfast. Diane wasn't sure she was ready to face Domenico already, but it wasn't as if she had a choice. She was in his house. His guest.

His wife.

No, not his wife. She'd been declared dead. So what did that make her? She didn't know.

Shaking the uncomfortable thought away, Diane headed for the morning room dressed in navy wool pants and a incredibly soft V-neck cashmere sweater. The sweater was warm and it made her feel safe—something she definitely needed as she faced Domenico in the bright light of day.

The morning room had always been one of her favorite rooms. Its high frescoed ceiling was incurably romantic, and the view of the Grand Canal from the four tall windows was simply stunning.

As she entered the room Domenico rose from his chair at the round marble-topped table and pulled out a matching chair for her. A pot of hot coffee steamed on the table next to a plate of warm, fragrant Italian breakfast breads and pastries.

"You look lovely," he said as she took the seat he held for her.

Diane blushed at the compliment, hating how she suddenly felt shy. There was no reason for her to feel shy. She'd been married to Domenico for two years before the accident, and in those two years he'd made love to every inch of her body. There was no reason to be nervous or self-conscious, but her heart was racing and she smoothed her pants to hide her unease.

"I do love navy. I think most of my clothes are navy. Navy is so much more interesting than black."

A hint of amusement shone in his dark eyes. "Really?"

She forced herself to smile, hoping her light, bright chatter would convince him that all was well. "Think about it. Navy can be the color of a midnight sky, or the deepest part of the ocean. It's also found in a pair of sapphire earrings or a pair of well-loved jeans."

He sat down across from her. "I think you're babbling to avoid having a real conversation with me."

Ah, so he knew. Her blush deepened, making her cheeks feel fiery hot. "I'm not babbling."

"No?"

"And I'm not afraid of talking with you."

"Is that so?"

"Yes," she snapped, before glancing away, undone by his dark eyes—eyes that seemed to see too much. Eyes that felt as though they could see all the way through her, reading her thoughts, reading her heart.

"Then why do you avoid looking at me?"

Heavens. He'd noticed that, too. What didn't he see? Curling her nails into her palms, she forced herself to meet his gaze. "It's been five years since we've been together. I'm still getting used to the idea that you're alive. For five years all I wanted was to see you again, and now we're having a meal together. Definitely surreal."

He smiled faintly as he lifted the coffee pot and filled her cup. "Were you able to get any sleep?"

"Some. But I had a lot on my mind." She spooned sugar into her coffee and then stirred it a moment before adding, "I couldn't stop thinking about your mother."

One of his black eyebrows lifted. "Sounds like a nightmare."

She picked up the china cup, blew on it before taking a sip. "There's no excusing her actions, but I think I understand why she did what she did...hiding the truth from us."

"You mean lying to us? Tearing our family apart?"

Diane gulped her coffee before answering. "I think it was to protect you."

The hint of a smile at Domenic's lips was gone. "I didn't need protection from you!"

"The doctors thought I'd be brain-damaged—"

"I can't believe you're making excuses for her. Unbelievable." His laugh was low, bitter, and he studied her broodingly, his long black lashes creating shadows beneath his eyes. "Or maybe I can. That's so you. So quick to forgive. So determined to turn the other cheek."

She hated the bitterness in his voice, hated how harsh he'd become. "I feel better when I turn the other cheek," she answered quietly, seeing yet again the harshness in his features and the resolute set to his shoulders.

He'd always been handsome, athletic and fit, but he exuded power now. Power and strength. Everything about him was tough, intense, primal, as though he could survive anything.

And, from the thick scar on his right cheekbone, he had.

She exhaled slowly, feeling the blood drum through her veins and pound in her head. Her pulse had begun to beat erratically the moment she'd entered the room, and it felt absolutely out of control now.

Domenico leaned forward to stare into her eyes. "You must hate her. I think I do."

Diane sucked her lower lip in, bit down hard. Hate the late Contessa? Maybe. Maybe not. She didn't know. She hadn't processed all her feelings. There was still too much to absorb to have taken it all in. "Maybe she really did think she was helping."

He let out an impatient sound. "*Helping*?" His forehead furrowed and his dark eyes looked almost black. "She took you from me. Sent you to New York and left you there. Alone." He ground his jaw together. "It's a good thing she's gone, because if she were here I'd kill her myself."

"Domenico!"

"It's unforgivable. Inexcusable."

It *was* inexcusable, yes, and Diane remembered all too well her grief and loneliness as she'd battled through rehab, struggling to regain a modicum of independence. But sons shouldn't hate their mothers. She'd never want Adriano to hate her.

"Mothers protect their children, Dom."

"Then that is the worst sin of all. Because it's the man's job to provide for and protect his family. You take that away from a man and he has no purpose, no self-respect. He is nothing."

Was that how Domenico had felt when he'd thought he'd lost her?

Had he lost his self-respect? Had he felt as if he was nothing?

Unsettled, Diane took a pastry from the silver

platter, but couldn't make herself eat it. Instead she pushed it around on her plate with the prongs of her fork. "Can I ask you something?" She looked up at him, nervous.

"Of course."

"Did your mother ever give my engagement ring back to you?"

He shook his head. "No. Why? What happened to it?"

"It was cut off the night of the accident. My fingers were broken and swollen. I guess I put out my hand—" She broke off, shrugged. "I've missed it."

"I'm sorry."

She nodded, bit her lip, fighting emotion. Because of course there *was* emotion. She'd lost Dom, the baby, even her ring. It had been such a terrible loss, and so complete. And it had all been pointless. Dom wasn't dead. She could have been with him. Could have been with her son.

For a moment she couldn't speak, couldn't think, couldn't handle the rage and grief and heartbreak— and then she realized she didn't want to lose one more second of her life to pain. Didn't want one more minute or hour or day given over to sorrow or anger. She'd suffered so much. Not just with losing Dom and the past five years. But before that. With the loss of her mother. The loss of Adrian. Her life had been full of losses, stacked one on top of the other, and they'd bury her, smother her, if she let them.

She wouldn't let them. And she wouldn't be angry. Or bitter. She'd focus on the positives. On the future.

"So what happens now?" she asked, drawing a slow, deliberate breath. "How do we move forward from here?"

Dom regarded her steadily. "You'll live with us. Be my wife. Be Adriano's mother. It'll be an adjustment, but it shouldn't be too difficult. We were once happy. We'll be happy again."

But he didn't look or sound happy. He looked severe and he sounded stern, as if their relationship was all about duty rather than love.

She searched his face for an iota of the tenderness he'd once possessed but found nothing. In place of warmth was steely determination. Instead of humor there was simply resolve. He was a driven man, and it scared her.

He scared her. He was so different. So full of scars and shadows and hollow spaces.

Despite her churning insides, she forced herself to speak calmly. "Can we really pick up where we left off?"

"Why can't we?"

"We're different people now," she said, thinking that *he* was different.

"Then we adjust. We're adults."

Yes, they were adults. But Adriano was a child, and she worried about his emotional stability. He was in for a series of shocks, and shocks were just that. Jolts to the system. "Adriano isn't an adult. And we can't just force this new life on him—"

"You're not his stepmother. You're his mother. You should be with him."

She studied his fierce expression. He wasn't pleased, and it crossed her mind that he was accustomed to getting his way. She wondered if Valeria had ever stood up to him.

"I agree," she said carefully. "But at the same time I don't think moving in with you immediately is the answer," she added, hoping her voice sounded stronger than she felt, because fear lapped at her ankles, licking toward her knees, threatening to consume her. "You were engaged to be married. That relationship only ended last night. And I…I…haven't dated anyone since you—haven't wanted to. But, that said, I'm not ready to just pick up where we left off. I need time. We all do."

"So what do I tell our son? That his mother is alive but she doesn't want to live with him?"

"No! Dom, how can you be so cruel? That's not what I mean and you know it. I just want us to be smart. To take things slow. We have to make sure we're able to give Adriano a safe, secure and *loving* home."

She knew he'd noted the way she'd emphasized *loving*. And for a moment there'd been a flicker of anger in Dom's eyes, but it was gone now. His mask was firmly in place.

"Domenico, please—we have to make sure we protect Adriano from being hurt."

"Why would he be hurt?"

Dom wasn't going to make this easy, was he? Diane searched his dark eyes, hoping to find an ounce of tenderness, empathy. "Because you and I aren't children. You and I have gone through things and we remember those things."

"And what do you remember?" he asked softly, his intense gaze never wavering from her face.

She touched the tip of her tongue to her upper lip, moistening her skin. She was nervous, oh, so nervous. "I remember what we used to be like, and how happy we were," she said huskily. "I remember how much we laughed." Her throat ached. "You always could make me laugh, even when I was angry with you."

"And were you angry with me often?"

"No. Of course not. I adored you."

"And you don't think we can have that again?"

She wanted to be honest. She needed to be honest. But, oh, it was hard when he looked at her with those dark fathomless eyes, and with such unnerving intensity. "Not immediately, no."

"Why not?"

"Because…" She licked her lip, struggled for courage. "Because you don't seem like you laugh much, or even smile. And it makes me think we wouldn't smile much together."

"That's an awfully large assumption."

"You asked," she whispered, hating how he'd put her on the defensive. The old Domenico would never, ever have done that. He had been light and warmth, everything good and kind and lovely. "What do *you* remember, Dom?"

Emotion sparked in his eyes, contradicting the cool, quizzical smile on his lips. "Fire. A car engulfed in flames. And you." His smile faded. "I remember hurling myself into the fire to save you. I didn't realize you'd been thrown free of the car, and I wouldn't leave the car without you."

Her eyes felt gritty. Her heart ached. "Is that what happened?"

"To my face?" he asked, his tone faintly mocking.

"No." *Yes.*

His smile returned slowly, humorlessly. "I'd do it again. I have no regrets."

"It's too awful—"

"Living without you was even more."

"Don't," she begged him, pressing her palms to her eyes, pressing back the image of him in flames. For her. Her, Diane Mayer, who was no one and nothing. Not rich, not famous, not even a true beauty. "I can't stand this. Can't bear to hear how you sacrificed yourself for me—"

"It was no sacrifice. It was the only thing I could do. You are my wife. You have always been everything to me—"

"No, no, *no*. This is exactly what we can't do. We can't go back, live in the past, torture ourselves over a time that's gone and buried. We must start over. Start fresh."

"Impossible."

"No, not if we take our time—which is why I think it's best if I have my own apartment while we get to know each other again. We can date. Take things slow—"

"And what about Adriano? Are you going to *date* him, too? See him just once or twice a week until you're ready to become a full-time mom?"

Two spots of color burned in Diane's cheeks. "You're being deliberately cruel."

"I'm being deliberately practical. We have a five-year-old son who desperately needs a mother and you're telling me that I have to play the doting suitor and court you, woo you, to make us a family again?"

"That's not it! I *want* my child. I need my child—"

"But you don't want me?" he interrupted softly, turning his face away from her to the window.

He was right. He'd nailed it on the head. She didn't want him. Not like this. Not when he was determined to be so hard, so unfeeling.

And yet with his face in profile, the scarred features hidden in the shadows, he looked like the Dom she'd known and loved. But that very same moment he turned his head and fixed his dark eyes on her, and he was the new Domenico. The one who harbored a beast.

Do not be intimidated, she told herself. Do not be afraid. "Adriano deserves a real family," she said, finding her voice. "He deserves real happiness. And the only way he is to know real happiness is if we are to be not just loving parents, but loving partners."

Dom's expression turned mocking. "So you do *want* to love me?"

"I want what I lost. I want love. And, yes, I want you. But not this strange, angry you. I think the kind Domenico is still somewhere inside of you, and I think if we tried we could find him again."

"You're giving me an ultimatum?"

"There's no ultimatum. Just a wish. Hope. Hope that we can find a way to make this work. Because right now it wouldn't work. There's no you and I.

We've changed. God knows, *I've* changed." Her eyes burned, but she wouldn't cry. "Something happened to me in the months and years following the accident. Knowing you'd died. Knowing you could be taken from me like that…. It made me…it made me—"

"Hate?" he supplied softly.

Her gaze jerked up to meet his. Hate him? Never. Ever. But mourn him? Grieve for him? Yes. Oh, yes.

The corner of his mouth curved. "Do you think you were the only one to suffer?" he demanded. "Do you think I let you go without a fight? You were my wife. My *world*. I couldn't accept that God would take you and leave Adriano with me."

His dark eyes glowed at her, and what she saw in their haunted depths stunned her. "I understand," she breathed, finally seeing what she hadn't before. "*You* hate *me*."

"I don't," he denied.

But he did. He hated her for "dying." Hated her for hurting him. Hated her for having that kind of power over him.

Diane drew a quick, ragged breath. If he hated her, what hope was there?

If he hated her, how could they possibly save their marriage?

CHAPTER SIX

DIANE left the table the moment she could, panic weighing on her chest, clawing at her throat.

This new Domenico terrified her. He was cold, so cold, and so deeply, tragically scarred.

It wasn't the burn on his face that bothered her, it was his iron-plated heart.

He didn't feel anymore, did he? It was all about duty. Necessity. Practicality. Nothing, absolutely nothing, about love.

Desperate for fresh air, Diane changed in her room, donning coat and boots, and knotting a soft violet scarf around her neck, before heading out of the *palazzo*. For hours she walked the narrow, damp streets that wound behind Ca' Coducci, her mind as foggy as the mist rising, shrouding the old buildings, turning the lagoon into veils of gray.

For years all she'd wanted was Dom. To have him back. To be with him again. For years she'd dreamed of finding him, loving him, living with him. And now that she had the chance she didn't want it. Didn't want *him*.

The Dom she'd dreamed of wasn't the man she'd left in the *palazzo*. The Dom she'd loved was gentle. Kind.

The Domenico of today was savage. Albeit an elegant savage.

Her forehead creased as she walked, and she balled her hands into fists inside her coat pockets.

Maybe savage was too severe. Perhaps *dangerous* was a better word.

Could she love this new Dom? Could she live with this man?

Picturing his forbidding expression, Diane shivered again.

But Adriano… Adriano deserved both mother and father. He deserved all the happiness in the world.

Thoughts heavy, heart heavier, she climbed a small bridge's five stone steps and, lingering at the top, watched a small motor boat approach and then pass beneath before disappearing into the fog.

Lots of couples raised children without living together. She and Domenico could find a way to share custody. She'd move to Rome, get an apartment not far from Dom's. Adriano would be happy. She'd be sure of that.

And what about Dom? This stranger who was her husband?

He was fierce, distant, sharp, demanding.

And yet somewhere underneath that gruff, impatient exterior had to be the man she'd fallen in love with. The Domenico who'd wooed her and wed her and loved her so dearly. That good, gorgeous, sensual man had to be there somewhere. The challenge, then, was to find him.

Domenico emerged from the library at noon to learn that Diane had gone for a walk earlier that morning but had yet to return.

Glancing out the window, he saw that instead of lifting the morning fog had just grown thicker, and he wondered if she'd perhaps gotten turned around and was lost. Venice was a beautiful and mysterious city, but difficult for visitors to navigate.

He grabbed his coat, and had just finished requesting that his elegant speedboat be brought around when the front door opened and uneven footsteps sounded on the grand staircase. She sounded tired, he thought, going to meet Diane midway.

"Going out?" she asked him, a little out of breath.

"I was just going to look for you."

One of her dark eyebrows arched. "Thought I'd run away?"

"It never crossed my mind," he answered, noting

how the glow of her pink cheeks made her eyes even bluer. "But I did worry you'd gotten lost."

"Oh, I did," she confessed with a grimace. "And I was so flustered that I tripped on a cobblestone and fell. Two elderly women rushed to my side to help me to my feet."

Domenico, who rarely smiled, laughed out loud, the rich sound filling the soaring *palazzo* stairwell. "Your rescuers were elderly women?"

"Very elderly. I was mortified."

Lips still twitching, he reached out and touched a glossy strand of her hair that had come loose from her ponytail. The tendril was cold, a little damp, and he slid his fingers down the silken length. "You must be freezing. You were gone for hours."

"I am a little cold."

"I know just the cure," he answered, drawing her against him to clasp her icy cheeks in the palms of his hands.

He heard her swift intake of breath as he dipped his head to brush her lips with his, and it was like stoking banked embers. His body and senses erupted into flames.

His woman. His beautiful woman. *His.*

He'd die for her. He would. And he'd died without her. He had. Still not able to believe she was really here, he brushed his mouth across her lips again.

It was the lightest of caresses, not even a kiss, but it sent a shudder through him.

She felt unreal and yet fit to him perfectly. His lips brushed her cheek and he breathed her in, savoring the satin texture of her skin and the smell of her, a smell he loved more than anything. It was sweet, spicier than vanilla, floral, musk. It wasn't shampoo or soap but *her*.

Oh, how he had missed her.

Desire torched his veins, consuming him, and he captured her lips to drink her in better. Her soft, lush lips quivered beneath his, stoking the flame even hotter, brighter. He ran a hand down her spine, molding her slim frame to his. She felt perfect. So impossibly right.

And it hit him then that he did feel. She made him feel.

Maybe there was hope. Maybe she could help him find his way back. Home.

Diane was home, and he'd been lost these past five years without her.

"Il mio cuore. La mia vita," he murmured, deepening the kiss. *"My heart. My life."*

She reached up to gently touch his chin, his jaw, and her touch was so soft and light it made him hot, made his body so hard he felt close to exploding. But then her fingers brushed up over his right cheek, fingertips stroking the scar, and he stiffened as if she'd thrown ice water over him.

Abruptly he pushed her away. "Don't," he gritted, a lock of hair falling forward on his brow as he thrust her away. He was rough, knew he was rough, and she let out a cry as he pushed her off-balance.

Swearing, Domenico grabbed for her, righted her. "Don't touch me there." His voice sounded as ugly as he felt. *"Please."*

"Did I hurt you?" she choked.

"I ask that you never touch that side of my face. Understand?"

"Dom—"

"Do you understand?"

He waited for her to nod, and then swiftly descended the staircase to the waiting speedboat.

Diane watched Domenico take the stairs two at a time, as if he couldn't get away from her fast enough, and it made her eyes and throat burn.

And then, instead of just letting him go, she raced down the stairs as fast as she could.

She reached the pavement just as Domenico was steering the boat away.

"You can't treat me that way," she shouted to him, not caring who might be listening. "I won't be bullied."

He didn't hear her. Or he just didn't care. Either way it hurt.

She'd lost him once and had learned to live without him. And just when she was okay again, whole again, he returned to her life—only nothing like before. The old Dom had made her feel safe. Cherished. But this man... He'd take her and break her heart every day and wouldn't even care.

Angry, so angry, she stood there on the pavement, watching the luxury speedboat accelerate and smoothly cut through the water to join the traffic on the Grand Canal.

He's not worth it, she told herself. He's not.

Let him go.

Let him go totally.

The baby didn't know her. The baby didn't need her. Domenico would find another woman to be the missing wife and mother. He certainly didn't need her.

But her thoughts were worse than the boat speeding away. Her thoughts were like a cleaver tearing meat from bone.

She was Adriano's mother. She wouldn't go. She couldn't go. Which meant that she had to make this work. Make this right. If not for her, then for the child who'd never known a mother. And she would be a good mother. She'd be a very good mother.

God help me.

God help me.

God...

And suddenly in the mist she saw the burgundy and gold speedboat make an abrupt turn and head straight toward her.

She shifted her cane between her hands and rubbed her cold pink nose while waiting nervously for the boat. Dom stood tall against the pale mist, his broad shoulders set. He looked angry. And fierce. She trembled on the inside but wouldn't run. Dom was right. She'd never run. Not from him. Love was stronger than that.

Diane held her breath as the sleek boat pulled up alongside the quay, water splashing. The pressure in her chest moved into her throat, and it was hard, so hard, to breathe.

Dom killed the engine and stared up at her, his dark eyes glowing with that strange secret fire.

"You scare me," he said roughly, his dark eyes glowing. "You make me doubt my own sanity. And yet, as difficult as it is to be with you right now, it is a hundred times worse to be without you."

She swallowed hard and blinked back tears. "You were doing a good job of leaving."

"And look how far I got," he answered, extending a hand to her. "Come with me. Please."

She hesitated just a moment before putting her hand into his, leaning her weight onto him as she carefully stepped down into his boat.

* * *

Domenico drove relatively slowly until they passed St. Mark's plaza and hit open water. Then he accelerated, sending the boat flying. He'd barely looked at her since she'd boarded the boat, but Diane didn't press for conversation. It was enough that she was here. Enough that he'd come back for her.

He might not love her, but it seemed he couldn't live without her.

She understood only too well.

They were quickly crossing the lagoon, heading toward the Lido, the slim Venetian island which protected the rest of the lagoon from the open sea.

Away from the city the fog was lifting, and the water glimmered like a pearl beneath the wan sun. Venice in the winter was perhaps even more magical than in the summer, when Diane had been here last on her honeymoon with Domenico.

They'd stayed in Venice for two weeks, with four of those days at one of Dom's friend's villas on the Lido. The eighteenth-century villa fronted the sea and boasted its own private beach, and the villa staff had spoiled them endlessly: pouring champagne, serving exquisite fresh seafood lunches on the terrace, treating them to delicious homemade *gelato* as they sunbathed.

Those four days had been the most extraordinary of Diane's life. They'd been absolutely perfect—lazy, sexy, happy. During the day they'd swum and laughed and kissed and napped, as the nights had been given to lovemaking.

Domenico had loved her so well, too. In his arms, against his body, close to his heart, she'd become beautiful. She'd become who she was meant to be: Diane Mayer Coducci.

"It didn't hurt." Dom finally spoke, breaking the silence.

But he spoke quietly, his deep voice pitched so low she had to listen closely to catch the words over the hum of the motor.

"It doesn't hurt," he added. "Most of the nerve-endings are gone."

The wind was catching at her hair, blowing it around her face, and she pushed a handful back. "Then…why?"

His gaze narrowed on the horizon, where the Lido's buildings and boats were coming into view. "It's not—" He broke off, frowned, shook his head before trying again. "It isn't—" Once again he couldn't finish the sentence.

"Tell me," she pleaded.

He turned his head, glanced at her. His gaze traveled over her face and his expression made her ache. "It's ugly. It makes me uncomfortable for you to touch…it."

It. Him.

Her heart squeezed inside her chest. "A little scar does not change who you are."

"It's not a little scar. I know what it looks like. It takes up a third of my face."

"Well, that's better than half!" she flashed, because there was no way she'd feel sorry for him. He'd burned himself trying to save her. He'd acted bravely, nobly. He'd acted on love.

"You say that now, but I see how you look at me. You can hardly bring yourself to do it, and when you do it's with a shudder of distaste."

"Distaste?" Her voice rose even as she grabbed another handful of hair from her face. "You think it's your scar that makes me uncomfortable? Heavens, no. Your scar is nothing. Just a little bit of skin. It's *you* that scares me. You, Domenico. You. You're harsh and angry and cold. So very cold."

He looked at her, really looked at her, his eyes searching hers. "I'm sorry I disappoint you." But he didn't sound sorry. His tone smacked of arrogance. And pride.

Furious with him, she tipped her head back to stare him in the eye. "You're not sorry. You like being cold. It gives you power and protection."

"Protection from who? Protection from what?"

"Protection from me. From love. From loss. From ever getting hurt again." She held his gaze. "No one can hurt you if you don't let anyone close to you."

"You're talking nonsense."

"I'm not, and you know it." Her voice throbbed with emotion. "What we are discussing right now is the very foundation for our future. Can we survive the accident that nearly killed us? Can we overcome the pain? Can we rise above the fear? It was a terrible, traumatic accident. It devastated both of us. But if we are to give Adriano the life he deserves then we must put it behind us and love, and hope, and trust."

He looked at her for so long that she thought he wasn't going to answer, and then he finally exhaled, a long painful whoosh of air. "Can you do that? Can you love and hope and trust again? After everything?"

She reached out for his hand and lifted it to her lips, where she pressed a kiss to the back. "If you help me."

CHAPTER SEVEN

THEY docked at Alberoni, parking at a boat slip filled in the summer months with luxury sailboats, speedboats and yachts. But the slip was nearly empty now, due to winter.

Domenico lifted her from the boat and onto the dock, and then took her hand as they started walking. Surprised, Diane glanced up into his face.

Domenico caught the look she gave him and wrinkled his brow. "You asked me to try, didn't you?"

He seemed so pained, she thought, which nearly made her smile. "Yes."

"Hope you're a little bit hungry. I thought we'd have lunch here in Alberoni and then head home. Does that sound okay?"

Hand in hand they walked three blocks to a charming but shuttered main street, and then down a quiet side street, and then an even quieter alley, where they ended up at a small restaurant. The restaurant was on the ground floor of a two-story gray stone building. Empty window boxes fronted the picture windows, but lights shone inside. Diane could see a dozen empty tables, with white linen cloths, scattered beneath the rustic iron chandeliers.

"You're sure they're open?" Diane asked as Domenico reached for the brass doorknob.

The green front door opened, and as she crossed the threshold she got a tantalizing whiff of sautéing garlic and white wine.

"Mmmm," she said appreciatively, suddenly very hungry. "Smells so good."

"My favorite restaurant in all of Venice."

Diane peeled off her scarf as she glanced around. "It's just a little place."

"One of those hole-in-the-wall restaurants that only insiders know about—which means during the Film Festival it's impossible to get a table."

She arched her eyebrows as Domenico helped her with her coat. "*You* can't get a table here, either?"

His broad shoulders shrugged carelessly. "Well, I can, yes, but it's not easy for most people."

Her lips twitched. "Must be nice being Conte Coducci."

He gave her a look as the restaurant owner emerged from the kitchen to greet them. The owner—who was also the head chef—greeted Domenico effusively before seating them at a corner table. There was just one other couple in the restaurant, and they sat at a table on the opposite side of the room.

"You still like fish, yes?" Domenico asked as she unfolded her embroidered linen napkin and spread it on her lap.

"Very much. And I haven't really had good seafood since arriving."

As an antipasto Domenico instructed the owner to bring them the restaurant's signature mixed seafood platter and a bottle of white wine. The seafood platter was followed by the house's zuppe di cozze, the classic Venetian dish of mussels cooked in white wine, garlic and parsley. A heavenly saffron and lobster risotto followed, and when Domenico moved to order yet another course—a pasta dish—Diane raised her hands in surrender.

"No, Dom. At least not for me. I couldn't eat another bite even if I tried," she protested, groaning. "But, oh, that was good. So very, very good. I can see why the locals want to keep this place secret. It's phenomenal."

"Coffee, then?" he asked, leaning back in his chair, his gaze skimming her flushed face before resting on her lips.

Diane grew warmer beneath his lazy inspection. "I think I'm happy with the wine," she answered, trying to ignore the frisson of excitement she felt every time he looked at her. When he wanted to be charming he knew how, and all through lunch he'd been the perfect companion—intelligent, interesting, witty, amusing.

Sexy, the thought came, unbidden.

She immediately pushed it away as she didn't want to go there. Didn't want to remember what it felt like to lie beneath Domenico, his strong, warm body against hers, possessing her. Domenico was an amazing lover. Too amazing. And the last thing she needed was sex clouding her thinking.

But it was hard not to think about sex when Dom sat so close to her. Yes, there was a wooden table between them, but it was a very small table, tucked into an intimate alcove, with velvet drapes framing the picture windows. The drapes made her think of a bedroom, and the candle on their table made her think of romance.

Foolishness. That was all it was.

If only Domenico wasn't quite so muscular, or quite so imposing. He filled their alcove, his broad shoulders blocking the light, his long legs stretched out close to hers.

She tensed every time he shifted, his thigh nearly brushing hers, and she'd never been more aware of anyone than she was of Dom right now.

She could smell him—man and soap and just a hint of cologne—and feel his warmth. She was conscious of the shape of his jaw, the light glinting in his dark eyes, even the sardonic tilt of his lips. Everything about him right now seemed sexy. She blamed the wine for the fizzy feeling inside her, but that didn't stop her from responding to him.

Yes, he was sexy.

He was also her husband—but not. Familiar and foreign. Dangerous but desirable.

What would it be like to make love to him after all these years? How would she respond to him? Would it feel comfortable, natural? Or would she be nervous and shy?

Nervous and shy, she thought, gulping a breath as Dom's gaze met hers and he smiled ever so faintly, making her feel as if he could read her thoughts. And well he might. He'd always been able to read her before. She wasn't a game-player, had always been transparent, and Diane wondered if she looked as aroused as she felt.

She prayed she did not.

Because if he kissed her, touched her, wanted her, she didn't think she could resist him.

She'd missed him so much. Missed his body and his warmth and the way he made her feel…beautiful, so beautiful.

Domenico smiled that lazy smile into her eyes. "I don't think, my love, you need more wine."

She felt her warm face grow hotter. So he *could*

still read her. "No?" she answered, trying for a non-chalance she didn't feel.

He gave his head the smallest of shakes. "You are still a lightweight, aren't you?"

He thought she was tipsy. Maybe she was. She certainly did feel more relaxed than she had since arriving in Venice. "I don't drink often, if that's what you're asking."

His lips curved slightly. His dark gaze seemed to caress her face. "Would you mind answering another question?"

His voice sounded deeper, huskier, and she felt that sizzle inside her again. Attraction. Curiosity. Desire.

Desire for Domenico, the lover who had loved her, possessed her, so completely.

He'd known her body.

He'd known her mind.

He'd known her heart.

"And what is that?" she asked, trying to hold his gaze even as her skin felt hot, electric.

"Have you really been with no one else? Has there been no other man in the past five years?"

Suddenly the intimate atmosphere felt charged, even tense, and Diane carried her wine glass to her mouth to wet her lips before answering. "There's been no one else, no."

"In five years?"

She lifted a brow. "Is that so surprising?"

"Five years is a long time."

"I loved you. I didn't want anyone but you."

"You weren't…lonely?"

She sighed impatiently. "Of course I was lonely. I have no family left in America. I had no job. I'd lost contact with my childhood and college friends. And after seven years in Italy I couldn't exactly call up old school chums and say, *Hey, I'm in a wheelchair, at this rehab facility in New York, but I'd love it if you'd stop by and talk to me. Make me feel a little less lonely, a little less crazy.*"

Except for the tightening of his jaw, Domenico's expression didn't change. "Did you feel crazy?"

"Terribly." Diane smiled then, slim shoulders lifting. "But I'm here now. I survived. And I learned something, too. Love is the only thing we have. Love is really all we have."

She could see from the hardening of his features that he didn't agree.

"How can you say that when we both know love can be taken away at any time?" he asked, bitterness tingeing his voice. "Love is temporary, at best."

For a moment she felt a rush of anger. They'd had such a wonderful love story, such a good marriage, and they'd become each other's best friends. How could he become so bitter? So stubborn and blind? She opened her mouth to say that very thing when a little voice whispered in her head—*he doesn't mean it.*

He's hurt.

He's afraid.

And men never like to be afraid.

Like a balloon deflating, all her anger disappeared, leaving her tender. Protective. This was her man. He'd always been her man. She needed to help him find his way back to her. Back to love.

And he could. They could.

Diane looked down at the table, where she'd been rubbing at the starched linen cloth. "I wouldn't have made it through the surgeries and rehab if it hadn't been for you." Her eyes burned and her lips curved, tremulous. "Even though you were gone I still loved you, and I still felt loved by you. I felt *you.* And, yes, I was lonely, but love got me through. I wouldn't have survived if I hadn't believed you'd want me to. I wouldn't be here now if I hadn't heard your voice in my head saying, *Don't give up, Diane. Don't give up. Be strong.*"

Domenico turned his head away, but she could see how he struggled to keep his emotions under control. She was just beginning to understand him again. He was so determined not to feel. He didn't want to feel.

But Domenico—her complex, passionate man— couldn't stay numb, frozen, around her.

"I hurt you," he said roughly.

"No, you saved me. I knew you'd want me to live. I knew you'd tell me to fight. I knew exactly what you'd say. And having your love in my heart and your voice in my head kept me together." She blinked back the tears filling her eyes. "And look—here I am. With you."

She reached up to wipe a tear. "Who would have thought we'd end up at the same party on the same night after all these years? I've never been back to Italy since the accident. This is my first visit. And you said you've never been back to Venice since our honeymoon. Yet for reasons I don't fully understand we both attended the costume ball. I don't know what that is…magic, maybe?"

He stared at her in silence, his intense gaze unblinking. "Not magic," he said roughly. "Destiny."

Destiny.

Destiny.

The word hung between them, and as it shimmered there in mid-air it crossed her mind that perhaps there was a miracle in the making here.

It was almost Christmas after all.

Destiny. Angels. *God.*

"Believe, Dom," she whispered. "Believe in us. Believe in love."

Suddenly he was leaning across the table and cupping the back of her head. And with his fingers threaded in her hair he kissed her gently, so gently, as though she were made of sugar and spun glass. It was the sweetest of kisses. Holy. Redemptive.

A kiss to heal broken hearts.

A kiss to make angels weep.

She loved him. She did. She couldn't be Diane without loving him. And now his lips and breath warmed her, making her feel...

Full. Cherished. Beautiful...

Ah, he was doing it again. Transforming her from ordinary into extraordinary. Transforming her into glorious, gorgeous, exquisite.

Only Domenico had this magic, this gift. How could she ever want any other man? How could she ever love any other man? Domenico was hers...

She parted her lips, giving him access to her tongue, her lips, the inside of her mouth. She wanted him. Wanted him to have her, take her, love her the way he once had. The way only Domenico could.

"I want you," she breathed against his mouth. "Want you to make me yours again—"

"You've always been mine."

"Then show me. Now."

She felt his mouth curve against hers. "Here? In the middle of Marciano's?"

Diane pulled back to look into his eyes. His eyes were dark, nearly black, but he was smiling at her. "They have a W.C."

"My love, it's the wine talking. You don't want to make love next to the toilet."

"We used to sneak off and make love in little closets and corners."

His dark eyes burned hotter, brighter. "You want our first time to be a quickie?"

"After five years I just want to feel you. In me. Against me."

She heard his soft hiss and boldly reached beneath the table to cover his zipper with her hand. He was hard. Very hard. And his erection pressed against her hand.

"Diane," he warned, his black lashes dropping to conceal his eyes as she stroked him with the palm of her hand.

"Don't you want me?"

"So bad I could rip off my skin."

He was no longer distant or detached. And if making love would bring them together, help them connect, then that was what she wanted. "Show me."

"You're tipsy."

"I missed you." She looked into his eyes, holding his gaze. "I missed making love with you."

He stared deeply into her eyes a moment, before rising to walk to the kitchen. He disappeared through the swinging door. He was gone maybe two minutes, but then he returned, and as he emerged into the dining room a door could be heard closing in the back. Dom walked to the front door and turned the deadbolt, locking it.

He moved from window to window, drawing the velvet curtains across the chilly glass until the dining room was cocooned in velvet and candlelight.

"If this is what you want—erotic play—then I can take you here. On this table. In this room. I'll feast on you as if you were my meal."

Oh, God. She'd forgotten how sexual, how sensual Domenico could be, and her stomach flipped and fell in a flurry of frantic butterflies.

"What about Marciano?" she breathed, referring to the restaurant's owner and chef as her heart raced. What had she started here?

"He's gone. Left through the back door, and locked it nice and tight so no one will disturb us." One of Dom's black eyebrows lifted mockingly. "Ah, now you're looking awfully nervous, *il mio amore*. Second thoughts?"

CHAPTER EIGHT

SECOND thoughts? How about third and fourth? But she wanted to reach out to Domenico, to show him how much she cared for him. And so, even though she quaked a little at her boldness, she met his gaze directly.

"No," she answered, telling herself it was only a little fib, because she *had* missed him, and for years she'd dreamed of being in his arms again, making love with him again.

But she gasped as he lifted her from her chair and placed her on the edge of the square table.

His eyes on her face, he slowly parted her knees, pushing her legs open wide. "Sure?" he murmured, watching her response as he ran his hands up the inside of her thighs and then across her hipbones.

Sure? No, not at all. Because this didn't feel like love, it felt like sex. And sex was all very nice, but what she wanted, needed, was Domenico's heart.

Ironically, her body didn't seem to agree, as every

place he touched burned. And every place he didn't touch ached for his attention.

Even though part of her mind was protesting that they weren't at all ready for this, another part of her didn't care. She was so very turned on that it became a battle between logic and passion. And passion appeared to have the winning hand. Five years was a long time to wait for comfort, never mind pleasure.

She was feeling pleasure, too. Her heart, oh, it was warm, and her body was hot, so hot, and getting hotter by the moment as Domenico ran his hands up from her hips over her stomach to cup her breasts.

She shivered against his hands, her nipples tightening, breasts swelling. How could such a light touch make her feel so much in so many different places? Her breasts tingled, nipples excruciatingly sensitive against the friction of his hands, while between her thighs she felt aching, wet.

Reaching out for Domenico, she caught his shirt in her hand, crushing the fabric, and dragged him closer.

His lips brushed her brow, then her nose, and finally across her mouth.

She moaned and arched against him as he pinched one of her tender nipples. She wanted more. Needed more. Where was the relief?

He lightly pinched the other nipple, getting the same response, and she felt positively wanton as she wrapped her legs around his hips, bringing the hard ridge of his erection firmly against the small sensitive spot between her legs.

Domenico reached for the hem of her cashmere sweater and tugged it off over her head, and in the next motion unhooked and disposed of her white cotton bra. He captured her full bare breasts in his hands, kneading, licking and then sucking the taut nipples, one and then the other.

Diane squirmed against him, unable to resist rubbing against his erection through the thin fine wool of his tailored pants.

"Can't we get rid of the rest of the clothes?" she panted, her hands already at work on his belt buckle.

"I think so," he answered, unzipping her navy wool pants and pushing them off her hips and down her legs.

She shuddered as her panties were stripped off next, leaving her naked and very vulnerable on the edge of the dining table. Self-conscious about her own scars, she put a hand on her hip, as if she could hide them.

"What about you?" she asked awkwardly, realizing that Domenico was still fully dressed.

"This is perfect."

"No." She reached for him, grasping his shirt and trying to unbutton it. "Not like this—"

"But you didn't want to wait. You wanted sex."

Diane cringed. *Sex.* How foolish she was. How desperate. Because of course Domenico was right. She'd deliberately tried to seduce him. She was using sex to reach him. Using sex to make him care for her. How pathetic.

"And you look beautiful," he added. "Your waist is so small and your breasts so full. You're exquisite."

His compliments left her cold. She felt cold. And lonely. Her plan had backfired.

"I'm enjoying myself, enjoying your lack of inhibition." He dipped his head, kissed her neck and the hollow behind her ear. "You *are* a different woman, aren't you?"

His mouth was so warm against her skin, but instead of pleasure she felt only pain. This wasn't right. This wasn't how their first time should be.

But he was pushing her back, stretching her out on the table, exploring her body with his hands and then his mouth. She closed her eyes as he kissed the underside of her breast and then down to her belly, and then the scar etched deep on her hip, before pressing a kiss to her inner thigh.

He kissed her again, closer to the apex of her thighs, and then again between her inner lips. His mouth was hot, and she was wet, and she felt intense sensation—but it was all centered between her legs. The rest of her was frozen.

"Diane?" He lifted his head, looked at her questioningly.

He still knew her, she thought. He knew she'd shut down. Gone cold.

Chilled, she sat up, covered her breasts with her arms. His hand still rested on the scar on her thigh, and she glanced down at where his fingers covered the long thin line running parallel to her femur. He hated his scar but was so comfortable with hers.

She jerked her head up, met his eyes, but she could see nothing but herself in the dark reflection. He, too, had shut down. He could have been a stranger in that moment.

Wordlessly she slid out from beneath his hand, carefully stood, and then even more carefully stooped to pick up her cane and gather her discarded clothes.

"Do you need help?" Domenico asked, his voice flat, devoid of all emotion.

"No, I've got it. Thank you."

She was grateful when he turned his back as she struggled to step into the panties, her pants, and then hook her bra. Her hands were shaking as she tried to hook the bra clasp, making the task more difficult.

Domenico silently came to her assistance, hooking the bra for her, his fingers briefly brushing against her back. She bit her lip, fighting the most ridiculous urge to cry.

Even almost dressed she still felt naked. Naked and ashamed.

There was a place for desire, and she and Domenico had always enjoyed a very physical relationship, but it didn't feel right today. It felt empty, carnal. Lust, not love. Maybe with someone else it would be okay, but not with Domenico. He was her husband. Her other half. She needed his heart, not just his body.

He'd disappointed her again.

Domenico was careful to keep his expression neutral as they walked the seawall promenade back towards the slip where they'd left his boat, but his gut churned.

He felt sick. Sick to his stomach. Sick with himself.

He'd tried so hard to please her. It had been her idea to make love at Marciano's, and he'd been surprised by her request but thought perhaps this was the new Diane, a less inhibited Diane, and so he'd tried to show her how beautiful she was and how much he desired her.

But he hadn't satisfied her.

Instead she'd withdrawn. Shut down. And now, as they walked, her cane softly tapping against the pavement, she looked as if she wanted to be anywhere but here, with him.

Domenico's chest hurt, and he grimaced at the

tightness around his ribs. Involuntarily he flashed to
the night he'd gone into cardiac arrest in the hospital's
burn unit. His mother had just given him the news
that Diane hadn't made it.

'Code Blue!' he'd heard someone shout. He'd
known he was dying. He'd wanted to die. It was the
only answer.

Dom's chest squeezed tighter, and he ground his
teeth together as he pictured the pink scars on Diane's
pale hip and thigh. He'd wanted to kiss those scars.
He'd wanted to heal them. Comfort her.

He wished he'd been there for her as she went
through all those surgeries and the months of re-
habilitation. He wished she'd been there for him. It
would have been so much easier to endure his burn
treatment if he'd had her there at his side.

"Adriano is like you," he said abruptly, glancing
down at her, his voice rough with emotion he couldn't
understand, much less control.

She was looking up at him with those stunning
blue-green eyes, and he nearly put a hand to his chest
to ease the pain throbbing there.

"He's smart," he added. "He can read already, and
he's fluent in English and Italian. I made sure of
that." He tried to smile, but his lips wouldn't curve.
He didn't know why. He also didn't know why his
eyes were gritty and his throat felt raw. "His mother,
after all, is American. And a scholar."

Diane took his arm as they walked, held it tight. "Thank you. Thank you for not forgetting me."

He glanced down at her. The top of her head didn't even reach his shoulder. She was so small, and yet so strong. "Couldn't forget you," he answered gruffly, covering her hand with his. "Ever."

In the boat Diane lifted her face to the sky, soaking in as much of the weak winter sunlight as she could. They were heading back to the *palazzo*, but she wasn't ready to return. Even though her right leg ached she wanted to move. Walk. Be outside.

It was nerves, she knew. Nerves and fear and dread all bundled together, giving her this terrible restless energy. Too bad her leg wasn't stronger. She and Domenico could climb the Campanile of San Marco like they had on their honeymoon.

Wistfully she looked to the famous bell tower in the *piazza*. It dominated the city skyline, startling red against the regal white Palace of the Doges and the dark sapphire water.

Venice was even more beautiful than she remembered. When she'd come here on her honeymoon she'd known she'd fallen in love forever. With Domenico, yes, but with Venice, too. She might have been born in a Chicago suburb, but home was Italy.

With her Italian husband and her Italian child. Little Adriano Coducci. She smiled. She'd meet him tomorrow night. And in another four days it would be Christmas.

"Dom?" she said, turning toward him. "It's almost Christmas and there's no tree at the *palazzo*. Nothing's been decorated. We have to get the house ready for Adriano. Children love Christmas."

"Adriano doesn't expect decorations. Most of us in Italy don't do Christmas trees or lights. Our Christmas is very simple. Adriano and I always put up the *presepio*," he said, referring to the traditional nativity scene, "and we have a special feast on Christmas Eve. And then of course on January sixth La Befana comes with gifts if he's been a good boy, but our Christmas is far more simple than yours in America."

Diane's forehead furrowed. "But in Rome you and I always had a tree, and we celebrated with stockings on Christmas morning."

"That was because you were there. We celebrated the holiday your way."

"You didn't like all the packages and decorations?"

He shrugged. "It was for you. It was what you knew."

She waited for him to say something else—perhaps suggest that they get a tree now that she was here, or decorate and make things festive—but he didn't. Instead he stared straight ahead, his attention on the lagoon. They were approaching the entrance to the Grand Canal, and on their right the beautiful domes of the Basilica of San Marco rose from behind the Palace of the Doges, yellow winter light gilding the white domes silver and gold.

"Do you mind if I get a tree?" she asked after a moment. "I'll spend my own money—"

He looked at her over his shoulder, his expression bewilderingly hard. "Is that what you want? Is that what will make you happy? A Christmas tree? Gaudy lights? Cheap decorations?"

Diane flinched. "I just wanted to do something for Adriano. Surprise him—"

"Oh, he'll be surprised when he returns tomorrow night, even without a tree or decorations. He thinks you're dead, Diane. Finding you here, alive, is going to be shock enough."

CHAPTER NINE

DIANE bit down hard into her soft bottom lip to keep from saying something she'd regret. Because right now she was full of anger and resentment and regret. She wished she'd never come to Ca' Coducci for the Christmas fundraiser. She wished she'd never discovered that Domenico lived. But oh, if she hadn't done that, she wouldn't have known about her son.

Adriano.

Who'd be here tomorrow night. In a little over twenty-four hours.

She'd see the boy she'd made with Dom when they'd been so very much in love.

How could she go? Where could she go? This was her family, Dom was her husband, and yet reuniting with him promised only pain.

Domenico parked the speedboat in front of Ca' Coducci. It was a struggle for Diane to climb out unassisted, but, using her cane, she managed to do it without Dom's help. And it was important to do it without his help. She wasn't weak and she wasn't helpless and she wasn't going to let him treat her shabbily either.

Silently they walked into the *palazzo* together, but once inside the grand entry Domenico headed off in the opposite direction without a word to her.

Diane's patience snapped. She wasn't going to be treated like this. Maybe he didn't love her anymore, but he could still give her respect. "What's wrong with you?" she snapped at his departing back. "Why is it necessary for you to be so mean?"

Dom froze in place, his broad back rigid. "Mean?" he drawled, his voice dangerously low as he turned around to look at her. "Let me add that to my list of attributes," he continued, slowly walking back toward her. "You've begun to put quite a list together for me. How does it go? I'm cold, hard, scary and *mean*."

She held her place, chin lifting. "You're being mean right now."

"And you're impossible to please."

"I just want you—"

"The way I used to be?"

Diane notched up her chin another fraction of an inch even as she told herself she could not cry. "Yes."

"Why can't you be happy with me as I am now? I'm not a bad person. I love my son—"

"But I *know* you, Domenico. I know who you were. I knew *how* you were—"

"You're the one who said we can't live in the past. You said we have to move forward. So why can't you start again now, with me as I am?"

Because she knew the old Dom, and she knew how much he'd loved her. She needed that love, too. She needed to be loved. "I want to accept you," she whispered. "I do."

"Then give me—the man standing here—a chance."

"I'm trying to, but the man standing in front of me is short-tempered and rough and hurtful—"

"God help me, Diane, I'm a man. I'm human."

Fire surged through her, licking her heart, reminding her of what they'd had, what she'd lost. Him. Them. Their baby. Everything.

"I know you are."

"Then why can't you see I'm trying my best? I'm trying so hard to give you what you want. What you need."

"All I'm asking for is tenderness. Patience. Love."

"And I'm not giving you that?"

She hesitated, wondering how to answer him.

Because maybe he did think he was. Maybe it had been so long since he'd been warm or gentle with anyone.

"What about at Marciano's?" he demanded. "That was all for you. You wanted to make love—"

"It was sex."

"What?"

"It wasn't making love. It was just sex."

Domenico stared at her for a long moment, and then he gave his head a shake. "I have to go. I can't do this."

"Where are you going?" she asked, panic rushing through her as he turned away and headed back for the door they'd just come through.

"Out. Away."

Terror clawed at her heart, making it impossible to breathe. She lunged forward, grabbing his sleeve. "Why?"

He pulled away. "Because being around you makes me hate myself. I know I caused the accident. I know it's my fault—"

"It's not your fault! It's never been your fault. We're just people, Domenico. Things happen—"

"Yes, they happen. Because I was careless and I let them happen. But I can't change the past. I can only try to fix things now, and I'm trying my best. I am. Only nothing I do is right. Nothing is enough—"

"That's not true."

"It is true. Even at Marciano's I couldn't please you, couldn't give you whatever it is you want—"

"I just want you to love me."

"That was what I was trying to do!"

"You weren't. You were going to *service* me. Your heart wasn't in it."

"How do you know?"

"I can tell."

"How?" he thundered.

"Because I know you!" she practically screamed back.

"Then explain this," he answered, ripping his shirt open with a violent tear, sending buttons popping, flying through the air. He closed the distance between them, his shirt held open by his hands, exposing his wide muscular chest. His wide, muscular chest with its ugly scar at the breastbone. "What do you know of my heart, Diane, hmmm?"

Breath bottled in her lungs, she stared at the scar for a moment before looking up into his eyes. "What happened?"

"I died when they told me you were gone." His dark eyes burned. "My heart stopped. They couldn't get it going again. They brought in the defibrillator. Put the paddles on me. Shocked me again and again. But I wasn't coming back. I wanted to be with you. I wanted to go where you were. But the doctors wouldn't give up. They cracked my ribs, opened me up and massaged my heart." His voice dropped, deepened. "So don't tell me about my heart. Don't tell me I don't feel. Because when it comes to you I feel *everything*."

And then he did leave.

Dom's sister Juliana and her family returned with Adriano a day early. They arrived at the *palazzo* two hours after Domenico left, with Domenico still gone.

Diane was in the sitting room, slowly pacing back and forth before the fire, when the doors opened and Juliana entered the salon with Leo, her tall, blond husband, and three laughing children.

The two older children were blond, a boy and a girl aged close to eight and eleven. The other child was young, with a mop of black hair and a handsome olive face made even more arresting by startling blue-green eyes.

Diane stared at him, stunned. Adriano. And he had her eyes. She hadn't expected that.

She couldn't look away, even as her heart beat harder, faster. He was all Coducci—thick jet-black hair, impossibly long black eyelashes, pure olive skin—except for those eyes. How funny genetics were. How bittersweet. Her brother Adrian had had the same eyes, and now here they were in her son.

Her and Dom's son. She felt a pang. Domenico should be there. Domenico needed to be there.

But Dom hadn't been exaggerating. Adriano was beautiful. Gorgeous.

A lump filled her throat and she had to blink hard, her eyes hot and gritty.

"*Santo Cielo!* Diane?" Juliana exclaimed, clapping a hand over her mouth, her brown eyes wide with shock

"Yes."

Juliana moved towards Diane, hands outstretched. "What… How…?"

"A long story," Domenico answered gruffly from the doorway, glancing from his sister, who was hugging Diane fiercely, to Diane.

Diane didn't know why Domenico hadn't prepared his sister for the shock, but she hugged Juliana back. "It's good to see you," she said. "I've missed you."

"We've missed you!" Juliana cried, as Adriano ran to his father, and threw himself into Domenico's arms.

"Papa! Papa!"

Domenico scooped him up, kissed him on each cheek. "*Comme vanno le cose?* How's my boy?"

"*Buono!* Good. I can ski!"

Domenico grinned and kissed him again, before setting him back on his feet. "Next time you and I can ski."

Juliana gestured toward the door. "We're just going to go and unpack. Settle in. That is if we're still welcome for Christmas?"

"Of course," Dom answered firmly, his hand still resting lightly on Adriano's dark head. "We'll see you at dinner?"

"Yes." Juliana shot Diane a brief, curious glance before herding her family out of the sitting room.

Diane heard the doors quietly close. She looked at Domenico and Adriano. They looked so alike. Definitely father and son.

"How are you, Adriano?" she asked, speaking Italian for her son's benefit.

"Good, thank you," he answered in perfect English.

She blinked in surprise. Her Italian was fluent, her accent flawless. "How did you know I spoke English?"

"You are my angel." He tipped his head, studying her intently. "I have your picture next to my bed."

Domenico cleared his throat. "This is your mother," he said.

"I know," Adriano answered with a hint of impatience. He shook free of his father to approach her, his striking eyes searching her face. "Are you real? Or are you still an angel?"

Diane's eyes stung, and her throat felt thick, but she smiled down at him and extended a hand toward him. "I'm real. You can touch me if you want. Just an ordinary person like you."

Adriano tucked his own hands behind his back, but he looked closely at her outstretched hand before looking up into her face. "Why aren't you an angel?"

She gazed into her son's eyes and struggled to think of an appropriate answer, but nothing came to mind.

"Because God had so many angels," Domenico said after a moment, filling the silence, "and even though your *mamma* was one of God's favorites, I think He knew we needed her more."

Adriano had been very serious, his expression almost grim as he looked from her to his father and back again. But then little by little he began to smile, until his eyes danced. "Because it's Christmas?" he whispered happily.

Diane blinked hard to hold back tears. "Exactly."

She moved toward Adriano at the same time as he came toward her, and, shifting her cane, she carefully crouched down and wrapped her arms around her son. He was warm and small and fit against her perfectly.

My baby. My boy. Finally. After all this time. Who would have thought such a thing was possible?

Destiny, she thought, overcome by joy even as Domenico's word echoed in her head. Destiny. Had to be.

CHAPTER TEN

THE rest of the afternoon was spent with Adriano and Diane, getting acquainted. Domenico stayed with them for the first hour, and Diane glanced at him now and then, wondering what he was thinking, wondering what he was feeling. But before she could ask him anything he slipped away, leaving her and Adriano to spend some time alone.

After Domenico left Adriano wanted to show her his favorite room—the kitchen—where the cook spoiled him with freshly baked biscuits and hot chocolate and whipped cream. Diane shared his snack as they sat at the vast kitchen counter, and then they went to Adriano's bedroom.

They sat facing each other on his small bed as he told her about his toys at home in Rome, his favorite books, and his favorite sport—which of course was football. He did like skiing, but next time he wanted to try snowboarding.

"Do you have an electronic game you like?" she

asked him, entranced by this bright, curious little boy. Domenico was obviously a devoted father. Adriano clearly felt confident and loved.

"I do, but I actually like reading better. You can get better pictures in your head."

Diane smiled down at him. "I think so, too."

He snuggled closer to her then, resting his head on her chest. He sat that way for several minutes, quiet. Diane didn't try to fill the silence. It was nice to just sit with him, be with him, be there for him.

"My birthday's almost here," he said after a moment.

"January first. New Year's Day."

The morning following the accident. She hadn't even been aware that they were delivering him. But she would keep that from him. It wasn't something he ever needed to know.

"You'll be five, won't you?" she said, reaching up to touch his head. His dark hair, so like Dom's, was soft and cool beneath her fingertips. Gently, gently, she stroked the hair back from his brow. "You're so big and smart. I'm very proud of you."

Adriano fell silent again for another moment. When he spoke again his voice was low, uncertain. "Do you think God will let you stay here with us until my birthday?"

How honest. How innocent. He really was just a baby.

Diane briefly closed her eyes against the whip of pain and the lash of emotion. They'd all suffered so much. Too much. "I'm not going anywhere, Adriano," she said huskily. "I've come home. I'm here to stay."

"What if God wants you back?"

Her heart squeezed again. Carefully she ran her hand over his hair, feeling his warmth, cherishing his honesty and innocence. "He will someday, but not for a long, long time."

"How long?" he asked, turning his head to see her face.

"At least seventy years," she answered, wrinkling her nose at him to make him smile. Of course she didn't know how long—but she could hope, couldn't she?

"Seventy years?" He laughed. "That's forever!"

Agreeing, she held out her hand to him, and together they went off in search of his cousins.

And soon it was time to dress for dinner.

Knowing that Adriano was happily playing, Diane slipped off to her room to change. In her suite, she took a quick shower, and then dressed in an elegant black beaded top and a slim-fitting black skirt that skimmed her knees. The skirt was a tad conservative, but the longer hem hid the scar running down her right thigh.

Standing before the mirror, she gave her auburn

hair a good brushing before pulling it into a high ponytail to keep it off her neck. With small diamonds at her ears and a little mascara and lipstick she knew she looked well, and with a deep breath for courage she headed downstairs to join the Coducci family for dinner.

Diane glanced at Domenico as they took their places at the elegant dinner table. They were seated at opposite ends of the table. He at the head, she at the foot, just as they'd always done at dinner parties during their marriage.

He looked impossibly handsome tonight, in a hand-tailored dark suit and one of the crisp white Egyptian cotton dress shirts he'd always favored. His dark hair was slicked back and he wore no tie. Instead he wore his collar open at the throat, giving her a glimpse of his gleaming olive skin. That glimpse of skin reminded her of the scar he'd flashed her earlier, the one above his heart.

She loved him.

It was that simple and that complex. She didn't want to live without him, had never wanted to live without him, and yet now she didn't know how to live with him. But she knew this. She had to try. Couldn't quit. Couldn't accept failure. Not when so many people's happiness was at stake.

She glanced at Adriano, who was laughing at something his cousin Sophia had said, his eyes crinkling with good humor, then back at Domenico, whose eyes had used to crinkle when he laughed, too.

But, ah, there she went again, going to the past, remembering how it had been, comparing Domenico then to the man before her now.

How fair was that?

Not at all.

Domenico suddenly looked down the table at her, his gaze meeting hers over the yellow glow of candle-light. He'd been so distant ever since their fight. She understood why.

She'd hurt him. Even though she hadn't meant to. But she had hurt him and that gave her pain now. He was such an extraordinary man—so brave, so strong—and he'd wanted to please her. Had thought he was pleasing her.

I'm sorry, she mouthed, genuinely contrite.

Dom looked at her, his dark eyes fringed by those dense black lashes, his expression somber. And then, little by little, he smiled, until her breath caught in her throat.

He was still so beautiful. The scar, the burn—it didn't matter. Nothing mattered except that they were together, and they were a family again.

It seemed like forever before dinner ended, and then there was coffee in the sitting room, but finally

Juliana, Leo and the children said goodnight. Adriano
wanted to sleep near his cousins, so Juliana took him
off with her to their rooms on the fourth floor, leaving
Domenico and Diane alone together.

"I thought they'd never go to bed," Domenico said,
walking toward Diane.

There was something in his voice and expression
that made her pulse quicken. "Were you bored?"
she teased breathlessly, feeling that sizzle inside her
again. Attraction. Curiosity. Desire.

Desire for Domenico—the lover who had loved
her, possessed her, so completely.

He'd known her body.

He'd known her mind.

He'd known her heart.

"You and I have a few things to settle between us,"
he said, leaning over her chair, his face just inches
from her own. "Quite a few, as a matter of fact."

She could smell the heady scent of his cologne and
skin, and it made everything inside her turn inside
out. "Such as?" she murmured, trying to hold his
gaze even as her senses swam and her skin felt hot,
electric.

He wasn't touching her, and yet she felt him
anyway, felt his strength, felt his intensity. Despite
all they'd been through, the physical attraction, that
powerful connection, remained. That spark of desire

had been there that first day they'd met at the library, and it still hummed between them now.

"Apparently I can't please you," he continued.

"Now, Dom—"

"But I intend to prove you wrong."

"Not necessary."

"Very necessary. You pricked my male pride."

She laughed softly, blushing. "Considerable, is it?"

"Of course. I am a man."

Her heart beat harder, blood drumming in her veins. "And Italian."

"A noble man."

"Handsome."

He grimaced. "I would have said wealthy."

She smiled up into his eyes, absolutely delighted that he'd play with her. She so loved this side of him. He'd always been both lover and best friend. "And how will we know when you've proved your point? Is there something I'll do...something I'll say?"

"You'll cry surrender."

"Will I?"

His leisurely gaze swept her face, moving from her eyes down to her mouth. "Mmm, you will."

She pressed her knees together, her body so warm she felt as though she was melting. Oh, she wanted him. She'd wanted him earlier, but then she'd got scared. Panicked. Insecurity getting the best of her. What if he didn't love her? What if he couldn't?

But what ridiculous doubts. He'd always loved her. He'd always protected her. No one would ever love her more.

Diane's hand shook as she reached out for him. She wanted him. Wanted him to touch her. But even more she wanted to find him, explore him for herself.

To rediscover the body she'd loved so well.

To learn the new scars.

To cherish the burns.

"Then maybe it's time you proved your point," she murmured, reaching up to run her finger across his lips.

He carried her up the stairs to his suite, the master suite, with its high ceiling and enormous canopy bed. He locked the door behind him and then turned around to face her where she stood in front of the fire, her cane clutched in nerveless fingers.

"Nervous?" he asked, moving toward her.

"A little. But also excited."

"Why are you nervous?"

She felt herself blush. "If I remember correctly, you're very well endowed."

He laughed quietly, his dark eyes gleaming. "That shouldn't scare you. It's supposed to give you pleasure."

Her blush deepened. "It's been a long time."

He began unbuttoning his shirt as he approached. "Yes, five years."

His shirt fell open, revealing that hard chest with the thick plane of muscle and the whittled torso. He was in phenomenal shape, and she flashed to the masquerade party where she'd first seen him in the winged lion costume. His body had dazzled her then, too, and she hadn't even known it was him.

"I didn't see your scar at the party," she said as he slid an arm around her waist.

"Valeria had me cover it up," he answered, dipping his head to kiss the side of her neck. "She thought it detracted from the costume."

"I think it would have added to the effect," she said, sighing helplessly as he kissed her again, setting off every nerve-ending, making her come alive. Oh, how she wanted him. Wanted his hands, his skin, his skill at making her feel. Feel loved.

She blinked, and was surprised to discover that her lashes were wet.

Dom reached out to wipe the tears from beneath her eyes. "Why are you crying?"

"Because I never thought I'd be here, with you, again."

"It's been hard, hasn't it?"

She bit her bottom lip and nodded.

"But it's over now. That was a different life. A different world."

It *had* been a different world, too. A darker world, a harsher world, a world empty of light and warmth and love. "I couldn't go through that again," she whispered. "I can't lose you again—"

"You won't."

"You can't say that. I could lose you. I might. Everyone dies. We're mortal, after all. You and I know that better than anyone—"

He cut her off with a kiss, his cool lips covering hers, silencing her painful words. He kissed her until her head spun and her legs went weak.

Domenico undressed her as he kissed her. He unhooked the beaded top, slid it off her shoulders, and then unzipped the skirt, sending it pooling to her feet. But he stopped there, leaving her in her heels and black lace bra and panties.

"Is this what you want?" he asked, pushing a heavy wave of hair back from her face. "Because I love you too much to have you uncomfortable, or to have you do something you don't want."

"You don't think I want to be with you?" she replied, even as her heart repeated his words—*he loved her too much.*

He loved her.

Of course he loved her. But still…still…

She rose up on tiptoe, holding on to his arms for support, and kissed his chin and then his mouth and then his mouth again. "There's nothing I want more. You own me, Domenico. Heart, mind, body and soul."

She reached for his belt buckle while talking, and unfastened the belt and then unzipped his pants. With his pants falling to his feet, she put her hand on the front of his briefs and freed him from the fabric.

He was indeed large, and she stroked him, delighting in the silken feel of his hard thick shaft and the soft knob at its tip. He had the perfect body, she thought, tightening her palm around the tip and stroking down more firmly than before.

Domenico inhaled sharply as she caressed the length of him, and Diane smiled wickedly, delighting that she could bring him pleasure. Knowing that he was so very hard and very aroused made her hotter, wetter, and she felt her womb clench, empty, aching—aching to be filled by him.

With a muffled oath Dom scooped her into his arms and carried her to the bed, where he peeled her lacy black bra off, and then the matching panties, before stripping off his own briefs.

She watched him as he joined her on the bed, his thick shaft jutting out. He was so very impressive that she couldn't help a shiver of anticipation. Five years without him. Five years of missing him.

Dom caressed the length of her, his palm molding her body, shaping her flat tummy and then up to her full breasts, over the taut rosy peaks, before stroking down again, this time over her hips to the juncture of her thighs.

He dropped his head to kiss her as his palm rested against the dark curls. She closed her eyes as he pressed down through the curls, the heel of his hand rubbing ever so lightly over her clitoris, wakening every nerve.

He was very good at what he did, too. The lighter he touched her, the more she needed him.

"Dom," she protested hoarsely, skin flushed, prickling, her pulse absolutely wild as he used the pad of his fingertip to circle the tiny sensitive bud, teasing, rubbing, pinching until she wanted to scream for relief.

He kissed her deeply, making her head spin, and stroked lower, caressing the slick silken skin before slipping his finger inside her.

She nearly gasped at the pleasure of it. "Make love to me, please," she panted, her thoughts close to splintering as he drew his finger out and then pressed in again, a deep, steady rhythm that had her writhing against his hand.

"Diane, you forget my injured pride," he murmured, kissing her again as buried his finger even deeper inside her. She was hot, wet, and desperate.

Desperate.

"You want me to surrender?" she choked, skin hot, glowing, body on fire. She'd never needed anything as much as Dom on her, in her, filling her, making them one again.

"I think I recall that I said you'd cry surrender," he answered, parting her knees and shifting his weight. He replaced his fingers with his mouth.

Diane whimpered at the feel of his warm wet mouth against her tenderness, and when he ran his tongue over the nub once, twice, she gripped the sheet, put a foot to his shoulder and gritted her teeth against the exquisite sensation which was equal parts pleasure and pain.

"Dom." She was caught up in something powerful, the pressure intense, the tension stretching her senses to breaking. She flexed her bare foot against his warm shoulder, pressing him down, pressing away, but he sucked her into his mouth, sucked her as his tongue stroked, and then she screamed as she came, body arching, bucking helplessly against his mouth.

As she climaxed Domenico sucked gently again, pushing her to that point of blindness and beyond. Diane screamed, "I surrender! I surrender."

He lifted his head, kissed her trembling inner thigh once, twice, before shifting his weight and stretching his legs between hers. "Will it hurt if we—?"

"No. I want you. Need you. Need. You."

Dom entered her in a slow, deep thrust, giving

her a moment to adjust to him before he withdrew to thrust even more deeply.

Eyes open, Diane watched Dom's face as he slowly made love to her in long, deep, steady strokes. His body was heaven. He made her feel like heaven. And she loved watching Dom's expression, his look of concentration. He was savoring every moment, giving himself over to pleasure, sensation, and she felt a wave of protective love.

He was hers.

He was everything she loved. Everything she needed.

"I love you," she whispered, feeling the tension in him. He was beginning to thrust faster, and she sighed at each stroke of his shaft going in, and then out, hitting that spot inside her that made sensation stronger, sweeter.

"I don't want to come without you," he gritted, his skin warm, damp.

She reached up to touch the bunched muscles in his powerful shoulders. "I don't need to come. I just want to watch you."

His features tightened, contorting. "I want you—"

"You have me, and I love you." He was close, so close, and she ran her hands over his shoulders, down his back, savoring his warmth and his muscles and the satiny texture of his firm skin. "You're my miracle, Domenico," she whispered.

And then he thrust deep, hard, harder. Groaning, he tightened his entire body, shuddered, emptying into her.

Spent, he lay down on his side and brought her close against the hard length of him. With his arm wrapped securely around her, one hand over her breast, he kissed her shoulder and then closed his eyes.

Diane knew the moment he drifted off to sleep and drew an unsteady breath, grateful, so grateful, for all her blessings. For the longest time she just lay there in the dark, thinking of all she had. So much. So very, very much...

Which meant it could all be taken away, too.

Diane's blood suddenly ran cold.

Bad things had happened in the past. More bad things could happen in the future. But she couldn't lose Dom again. It would kill her. It would.

And the accident hadn't been Dom's fault anymore than it had been her fault. Things happened in life because that was what life was. Accidents. Illnesses. Births. Deaths. Change.

Change.

But change meant that she could lose Dom again. And Adriano.

She whimpered into the crook of her arm,

overwhelmed by the reality of life. The truth of their mortality.

"*Amore*, my love, what is it?" Domenico asked sleepily, even as he leaned on his elbow to look down at her in the dark. "What's wrong?"

Chilled, frightened, she rolled against him, pressing her damp face against his bare chest. She couldn't stop shivering. It was all very fine to be brave in public—and she'd tried to be brave, tried to be the strong—but she'd been through too much. Hurt too much. Knew too much.

He kissed her cheek, and then, when she turned her face to his, her mouth. His kiss was deep, hungry, passionate, and she kissed him with blind desperation.

"I can't do this," she choked against his mouth, salty from the tears she'd cried.

"And what is that, my love?" he murmured, his thumb stroking her cheek as his lips moved gently to the edge of her mouth and kissed the corner, and then the bow of her upper lip.

"Want you. Need you."

"I think it's too late for that." He kissed the curve of her lower lip and it trembled, so sensitive. "We already know how we much we love each other. Never mind how we feel when making love."

"But I was just learning to live without you. I was learning to be independent. I could sleep through the night without nightmares. I could get through a month without crying. I had a new, prestigious job..."

"And now here I am?" he completed for her.

She nodded. "Yes. And you could break my heart all over again."

"By being cold and hard and cruel?"

She sniffed and wiped away tears. "No. And you're not that cold and hard and cruel. You're just a man."

He laughed softly, amused. "I promise you I won't ever hurt you, not again—"

"You can't say that. There could be another accident. You could have another heart attack."

"Someday, yes, but not today. And probably not tomorrow. Or the day after that."

She lay still for a long time, her face buried against his chest. She loved the smell of him and the feel of him and the steady, reassuring beat of his heart. "All we have is today, isn't it?"

"It's all we ever had. We just didn't know it."

And wasn't that the truth? There were no forevers. No guarantees. All they had was the moment, and they had to live in the moment. If they did that then they would have real love and, just maybe, all the assurances they'd ever need.

"Then you have to do something for me, Domenico," she said softly.

"What is that?"

"You have to stop blaming yourself for the accident. You have to stop hating yourself over something you couldn't control. It makes me too sad. Hurts me too much—"

"But I am responsible—"

"Because you're human. Just as I'm human. People make mistakes, and we have to learn to forgive ourselves for our mistakes or else we'll always suffer. We'll never know happiness. And that's not fair to Adriano and not fair to us. We deserve better, Dom. You and I, we deserve better. We deserve peace after all our pain."

"You make it sound easy," he said roughly.

She slid a hand slowly up his chest, over the ribs and across the plane of hard muscle. She felt the ridge of the scar at his sternum and the steady thud of his heart beneath.

What a good heart he had. A magnificent heart.

"Not easy," she answered. "Because I know what it's like to blame yourself. For years I blamed myself for my brother's death. If only I'd driven him to school that day. If only I'd woken him up before I went to my class he might not have been racing to school. If only I'd arrived at the hospital before he died…" Tears thickened her voice. "I know what it's like to hate yourself, and it's the worst feeling in the world. I hated me, hated my world, until you came along. And you made me smile and you made me hope and you made me love again. And that's what I want for you. Hope. Love. Joy."

He was silent, and gently she continued exploring his chest, caressing up toward the hollow at his throat, over the thick shoulder and then down again, savoring the miracle of him. The gift of life.

"Can you possibly forgive yourself? If you can't do it for you, do it for me. Please?"

He cupped her head, drew her face down to his and kissed her slowly, tenderly, as if she were the most beautiful thing on earth. "I love you," he said against the softness of her mouth. "And I don't want you to cry anymore. I don't want to see you sad. It breaks my heart—"

"Then forgive yourself. And love yourself. Just as I love you."

"Okay."

Her mouth trembled at the corners. "Okay?"

"Yes. I will try."

"Promise?"

"I promise." And then he drew her down into his arms, tucking her against the strength and warmth of his chest. "I love you, Diane. I will always love you. You can count on that."

And, with his assurance repeating in her head, she fell asleep tucked safely in his arms.

* * *

The next few days passed in a flurry of Christmas activity. Domenico built the nativity scene in one of the sitting rooms with the help of the children. The cook worked with Diane and Juliana to plan the seven fish dishes that would be served at the Christmas Eve feast. And Diane spent the afternoon of December twenty-third shopping for gifts for everyone.

That evening, when Domenico and Leo took the children to see the live nativity scene at St. Mark's *piazza*, Diane wrapped her gifts and decorated them with elaborate bows, candies, glass beads and ribbons.

That night she and Dom made love, and then, as they were just about to fall asleep, he surprised her by asking if she was happy.

Sleepily she turned to face him in the dark. "Do you doubt it?" she asked.

"I just want to be sure."

"I am happier than I've ever been."

"Would you marry me again?"

"I thought we were already married."

"But you'd do it again? Even after everything we've been through?"

"In a heartbeat. Right now. This very moment."

She could feel him smile. "We've no priest here, my love."

"Good thing," she teased, snuggling up to him.

"He'd probably find it rather awkward. We *are* both naked."

Dom laughed his husky laugh. "So tomorrow you'd renew your vows?"

"Yes. Of course."

"Okay."

She waited for more, but he said nothing else, and yet it felt as if there was quite something else behind that one little word. *Okay.*

What did okay mean?

"Is there something happening tomorrow I should know about, Dom?"

He kissed the top of her head. "Mmm, a small ceremony. You do have something you could wear, don't you?"

"For a ceremony?"

"A renewal of vows."

"But that's essentially a wedding."

"Mmmm." His kissed her again. "Yes. I suppose it is. Goodnight. Sweet dreams."

CHAPTER ELEVEN

SHE wasn't really a bride. They were just renewing their vows. And yet in her bedroom, as she smoothed her ivory and gold couture gown over her tummy, Diane's butterflies felt out of control.

There was no reason to be nervous. She'd been through this before—had married the same man seven and a half years ago and loved him more today than she'd loved him then. But still, ceremonies were ceremonies and vows were vows, and today would be filled with emotion.

A knock sounded on her door and then the door opened. Domenico. His dark hair had just been cut, cropped close, emphasizing the perfect line of cheekbone and jaw. As he took her in, his lips curved in a slow, appreciative smile. "You get more beautiful every day."

"Thank you for my dress. I've never had anything quite so glamorous before. I feel like a princess."

"Sadly, you're just a *contessa*."

She laughed, and Domenico grinned, his teeth white, dark eyes lit with humor.

This was Domenico, her Domenico, and her stomach did a crazy somersault as he walked toward her.

Reaching her side, he drew a small jeweler's box from inside his tuxedo pocket and snapped it open, to reveal a sparkling marquis-cut diamond set in platinum.

"Your engagement ring," he said, taking her left hand and slipping the ring onto her third finger. "I had it remade, exactly as it was before."

Her eyes burned, but she wouldn't let herself tear up. Juliana had just spent a half-hour doing Diane's make-up, and Diane could not ruin Juliana's efforts. Instead she held her ring up to the light and turned her hand this way and that, transfixed by the stone's radiance.

"It's not exactly as it was before, Dom. It's twice as large and twice as brilliant. Look how it sparkles."

"It's the way it was cut," he said, watching her, not the ring. "The hard cuts reveal the diamond's true beauty." He leaned toward her, kissed her. "Like you," he added huskily, before kissing her again, his lips lingering. Reluctantly he lifted his head and extended his arm to her, supporting her so that she didn't need the cane. "Come, our guests await."

Domenico had told her the ceremony would be

simple. He'd said it would be in the grand salon on the second floor. She'd expected a priest and their family, but was surprised by the magical world that awaited.

Banks of Christmas trees with white fairy lights filled the room, and Diane glanced up at Dom, her dark eyebrows arching. "Christmas trees are such silly things," she teased him.

"Yes, but my wife loves them."

She laughed even as her heart ached. How wonderful and impossible and joyous all this was.

Juliana stepped forward, kissed Diane, and handed her a lush white, gold and green bouquet that complemented Diane's gown perfectly. The lights were dimmed, leaving them in a soft halo of candlelight as a string quartet began playing "The Wedding March."

The ceremony wasn't particularly long, but the vows were sincere and heartfelt. Diane felt Adriano's rapt gaze as she and Dom exchanged rings. Turning her head, she caught sight of him, dressed in a little black tuxedo, one that matched his father's. His blue-green eyes were wide, his expression serious. He knew this was a monumental occasion.

He was, she thought, the heart and soul of the future.

Reaching out, she drew him forward, and held his hand in hers as the priest blessed them. This wasn't just a wedding, a renewal of their marriage vows, this was a homecoming, and Adriano belonged there with them.

When the elegant candlelit ceremony ended the real party began. Dinner was the traditional Christmas Eve feast of fish, as meat was not served in Italy on the night before Christmas. The dishes came one after the other—eels, clams, shrimp, calamari and more. The meal was interrupted again and again with toasts, and it ended late with cake and chocolates and after-dinner drinks.

It was midnight before the children were tucked into bed, and then she and Domenico were in his room, which was now officially *their* room.

A fire was burning in the hearth and the lights had been turned down, as had the covers on the luxurious canopy bed. White roses and lilies scented the room, and a small table sat next to the bed with two crystal flutes and a bottle of champagne chilling in an elaborate silver bucket.

Diane looked at the fire, the flowers, the champagne, and then smiled shyly at Dom. "Well, husband…"

"Well, wife…"

She laughed at his tone, and Dom leaned against one bedpost to study this woman who'd twice promised herself to him.

She was extraordinary. Beyond beautiful. She

was a woman to cherish. "Any regrets?" he asked softly.

"Absolutely none."

"You've made me a happy man. Thank you."

Pink color stained her cheeks and her eyes were bright. "We're lucky."

"Very." And then he moved to sit down on the edge of the bed. He beckoned her. "Come, join me. We must thoroughly consummate this renewal of ours."

Diane blushed. "Thoroughly, is it?" she repeated breathlessly as she walked towards him.

"I'm Italian."

"And male."

"Powerful."

"And very well endowed."

Dark eyes glittering, he proceeded to kiss her, undress her, and make love to her for hours. And hours. After all, there was only one wedding night.

Or two, if you were lucky.

Diane fell asleep to the sound of freezing rain drumming on the roof and pinging against the windows of their bedroom, but the glow of the fire and the heat of Dom's body kept her warm well into the night.

She slept deeply, more content than she'd been in years and years. But later she stirred in Dom's arms and, sitting up, noticed the fire had gone out and the covers had fallen off their bed.

Taking her cane, she slid from the bed to pick the duvet off the floor, and as she did so something caught her eye at the window.

Fat white flakes drifted slowly, lazily, past the tall paned glass.

Snow!

Astonished, Diane crossed to the window and pushed the heavy brocade drape back, exposing the thick Venetian pane of glass.

Dazzling bright snowflakes tumbled from the sky, powdering the banks of the Grand Canal and the bows of the tethered gondolas in shimmering white. More snow piled on the colorful poles.

"Snow," she whispered, touching the chilly glass, as delighted as a child by the wonder of this fairytale water city glittering in snow and ice.

"It doesn't happen often in Venice." Dom's deep voice sounded from bed. "But it's beautiful when it does."

"So beautiful," she breathed, eyes wide, turning to look at him.

"You're beautiful," he answered.

"No—"

"You are. I've never met anyone more beautiful than you."

Her smile grew even as happiness bubbled up

inside her, so big, so warm, so full. "Let's wake up Adriano. He should see the snow."

He curved his lips, amused. "It's four in the morning. Come back to bed. He'll be awake soon enough. Trust me."

"But shouldn't he see this? Shouldn't he see Venice in the snow?"

Dom threw back the covers. "I've a better idea. How about you and I just slip out together? The city will be deserted and we can have our own Christmas morning, just the two of us."

Her heart turned over. He was back. The Domenico she'd always loved. The Domenico who'd loved her better than anyone in the whole world. "Yes. Let's."

Quietly they dressed, and even more quietly snuck from the *palazzo* out onto the banks of the Grand Canal, where they walked towards the Rialto Bridge, and then on toward St. Mark's Square. The world was so silent, so white and serene. It was a dream world. Perfect. Glistening. Pristine.

As they approached the square Diane's cane hit a patch of ice beneath the snow and slipped, throwing her off balance. She would have fallen if Domenico's arm hadn't swiftly wrapped around her and pulled her to his side.

"Good save," Diane whispered breathlessly, tilting her head back to look up into his face.

His dark eyes held hers as he gently reached up

to dust delicate snowflakes from her hair and lashes. "Always. Always when it comes to you."

He sounded so grave, so serious, that it made her heart turn over. Rising up on tiptoe, she touched her mouth to his. His lips were cool and yet his breath was warm, and she clung to him, and their tentative kiss turned fierce and hot and demanding.

Her arms wound round his neck and his hand settled low on her back, molding her slim frame to his. She loved him and needed him more than she'd loved or needed anyone.

"Tell me this isn't a dream," she begged. "Tell me that it's real—"

"It's real."

"And we're together?"

"And very much in love."

Her eyes burned, and her throat ached, and she curled her fingers into a fist against his chest. "Five years, Dom. Five years…"

"I know."

"So how can it be? How did we find each other?"

He gave his head a slight shake and carefully brushed a stray snowflake from her cheek. "I don't know. But I thank my lucky stars."

Lucky stars, she repeated silently, tipping her head back to look up into the sky. Thick clouds obscured the stars, and yet she sent up a prayer. *Thank you, destiny. Thank you, angels. Thank you, God.* This was the most beautiful, miraculous Christmas ever.

Well, almost.

Domenico wrapped her even more securely in his arms and dropped a kiss on the top of her head, then the tip of her nose, before at last finding her lips. "Merry Christmas, my heart."

He was warm, and strong, and real, and he was hers. Hers to cherish forever. "Merry Christmas, my love."

And it was.

Snowbound with the Millionaire

Catherine GEORGE

Catherine George was born in Wales and early on developed a passion for reading which eventually fuelled her compulsion to write. Marriage to an engineer led to nine years in Brazil, but on his later travels the education of her son and daughter kept her in the UK. And instead of constant reading to pass her lonely evenings she began to write the first of her romantic novels. When not writing and reading she loves to cook, listen to opera and browse in antiques shops.

Look out for new novels from Catherine George in Modern™ in 2011.

Dear Reader,

For me Christmas means the joy of having my family around me to celebrate this special day. Hours, sometimes days, of preparation and cooking and gift-wrapping are a labour of love I enjoy every year, my ears glued to the travel news as I worry about the journeys our nearest and dearest must take to join us.

When they arrive we all gather round the festive table, happy to be together to drink toasts and pull Christmas crackers and laugh at the corny jokes in the mottoes as we enjoy roast turkey and herb stuffing and vast quantities of bread sauce (vital ingredient!) followed by much smaller servings of traditional Christmas pudding. And when, at last, no one can eat another thing, we finally get down to the joyous business of handing out presents.

In other words, for me, as for most fortunate people, Christmas means togetherness and family reunion.

In my story, however, the situation is very different. Both my main characters are determined to spend Christmas entirely alone. But fate and stormy weather bring them together to share an unusual, eventful Christmas, followed by a New Year happy with promise for the future.

With warm good wishes to you for Christmas and the New Year,

Catherine

CHAPTER ONE

DOUBTS crept in towards the end of her journey. Her brilliant idea began to feel like such a big fat mistake she was tempted to make a swift U-turn back to Pennington. But a stubborn refusal to admit she was wrong—plus the rain and gale-force wind buffeting the car—sent her off the Christmas-busy motorway at the next exit.

A few winding B-route miles later Georgia's headlights picked up a battered signpost which directed her down a steep, unlit side road. The car bucked like a runaway horse on its potholed descent to an ominously swollen river, but as she crossed the narrow bridge a solitary streetlight gave her a glimpse of a white cottage on a rise up ahead. With a sigh of relief she drove up to it through a layer of surface water seeping from surrounding fields.

Georgia parked the car in a converted outhouse at the back of the cottage, then hauled out her suitcase and dashed across the yard to the back door. After a struggle she got the big iron key into the lock, and fumbled for the light switch as she opened a door which led straight into a kitchen. She took a quick look round, then dived back out into the relentless downpour to unload the car. Breathless and drenched after the final trip, she dumped down a heavy coolbox and locked the kitchen door behind her in triumph. She'd made it!

Teeth chattering, she hung her dripping raincoat on a hook on the back door, and then switched on the heating and filled a kettle. She took a quick look in the small sitting room and finally sat down at the kitchen table with a mug of coffee, to text her safe arrival to her friend and flatmate. Amy Conway thought Georgia was totally crazy to come here for the Christmas holidays, instead of spending them at the Conway family home in Pennington. And right now, alone in a cold strange house, Georgia could see her point.

But as the temperature rose in the small farmhouse-style kitchen Georgia's spirits rose with it. For several reasons—some of them kept secret even from Amy—she had opted for Christmas on her own in peace. The plan was to go to bed early, get up late, and recharge her batteries ready for the coming year. The cottage had a television, and she'd brought her radio for company at night. She had a bag of presents to open on Christmas morning, a supply of food and, most vital of all, a stack of fiction plus a few text-books to get some work done. And on Boxing Day she would get some fresh air on the kind of long walk she never had time for in town.

Georgia heated soup she was almost too tired to eat. Afterwards, yawning widely, she filled a hot water bottle from the kettle and took her bags up the steep staircase. She shook her head in wonder at the thought of her mother and stepfather in this basic little cottage. But their home had sold so rapidly while Georgia was working in Northumbria that the Coopers had been obliged to rent somewhere in a hurry after shipping their belongings to Portugal. When Georgia had returned south to Pennington her mother and stepfather had spent a fortnight with her in the flat she shared with Amy, and then flown off to their new life in the Algarve—to the house that had once been their holiday getaway and would now be their permanent home. But at the very last minute at the airport Rose Cooper, tearful at parting with her daughter, had remembered something left behind in the rented cottage Georgia had never seen.

'It's just a box of sentimental things—photographs and so on—but I'd hate to lose them. You've got the key to hand over to the estate agent, but before you do could you pop down there, darling, and pick the box up for me some time before the lease is up at the end of the year? You can bring it with you when you come over in January for the almond blossom.'

Georgia smiled guiltily as she surveyed her sleeping quarters. Her mother had never intended her to spend more than an hour or two here, especially at this time of year. Nevertheless here she was, switching on lamps, making the bed, and preparing to sleep in a strange room in a house she'd never set foot in before.

It would be a very unusual Christmas. But at least she'd have peace on earth. And by the time she left she might even manage goodwill to all men.

She hung up the few clothes she'd packed for her brief stay, and got ready for bed in a hurry, grateful to curl up with the hot water bottle under a heavy-duty duvet as gusts of wind lashed rain at the window. At least there was one comfort. The scary journey on top of a busy stint at Amy's shop meant she should sleep well tonight.

Georgia slept so well she surfaced slowly the following morning and stretched, savouring the rare luxury of a lie-in. After a hot bath she dressed in a warm shirt, heavy cable sweater, thick cord jeans and fleece-lined boots, and with time to linger for once enjoyed a leisurely breakfast. Later she switched on lamps in the cosy little sitting room, and thought about putting a match to the log fire in the horse-shoe grate. In the end she deferred that as a treat to look forward to later. As she settled down to work she received a text from Amy, which translated as *'late night, mega headache, shop packed, lucky you.'* Georgia grinned. She could just picture the scene in the hip little dress shop as party finery sold like hot cakes. But, having manned the shop alone for a while the previous Sunday, while Amy went Christmas shopping with her boyfriend, Georgia went on working, untroubled by guilt. It would be her first Christmas Eve without a frantic last-minute shopping session: one thing, at least, she was deliriously happy to miss in this weather.

Georgia spent the day with lesson plans and textbooks, and then went upstairs to look for her mother's belongings. Their move to Portugal had been in the pipeline for some time, and would have been made long since except for Rose Cooper's reluctance to leave her daughter behind in the UK. Once Georgia had graduated and her career was underway she had finally convinced her mother that she would be fine, and at last the Coopers had taken the plunge—but only after Paul had put down a generous deposit on a bigger Pennington flat for his stepdaughter. Amy had been delighted to move in as her friend's tenant, and Rose and Paul had finally gone off happy to their new life in Portugal.

Georgia soon gave up on the bedrooms. There was no cardboard box of keepsakes in either, nor in the bathroom. A thorough search downstairs had no success, either. Georgia thrust her hands through her hair, stymied. But she was so hungry by this time she gave up. If the box had been left in the outhouse, the search would have to wait for daylight in the morning.

With a sudden yen for the kind of meal frowned on in the flat, due to Amy's constant dieting, Georgia grilled bacon and tomatoes, fried an egg, made toast, and piled it all on a tray to eat in front of the television. She put a match to the fire, and then sat back to enjoy a carol service from Kings College, Cambridge. Fond though she was of Amy, it was rather restful to have time alone. Guilty at the discovery, she rang her friend to hear that the shop had done record business.

'Due to your brainwave of ten percent Christmas Eve reductions customers braved the rain in droves,' said Amy with satisfaction. 'The Saturday girls worked their little socks off, and Liam is now waiting to wine and dine me before delivering me to the Conway family pile to hang up my stocking. So what's happening with you? Are you all right? Really, I mean? Because if you're not, Georgie, promise me you'll drive straight back here in the morning.'

Georgia stated firmly that she was fine, sent affectionate messages to Amy's family, and rang off before her friend could get started again on the sheer lunacy of spending Christmas alone.

It was later that night, just as Georgia was wondering whether to go to bed early or add another log to the fire, when hammering on the front door, followed by a dog's deep-throated barking, frightened the life out of her.

'Open up!' yelled a man's voice.

Heart thumping, Georgia sucked in a deep, unsteady breath. 'Who—who is it?'

'More to the point who are *you*?' he shouted. 'Open this door!'

Praying that the stout safety chain would hold, Georgia darted into the sitting room to grab the poker. Brandishing her weapon, she opened the door the merest crack, then stared, utterly speechless, at the apparition on the doorstep.

Torch in one hand, the leash of a large, panting dog in the other, Chance Warner loomed tall in sodden caped raincoat and wide-brimmed hat.

'Georgie?' He eyed her in blank amazement through the narrow opening. 'What the devil are *you* doing here?'

Georgia lowered her weapon. 'I could ask the same of you!' She stiffened as the lights flickered.

Her visitor cursed under his breath. 'I was afraid of this. Get your things. You'll have to come up to the house.'

'*Your* house?' He had to be joking! She'd had quite enough of Chance Warner and his family—his brother Toby most of all.

'You certainly can't stay here. Who's with you?'

'No one,' she admitted reluctantly.

'You're here *alone*?' He eyed her suspiciously. 'Why? Though it's a damn good thing you are. I draw the line at a house party. And put that poker down. You're upsetting the dog!' A sudden gust of wind threatened to take the door off its chain, and her visitor lost patience and swung the torch beam over the garden. 'Take a look at that. Now, will you please get a move on?'

Georgia stared in horror at the water covering the lower half of the small lawn. 'Oh my *God*! Will it reach the cottage?'

'It might. So get your gear and let's move. Now!'

'I need to make the fire safe first—'

'Let me in, and I'll do that while you pack. Travel light,' he added as she unhooked the chain. 'The road down below is under water, so it means a hike up over the common to my place.'

The little hall felt crowded with the addition of a tall wet man and a large wet dog. Georgia frowned anxiously as he shut the door behind him. 'Shouldn't we move some furniture or carpets, or something? In case the water does come up this far?'

'No time. Get your things while I make the fire safe. Come *on*, Georgie.'

Her mind in a turmoil, she flew up the stairs, pulled on a long cardigan, tied a scarf round her neck, and stuffed her possessions in her holdall. She raced downstairs to pick up the bag of presents, and hesitated over the rest of her books. When the lights gave another ominous flicker she abandoned them and shot out to join Chance in the kitchen.

'Well done!' He took the holdall from her. 'Can you manage the other bag yourself for now?'

'Of course.' She zipped herself into her scarlet raincoat and fastened the hood tightly over her hair. As an afterthought she found some bin liners under the sink, tied the bag of presents securely inside a couple of them, then got out her keys and slung her handbag over her shoulder.

'I'll turn everything off.' He switched on his torch, then flipped the necessary switches behind the door. When he opened it he directed the torch beam at the path leading up behind the outhouse and let the dog loose. 'Home, Luther!'

Georgia stared in surprise as the dog went loping off. 'Won't someone be worried when he gets back on his own?'

Chance shook his head. 'Nobody home except Ruby, and he'll enjoy the run. He'll shelter in the

stable until we get there. Now, lock that door, Red
Riding Hood. Let's *go*.'

It was no easy task in a howling gale in the dark,
even with his torch trained on the keyhole. Georgia
finally managed it, dropped the key into a pocket,
picked up her bin bag and followed her rescuer across
the yard and up the steep, sodden path, apprehensive
now she was alone in the dark with Chance Warner.
Their sole previous encounter had caused such embarrassing trouble she'd done her best to forget it. Yet
now she was on her way to stay in his house.

And who was Ruby?

'Is my car safe in there?' she shouted at his broad
back.

'Have to be—no way to move it,' he yelled over
his shoulder. 'A gate up the top here opens onto a
narrow path up to the common, but it's very steep
and easy to stray from in the dark. Hook your free
hand in my belt and stay close behind me.'

Wishing passionately she'd never left Pennington,
Georgia had to trot awkwardly to keep up with
Chance's long-legged stride on the steep ascent. After
a while the world was reduced to a howling wet wilderness, with only the beam of the torch spearing
the dark. They climbed at such a punishing pace
the breath was tearing through her chest by the time
the path finally levelled out on to the common and
lights were visible in the distance. Georgia wrenched

her frozen fingers from his belt as Chance came to a halt.

'Civilisation in sight,' he panted, and shone the torch on her face. 'Are you all right, Georgie?'

She nodded dumbly, trying to catch her breath.

'Give me that bag. It's not far now. The going's a bit easier now we've stopped climbing.'

It was marginally easier underfoot, but the relentless wind blew such gusts of sleet in their faces Georgia's teeth began to chatter like castanets. The lights seemed to stay obstinately in the distance, but at last the torch beam picked up a stone wall lining the road, and a pair of tall gates came into view. Chance reached in his pocket and aimed a remote control; the gates swung open to let them through, and then clanged shut behind them as they trudged along a drive lined with trees and what appeared to be genuine old street lamps. Luther raced out to meet them as floodlights lit up the façade of a house so austerely beautiful Georgia made a note to take a good look at it some time when she wasn't drenched and exhausted and in a spin over the drastic change in her Christmas plans.

'Good lad!' said Chance, patting the dog. He turned searching eyes on Georgia as the light fell on her wan face. 'We'll go round the back to the boot room. You'll soon be warm.' He hurried her across a yard and unlocked the door of a huge utility room to a vociferous welcome from a Jack Russell terrier which leapt up, barking in shrill excitement, as Georgia put down her bin bag.

'Good girl, Ruby,' said Chance, patting her as he tossed his hat on a draining board. 'Now, let's get you out of that wet coat, Georgie. You must be frozen.'

'A bit,' she admitted hoarsely. 'That was quite a hike.'

'Sorry to drag you along at such a lick, but I wanted to get you home and dry.' He helped her off with her raincoat and hung it up with his own. 'Did you pack something to put on your feet?'

She nodded and bent to unzip her holdall, but her numb fingers refused to oblige.

'Let me. Are these what you want?' Chance took out the black velvet slippers she'd thrust on top of her clothes, and lifted her on to a countertop to pull off her boots. 'Your feet are like blocks of ice,' he muttered, rubbing them between his hands. 'Though I'm glad to see you go for sensible boots instead of useless things with five-inch heels.'

A good thing she hadn't brought the pair she owned exactly like that, then, thought Georgia, her pulse racing at the touch of his hands, which stilled suddenly as his eyes met hers. She scrambled down in a hurry, forcing a polite smile as she thrust her icy feet into the slippers. 'This is very good of you. I'm grateful.'

'But you wish it wasn't me you had to be grateful to?' he said bluntly, his hands shooting out to grab her as a wave of fatigue hit her so hard she swayed on her feet. 'Steady. You need a hot drink.'

He opened the door into a big kitchen, and let the dogs through to make for their beds alongside a dark blue Aga. Georgia revived enough to take note of creamy yellow cupboards and a central island with interesting cooking hobs as Chance led her across a gleaming floor to one of the chairs surrounding an oak table.

'Sit there to get your breath back. What would you like?'

'Tea would be wonderful,' she said huskily.

Chance raked his fingers through a mane of dense dark hair as he turned away to fill a kettle. 'Incidentally,' he said casually, 'if Toby intends visiting you over Christmas at the cottage you'd better ring him to warn him about the conditions.'

Her mouth tightened. 'No chance of that. I haven't seen him since just after his birthday.' Though it wasn't for want of trying on Toby Warner's part. He'd kept after her so relentlessly he was beginning to frighten her.

Chance turned, but his face, harder and more controlled than his brother's, gave no clue to his re-action. 'So who *is* spending the day with you?' he demanded.

'No one. I had a yen for peace and quiet on my own this year.' She smiled sardonically. '*Not* one of my better ideas. I should have kept to the original plan and stayed in Pennington with my friend's family.'

'Why aren't you in Portugal with your own family?'

'Not enough time off.' Georgia frowned. 'How do you know about that?'

Chance poured boiling water into a teapot. 'I met your parents when they stayed here. Ridge Cottage is part of this estate. You obviously didn't know that or you wouldn't have set foot in the place.' He looked her in the eye as he set a tea-tray in front of her. 'Right, let's get this out of the way. I'll apologise again for the infamous kiss just one more time, plus the fuss Toby made afterwards, but I'm damned if I'm going to keep on apologising.'

Her eyes flashed coldly. 'I'm not asking you to.'

'Good. Would you like something to eat with that?'

'No thank you.' She picked up the teapot. 'Are you having tea?'

He nodded. 'But I'll have a shot of Scotch in mine for a nightcap. How about you?'

The mere mention of the word *nightcap* brought the realities of her situation home to Georgia in a rush. While they'd been hurrying away from the cottage her sole thought had been escape. But now, about to spend the night in this big, beautiful house, alone with its dangerously attractive owner, she thought it might have been wiser to take her chances at the cottage.

'No whisky for me, thanks.' She smiled politely. 'Great kitchen. When did you move into the house?'

'A few years ago. Toby never mentioned it?'

'Oh, yes, he mentioned it often enough.' She eyed him steadily. 'Your brother resents your success.'

'I know—though to be accurate he's my half-brother. The resemblance comes from our paternal genes. His mother married my father when I was ten,' he added without inflection.

'Was that difficult for you?'

He nodded. 'Toby's arrival soon afterwards was the final straw. I was glad to go away to school.'

Georgia felt a pang of sympathy. 'Were you unhappy there, too?'

'No. I was big for my age, and good at sport, so I settled in fairly quickly.' He shrugged. 'It was better than trying to play happy families at home.'

'Toby mentioned a teacher who had a big influence on you.'

'He told you quite a lot about me!'

Her eyes flashed. 'After he'd surprised us *in flagrante*, he never stopped.'

Chance smiled crookedly. 'Hardly *flagrante*, ravishing though that sounds. When a beautiful woman kisses a man, the result is pretty inevitable, Georgie.'

'You know perfectly well that I mistook you for Toby,' she retorted hotly. 'I wasn't wearing my contacts, and a casual birthday peck on the cheek went horribly wrong.'

'Not for me. It felt like *my* birthday.' He shot her a look from thickly fringed eyes a darker shade of blue than his brother's. 'I reacted as any man with a pulse would have done and kissed your mouth.'

Georgia coloured hotly at the thought of those brief heated moments before Toby had burst in on them, hysterical with rage. 'The conservatory was dimly lit, and I thought Toby was just lurking there to surprise me—' She halted.

'Go on,' he prompted.

'He was an acquaintance more than a boyfriend, and he'd never kissed me at all—let alone like that.' Her eyes kindled. 'Only it wasn't him, it was you.'

'Guilty as charged. At what point did you realise it wasn't Toby?'

'I knew almost at once,' she admitted reluctantly.

'Yet you didn't push me away?' Chance gave her a look that set her teeth on edge.

'I soon wished I had!'

He smiled. 'Other than the ensuing row, and any distress it caused *you*, I look back on the episode with enormous pleasure—up to the point where Toby barged in and spoiled everything.'

'You needn't have hit him so hard!'

'I should have stood there and let him use me as a punch bag?'

'No. But breaking one of his teeth was a bit over the top.'

'Total accident.' He shrugged. 'You heard me offer to pay for the dental work.'

Georgia nodded glumly. 'It went down about as well as my attempt to explain my mistake. Toby was complaining too loudly about the nosebleed you gave him to listen to either of us.'

'He planted one on me, too,' Chance reminded her. 'I wanted to offer you support of any kind you would accept, but I did the decent thing and went off to have a drink with my father so you could kiss Toby better.'

She shot him a dark look. 'I hadn't the least desire to kiss him better. He actually had the gall to accuse me of dumping him to hit on the brother with money.'

'Something he took pleasure in repeating to me whenever possible,' Chance said without expression.

'Did he?' said Georgia indifferently. 'He said it

just once to me, but that was enough. I made my apologies to your stepmother and went home.'

'To my intense disappointment. When I came back with my father you'd gone, and Toby was still ranting.'

Georgia smiled coolly. 'I gather women have preferred you and your money to him before.'

'Only in Toby's imagination—which is why I keep well away from family gatherings. That night I turned up solely because my father asked me to.' He smiled sardonically. 'Elaine was so furious that I'd hurt her baby boy she ordered me out of her house for good.'

Georgia winced. 'You should have explained that it was my fault!'

He shook his head. 'The fault was mine, Georgie. Besides, my father reminded the lovely Elaine that actually it was *his* house and he wanted me to stay. At which point I gave him a grateful hug, handed over Toby's birthday card—with enclosed cheque—and gave Dad a break by taking myself off.' He met her eyes. 'And caught up with you in the lane, trying to start your car.'

She looked away. 'I was lucky you were able to get it going for me.'

'Even though I demanded a reward?'

Georgia swallowed at the memory of the second kiss, that had left her breathless and shaken as she drove away. 'Did Toby return the cheque, torn into dramatic pieces?' she asked, determinedly casual.

'Did he hell!' Chance exclaimed. 'He cashed it right away in case I cancelled it.'

She eyed him curiously. 'Would you have done that?'

'Certainly not! Toby's opinion of me, unfortunately, tends to be coloured by his mother's.'

'Have you seen your father since?'

He nodded. 'He visits me here pretty often. Dad and I have long since smoothed over the rough patches in our relationship. The worst of them was after I dropped out of college to develop my computer games.' His mouth twisted. 'He found that hard to understand.'

'Toby took much pleasure in telling me about that. He talked about you so much I almost felt I knew you. But he never mentioned the striking resemblance.' She considered him objectively. 'Though actually it's far less striking than I thought.'

'You mean I'm not as pretty as Toby?'

No one, thought Georgia, could ever think of a man like Chance Warner as *pretty*. 'No, you're not,' she assured him.

'Thank the Lord for that,' he said piously. 'Right. I'm a bit peckish after our hike. Let's have a sandwich. What would you like? Due to Christmas I'm stocked up with most things.'

'Whatever's easiest.' She got up. 'I can do it.'

'Not tonight.' He pushed her back gently. 'Just sit there.'

Georgia looked on as Chance sliced bread and ham with speed and dexterity. He was obviously very much at home in his vast, beautiful kitchen. The spotlights above the central island highlighted his bone structure with a clarity that made it extraordinary, now she had time for a closer look, that she'd ever mistaken him for his younger brother. His features were harder and more defined, with knife-edge cheekbones, a slight notch at the bridge of his nose, and a strength to the set of his mouth and jaw that Toby would never achieve. And the grace and muscularity of his tall body made it obvious he was used to physical activity of some kind. But most disturbing of all, when he looked up and found her watching him, the chemistry was still there between them, in full working order right here in his kitchen.

'You're very quiet,' he observed.

She looked away. 'I was just wondering why you're here. Toby told me you always go skiing at Christmas.'

'I was going to St Moritz this year with a party of friends, as usual, but I went down with the damned flu and had to cancel.'

'Are you spending Christmas Day with your family tomorrow instead?'

'No. Dad had lunch with me here yesterday instead.' The striking blue eyes hardened. 'I'm still cast out of Eden as far as my stepmother is concerned. Besides, I much prefer a peaceful day at home with Luther and Ruby.'

'Unaware that you'd be put to all this trouble.'

He shrugged. 'A few sandwiches are no trouble, Georgie, and there are empty bedrooms upstairs.'

'Surely you don't run a house of this size on your own?'

He shook his head. 'My excellent Mrs Dawson worked for the previous owner and, thank God, agreed to stay on with me. She cooked a fantastic meal for Dad and me yesterday: turkey with all the trimmings. Then her husband Ted drove her off to stay with their daughter and grandchildren until after New Year.' He sat down facing Georgia, and pushed the sandwich platter towards her. 'Odd thing about tonight—I don't usually walk the dogs that late, I just let them out in the garden, but Luther objected so strongly to coming back in I locked Ruby inside and took Luther on reconnaissance to see what was spooking him. And spotted lights down in Ridge Cottage, which should have been dark. The river had broken its banks and appeared to be rising fast, so we splashed up to the cottage to bang on the door.'

'And scared the living daylights out of me!'

He smiled. 'Sorry, Georgie. I didn't know it was a lone girl in there.'

She eyed him curiously. 'What would you have done if it had been a couple of heavyweight squatters?'

'Rung the police, and in the meantime hopefully sent the intruders packing with Luther's help. He's pretty effective as a bodyguard.'

'Tell me about it! That bark of his is blood-curdling.' Georgia smiled as the dog raised his head. 'But you're very handsome,' she assured him. 'What is he, exactly?'

'A Schnauzer.'

'But I thought they were smallish dogs!'

'Some are, but Luther is the full-size variety and, in spite of the blood-curdling bark, a gentle soul, though fiercely protective. It would take a brave man to lay hands on me in his company.'

'One look at him would be enough! I love dogs, but he certainly frightened me. I suppose it's because he's so big and solid—and black.' She laughed as Ruby got up to trot over, wagging her tail hopefully.

Chance waved her away. 'Now, then, no begging—back to your bed.'

'Poor Ruby!' Georgia took another sandwich, chuckling as the little dog obeyed her master reluctantly, one paw at a time. 'This is delicious ham.'

'Mrs Dawson roasted that, too. Before she left on

holiday she made sure the refrigerator was crammed with food.' Chance touched a hand to hers. 'It won't be the conventional Christmas dinner, Georgie, but we won't starve.'

She tensed as the fleeting touch sent trickles of fire skittering down her spine, and smiled brightly to cover it. 'This is *so* embarrassing. You obviously wanted peace and quiet over Christmas as much as I did, and now you're stuck with me.'

His eyes locked on hers. 'And you're stuck with me. So we'll just have to make the best of it. Have another sandwich.'

She shook her head. 'No, thanks, but I'd love more tea.'

'Georgie, you may have anything in my power to provide.' A statement which raised her body heat another notch.

'Why do you call me that?' she asked, getting a grip. 'Toby doesn't.'

'That's how your father refers to you.'

'Actually, Paul's my stepfather.'

'Then it's obviously a good relationship.'

'It is. I would try to be fond of anyone who makes my mother so happy, but with Paul I don't have to.' She shivered as a gust of wind blew great splotches of sleet against the windows. 'Do you ever get flooded here?'

'Ridgeway is pretty high up—right above the snow

line. So if *I* get flooded the surrounding countryside is in deep trouble!' Chance smiled as a sudden yawn engulfed her. 'You're exhausted, Georgie. I'll show you where to sleep.' He picked up her bag and went ahead of her to open the door into a long hallway. 'Dining room first right,' he informed her, 'my study on the left, cloakroom next, then the drawing room farther on beyond the staircase—but you can see those tomorrow.'

Georgia trailed wearily up the stairs after her host to a square galleried landing. He opened one of the doors leading off it, switched on lights, and ushered her into a pastel-painted room with satinwood furniture.

'The room had been newly decorated like this when I bought the place,' Chance informed her. 'It seemed so much in keeping with the house that I bought the furniture from the owner. Your bathroom is through the door in the corner. Sleep well.' He trailed a finger down her cheek.

She stiffened and backed away. 'Thank you for all your help,' she said frostily. 'Goodnight.'

The warmth in his eyes extinguished abruptly. 'A gesture of friendship only, Georgia,' he drawled. 'The rescue service came free.' He gave her a mocking bow and walked out, closing the door very deliberately behind him.

CHAPTER TWO

GEORGIA could have kicked herself. Chance had probably meant nothing by such a casual caress. Nevertheless the fallout from their brief, heated encounter on Toby's birthday was still right there between them, like the proverbial elephant in the room. She heaved in a deep, unsteady breath. No man had ever affected her in this way before. And since the man in question was Chance Warner, with all the baggage that came with him as Toby's brother, she would keep a tight rein on her inconvenient hormones. She bit her lip in frustration. Christmas Day would be awkward now, after her stupid shrinking violet act.

After the marathon hike from the cottage a long soak in hot water was a temptation too hard to resist. Georgia used some of her own bath oil, and lay back in the aromatic steam, resolved to be the perfect guest tomorrow. But soon her eyes grew so heavy that rather than nod off and risk a mouthful of bathwater she got on with washing her hair, and went out into the bedroom to find her hairdryer.

When she finally climbed into the inviting bed Georgia fell asleep almost at once, and woke to bright daylight and the unfamiliar ringtone of her new phone. Guilty when she saw it was her mother calling, to wish her Happy Christmas, Georgia thanked her for the presents she hadn't opened yet, and assured her anxious parent that she was fine. Then, after a chat about the Coopers' plans for the day, she sent Paul her love and disconnected, brushing a stray tear away as she crossed the room to open the curtains.

Her eyebrows shot up. No wonder the light was so bright. The gardens lay under a blanket of snow. She dressed quickly in tailored wool trousers and a newish sweater, the best she could come up with for the occasion, and sent a Christmas text to Amy. Then she paused for a moment outside her room, not sure what was expected of the perfect guest. With a glance at the closed doors on the gallery she went down to the kitchen—to receive a joyous vocal welcome from the little white terrier.

'Hi there, Ruby, Merry Christmas,' said Georgia, patting her. 'Do you think anyone would mind if I made some tea?'

Since Ruby obviously thought this would be fine,

Georgia made for the kettle and found a note propped against it.

Georgie, I've taken Luther for a tramp in the snow. Back soon. Help yourself.

Relieved to see she was 'Georgie' again, and that the table was laid for two, she filled the kettle, found a mug, and took her tea over to the window with a wagging Ruby following at her heels.

Ridgeway's gardens appeared to be on several different levels, and beautiful in a slightly untamed way she liked a lot. Georgia bent to fondle Ruby's head as she looked round the kitchen, which was an inviting place in the morning light—very different from her narrow galley at the flat. Her job took her away a lot, sometimes for months at a time, but with Amy's fervent blessing she did all the cooking when she was home. She sighed enviously. She could be really creative in a kitchen like this.

Suddenly Ruby raced, barking, towards the door of the boot room, and Georgia hurried to open it for her as Chance came in from the garden with Luther on his heels.

He kicked off his boots and gave her a friendly smile. 'Merry Christmas, Georgie. Hello, Ruby!'

'Merry Christmas, Chance.' She returned the

smile in kind and patted Luther's damp head. 'Sorry I slept late.'

'I'm glad you got some rest.' He shrugged out of a bulky down jacket. 'I have to be up early to see to the dogs. Ruby's legs are too short to let her enjoy the snow for long, but I took Luther with me to check on the situation. I'll report over breakfast,' he added, rubbing Luther down. 'Or have you had yours?'

'No, just some tea. I'll cook, if you show me where things are.'

'An offer too good to pass up,' he said with enthusiasm, looking windblown and so fit it was hard to believe he'd been ill. He held the kitchen door open for her. 'I took the liberty of putting your Christmas presents under the tree in the study with mine. Did you see them there?'

She shook her head. 'I didn't like to explore on my own.'

'What a polite little girl you are!'

'Not that polite!'

'And not a little girl either.' His eyes moved over her with frank appreciation. 'Toby was a total fool to break up with you.'

She gave an inelegant sniff. 'Is that what he told you? You may not believe this, but it was the other way round.'

'Of course I believe it! I knew damn well he was lying to save face.'

Georgia smiled, relieved. 'He's been such a total pest ever since, he's partly to blame for my runaway Christmas. He's taken to lying in wait for me outside Amy's shop, and the last time he resorted to caveman tactics—something which made me so furious I slapped him and told him to get lost. But he kept on ringing me afterwards, so I bought a new mobile phone. The answer-machine picks up his landline calls, but if my flatmate's in when he rings she picks up and gives him hell....' She trailed into silence at the blaze in Chance's eyes.

'The fool's been *stalking* you?'

'I wouldn't put it quite like that,' she said hurriedly, wishing too late that she'd kept her mouth shut.

'I'll have a word,' he said ominously.

She shook her head. '*Please* don't. I'd hate to cause more trouble for your family.'

His eyes hardened. 'But Toby's causing trouble for you, so it must stop. After the holidays I'll see to it.'

Georgia sighed unhappily. 'Perhaps Toby will have given up by then.'

'Or the minute you get back you'll have him making your life a misery again! I'll make very sure he doesn't, and at the same time keep him from causing any more trouble for Nicholas Warner Senior.'

'Senior? Is Nicholas Toby's first name?'

'No, mine. At least it was until I went away to school. I told everyone there I went by my middle name, Chance, and from then on I refused to answer to anything else at home.' He smiled crookedly. 'Chance was my mother's maiden name. It was a comfort on my first time away from home.'

Georgia felt a sharp pang of sympathy. 'Poor little boy.'

'Going away to school did me no harm. In fact I benefited enormously, due to John Gillespie, who encouraged my interest in things electronic.' Chance turned as Luther padded across the floor to him, with Ruby in pursuit. 'Sorry, chaps. I forgot.' He took a bag of dog biscuits from one of the cupboards and handed some out.

'How about their master?' Georgia asked. 'If a fry-up appeals, just show me where things are and I'll get started.'

'Yes, ma'am!' He bent to open cupboards in the island, and took out a couple of pans, leaving her to work out the switches for the hotplates while he rummaged in the fridge for the ingredients for a traditional English breakfast. 'The grill is in the smaller of the two ovens over there,' he told her, setting packages on the counter. 'I'll man that while you get started.'

As scenarios went, thought Georgia later, when they sat down to eat, this was one of the strangest.

To be having breakfast with Chance Warner, who had helped cook it, was a far cry from her original expectations of Christmas Day.

'This sort of thing,' he said indistinctly, 'is wonderful now and then—all the more for its aura of sin in our health-conscious times.'

Georgia smiled. 'Unfortunately I had more or less the same for supper last night, too. Amy would be horrified.'

'Who is Amy? And why the horror?'

'She's been my friend since nursery school and now shares my flat in Pennington. Amy's constantly on a diet of some kind, hence the horror.' She chuckled. 'I burned off last night's indulgence on the hike from the cottage, but I've sinned again this morning.'

His eyes glinted. 'If that's the worst of your sins, Georgie, you hardly need worry.'

'I don't,' she said serenely.

'Is the weight-conscious Amy a model?'

'In a way. She designs clothes—dresses, mainly—and sells them with the rest of the stock in a trendy little shop she manages in Pennington. She works hard to stay at a perfect size ten to show off her creations. I help there too, from time to time.'

He eyed her in surprise. 'I thought you were a teacher.'

Georgia nodded. 'I am. But at the moment I'm

attached to an agency as a tutor. I help students prepare for an exam, or catch up when lessons have been missed through illness.'

'Does it pay well?'

'Quite well, yes. And I help Amy in her shop between jobs. For the time being I prefer the variety of tutoring to a post in a school. My actual degree is in history, but I'm qualified to teach seven to fourteen-year-olds across the entire curriculum. They learn at an amazing rate with one-on-one teaching.'

'Lucky little devils!' His eyes gleamed. 'None of my teachers looked like you, Georgie.'

'Surely you went to a single-sex school?'

'Only from eleven.' He grinned. 'I had a huge crush on Miss Pargeter in the one before that.'

Georgia chuckled. 'It must have been a culture shock at a single-sex school. Did Toby grace the same one?'

'No. Elaine persuaded my father to enrol him at one of the local schools, so he could stay home with Mummy.' He smiled wryly. 'Personally, I think a spell away from the apron strings would have done him a whole lot of good.'

'I agree,' she said with feeling. 'By the way, what *are* the roads like out there?'

'Bad. The rain froze into a layer of ice before the snow came down on top of it overnight, so Luther and I didn't get very far. I meant to check on Ridge

Cottage this morning, but the roads are dangerous over quite a wide radius in this area. According to the travel news on the radio some are blocked, and more snow is forecast.' He touched her hand. 'I'm afraid that for the immediate future we're more or less marooned. But don't worry, Georgie. Thanks to Mrs Dawson we won't go hungry.'

'I'm not worried,' she assured him, 'just enormously grateful to you for rescuing me last night! Though I hope the snow doesn't last very long. I'm due at my next job just after New Year.'

'Where?'

'Happily it's in Pennington this time—' She broke off as her phone rang. 'It's Amy. If you don't mind, I must call her back. She's probably worried.'

'Tell her you're safe here with me.' The intent blue eyes held hers as he got up. 'Which you are, Georgie.'

She nodded briskly. 'Of course.'

'Come into the study. You can chat in peace there.' Chance led her into the room across the hall. 'It's a bit of a squeeze with the Christmas tree in here, but it seemed pointless to put it up in the drawing room where I would hardly ever see it.'

He switched on the tree lights and led her to a deep leather sofa in front of a stone fireplace, then left her alone.

Amy was deeply relieved to hear from Georgia,

and reported that the side roads were blocked in Pennington, and main roads only passable with care. 'It's a good thing Liam is staying right here with us for a bit because he can't move the car. But what on earth is it like in the back of beyond with you, love?' demanded Amy. 'We're worried sick about you.'

Georgia gave a brief, unembroidered account of the rescue mission the night before. 'And now we're pretty much snowed in here for the time being. On the plus side Chance is stocked up with food—'

'Whoa!' broke in Amy. 'Are you saying you're all alone with the man who caused all that trouble at Toby's party?'

'I caused the trouble, not Chance,' corrected Georgia. 'I'm very grateful to him for rescuing me.'

'Is—is everything all right, Georgie?' said Amy anxiously. 'I mean—'

'I know what you mean, and everything's fine.' At least she hoped it was.

'If you say so. Anyway, I thought you'd better know that your rescuer's pest of a brother rang here this morning.' She chuckled evilly. 'He went ballistic when I refused to give him your new phone number!'

'You are such a star, Amy. I owe you,' said Georgia fervently. 'Give your parents my love. I'll talk to you tomorrow.'

'Be careful!'

'Always am. By the way, I haven't opened any presents yet, but thanks in advance for yours. I shall start unwrapping shortly.'

'I just wish you were doing that here with us.'

'Stop worrying! I even have two dogs to play with, so I'll be fine.'

'As long as it's only the *dogs* you play with,' said Amy darkly.

Georgia put her phone away and curled up in a corner of the sofa, her eyes brooding. She'd done all she could to cut Toby Warner out of her life, unwilling to show even Amy that his stalking had begun to frighten her. Yet here she was, spending Christmas with his brother. Fate must be laughing up its sleeve.

She looked up as Chance came in. 'I've put Amy's mind at rest. She was worried about me.'

'Hardly surprising if she thought you were alone in this! My little brother has a lot to answer for,' he said grimly, and bent down to put a match to the fire.

'He rang Amy this morning, asking for my new number.'

Chance's eyes glittered coldly. 'Toby just has to learn to take no for an answer—something he's not used to. But where you're concerned he'll get used to it fast. I'll see to it personally. And don't worry,' he added, as her eyes narrowed, 'I shall use rhetoric this time, not force. I've just been speaking to my father, by the way. They're snowed in and Toby's in a black mood because some party's been cancelled. Dad was unusually keen to know if I'd opened my presents yet, so I'd better do that now. Do you want to open yours or leave them for later?'

'Now, of course!'

'Let's hope they survived our trek without damage.'

'Amen to that.' She smiled at him, and sat down cross-legged near the tree. 'Weren't you tempted to open yours beforehand?'

He shook his head and let himself down beside her. 'I get pretty much the same every year.'

'My parents left presents with Amy for me,' she told him, undoing one end of a parcel of clothes. 'Thank you, Mother, just what I needed,' she told the card gratefully, and smiled at Chance. 'I'll look at them later.'

He eyed his own parcels without enthusiasm. 'Elaine usually gives me some article of clothing I pass on to a charity shop. Toby invariably buys— or Elaine does—some kind of book. And here it is. Pictorial views of various cricket grounds round the world. Good choice this year!'

'You like cricket?'

'Big fan. And I'll enjoy the book all the more because it's obvious that my father chose it, not Elaine.

I doubt that my little brother had anything to do with it other than scrawling the label!'

'What did you give him?'

'A cheque—what else?' Chance shrugged. 'He prefers money to anything less than a Porsche.'

Georgia frowned. 'I never realised Toby was so immature. But then, I saw him only a few times socially before the birthday debacle.'

'And now you refuse to see him again, and Toby always wants what he can't have.' Chance met her eyes. 'If he does get it, he no longer wants it.'

Her hands stilled. 'Is that a warning?'

'No, just a statement of fact, Georgie.' He raised a wry eyebrow as he opened another parcel. 'I'm surprised Elaine gave me anything at all this year, but Dad probably put his foot down.' He shook out a square of black cashmere. 'Oh, God. Why has she given me a shawl?'

Georgia grinned. 'I think it's a sort of posh throw, to use on a long haul flight.' She took a peep at Amy's present and hastily thrust it back in its wrappings.

His eyes gleamed. 'Something I shouldn't see?'

'Absolutely.'

'Spoilsport!'

Georgia went through the rest of her presents quickly, smiling gratefully when she came to a card with a sizeable cheque from her stepfather. 'Paul never had children of his own and tends to spoil me,' she told Chance. 'So I gave him the best present I could come up with—his first Christmas alone with his wife in their Portuguese hideaway.'

Chance eyed her with respect. 'So the "no time" excuse was a white lie?'

'Right.' She sighed. 'But it's a really painful wrench to spend Christmas away from my mother for the first time.'

Chance was suddenly still as he looked inside the box he'd unwrapped. 'It's my father's pocket watch,' he said, clearing his throat. 'His wedding present from my mother.'

She leaned closer to look. 'What a gem!'

Chance touched it with a reverent finger. 'I thought Dad would just leave it to me in his will,' he said huskily.

Georgia gathered up her belongings and stood up. 'While you ring to thank your father, I'll take my stuff out of the way.'

She lingered in her room to go over her haul of book tokens, jewellery, perfume, and her mother's gift of a cashmere sweater and some dramatic wide-leg velvet trousers from Amy's shop. She grinned at the wisps of nude chiffon and lace from Amy. 'For extra-special occasions' her friend had put on the tag. Georgia rolled her eyes. No kidding!

Chance was waiting at the foot of the stairs in his bulky down jacket when Georgia joined him. 'It's not snowing—yet—and your boots are dry now. I thought you might like a walk round the garden.'

She smiled, delighted. 'I'd love it.'

In the boot room Chance produced a vintage sheepskin coat and helped her into it. 'This will swamp you, but it's warmer than your raincoat. If you fish in the pockets you'll find some gloves.' He began fastening the excited terrier into her harness. 'Luther's fine off the lead, but Ruby is an escape artist. I don't want her tearing off in this weather. She'd be hard to spot in the snow.'

'Unlike Luther.' Georgia patted the black glossy head, delighted when he stayed close beside her as they went outside.

'A flagged terrace wraps around the house, with paths leading down to various parts of the garden,' Chance informed her. 'Ridgeway dates from around 1825.'

Georgia gazed up at the classical façade of multi-paned windows flanking a pillared portico. 'It's beautiful. Have you had a lot done to it?'

'The kitchen has been done, but the reception rooms need work. The building's listed, so I proceed with care.' They walked on, sinking ankle-deep on the paths leading down to lawns blanketed with snow. 'The man who lived here lavished far more care on the gardens than the house. Too much, for my taste. I prefer a wilder, more natural look. There'll be a marvellous show of snowdrops on the terrace soon, and later on the beds and the walled garden will be full of daffodils. Then great swathes of bluebells arrive in May.' He shot a look at her. 'You must come back and see them.'

'I'd like to.' She shivered suddenly.

'You're cold. We'll go back to the house and watch a film or whatever.' He took her hand. 'Let's run for it.'

Their chase through the snow, with happily barking dogs for company, gave Georgia bright pink cheeks and sparkling eyes by the time they reached the house.

'What would you have been doing at your friend's house?' asked Chance as he took her boots off, his hands deliberately lingering over the task.

'Snoozing in front of the television at this stage, probably.' She smiled brightly to hide her heightened colour. 'But Christmas evening at the Conways' means party games. I hope Liam's up for that. He's Amy's new man—and yet another reason why I decided against joining the party.'

'Don't you like him?'

'I do—very much. But their relationship is fairly new, so I didn't relish playing gooseberry there, either.'

Chance eyed her searchingly. 'Wasn't there someone you could have brought to the cottage with you?'

'If you mean a man, no,' she said flatly. 'After the unpleasantness with Toby I'm steering well clear of men for the time being.'

He grinned. 'Does that include one who entices you with a log fire, hot tea and Mrs Dawson's prize-winning Christmas cake?'

She shook her head, laughing. 'Present company definitely excepted on those terms. Consider me enticed!'

CHAPTER THREE

IT WAS surprisingly restful, later, to sit facing the log fire and just talk for a while rather than watch a Christmas film. But eventually Chance turned to Georgia with a look of purpose which put her on the alert.

'After our second encounter that famous night, you drove off before I could ask for your phone number.' He held out his teacup for a refill.

She kept her eyes on the tea she was pouring. 'Why did you want it?'

'To apologise. But in the end, rather than cause more trouble for my father, I decided against it. He feels he was to blame in the first place for sending you to the conservatory to find Toby. Elaine, of course, insists that you broke her poor boy's heart that night.' He grinned at Georgia's look of horror. 'And Dad made it worse by assuring her that Toby's only casualty was his self-esteem.'

'Which endeared me to the lady all the more,'

said Georgia gloomily, and she took another sliver of prize-winning cake.

'Do you mind?'

'Yes, a bit. Not that it matters. I'm unlikely to meet up with her again,' she said, licking icing from her fingers.

Chance got up. 'Let's take the tray out and lay our plans for the evening, Georgie. An evening,' he added, 'I shall enjoy far more with you than on my own. I could hardly believe my eyes when I found you camping out at Ridge Cottage.'

'I don't blame you,' she said bitterly. 'I should have paid more attention to the weather forecast before leaving for my getaway Christmas for one.'

'But now it's Christmas for two and all's well,' said Chance.

Not sure she entirely agreed, Georgia bent to pat Ruby. 'When does *this* lady go out again?'

'I'll take them both out shortly, but you stay inside this time. I'll take you on a tour of the ground floor instead.'

Chance took her first into a big, empty room, with long windows looking out over the garden. 'This will be the dining room in time.' He led her out into the hall again, which eventually gave way to an open colonnade leading to a reception hall. 'The drawing room is over here on the left.'

He opened a door and switched on lights in a large

room with supremely comfortable furniture interspersed with antique pieces. 'This needs some final touches,' said Chance, eyeing it objectively. 'Any suggestions?'

Georgia gave it some thought. 'If it were mine I'd hang a couple of abstract paintings as contrast to the conventional furniture, add a mirror or two, and maybe some seasonal flowers to bring the room to life.'

He nodded. 'You're right. It's like Sleeping Beauty, waiting for the kiss.'

'It's a lot of house for one man.'

'True. My original intention was something on a much smaller scale. But when I was house-hunting Ridgeway came up on my computer screen. The shot was taken with the gardens in full bloom: a *Midsummer Night's Dream* of a house. One look and I was hooked. The feeling only intensified the first time I actually crossed the threshold. I knew I had to live here.' Chance smiled wryly. 'Friends thought I was mad, and Toby, of course, sneers about delusions of grandeur.'

'How about your father?'

'He loves the place.' Chance looked at his watch as they left the room. 'I suggest we go our separate ways for a while. I must take the dogs out briefly, and then shower and so on. I'll have drinks waiting in the kitchen about seven. Will that suit my guest?'

'Perfectly. Then I'll help put our Christmas dinner together.'

'I don't normally ask guests to prepare their own dinner!'

Georgia shrugged, smiling. 'I'll enjoy doing it.'

As they reached the stairs Chance tapped his watch. 'No later than seven.'

Georgia made good use of the time. After a quick shower, and a protracted session with her hairdryer, she pulled on the trousers and sweater her mother had bought from Amy's shop. The butterscotch shade of the cashmere was such a perfect match for her hair that contrasted so dramatically with her dark eyes she raised a wry eyebrow at her glowing reflection, well aware of what—or who—was responsible for her extra sparkle. Steady, she warned herself. Don't go there.

It was just after seven when Georgia went downstairs to the kitchen, to find the table festive with gleaming crystal and red candles in silver holders. She turned with a smile as Chance, impressive in a formal suit for the occasion, entered by the door from the boot room to the sound of clashing steel bowls in the background as the dogs enjoyed their supper. He took one look at her and stood deliberately still; the gleam in his dark blue eyes was all the reward for her efforts she could have wished for.

Chance kept looking at her as he shut the door behind him. 'I'll leave the dogs out there while we put the meal together; it'll keep Ruby's white hairs away from your velvet.'

'They'll brush off,' she assured him, and moved to the big refrigerator. 'What are we eating? In spite of all that cake, I'm hungry again.'

'So am I.' Chance joined her to throw open the double stainless steel doors. 'I'm afraid it's just ham, turkey and cold beef. Take your pick.'

'Very posh leftovers,' she commented.

He smiled crookedly. 'Leftovers or not, Georgie, I rather fancy my Christmas at home surpasses anything St Moritz can offer.'

'You've certainly got as much snow,' she said, flippant to hide her rush of pleasure. 'Now, are you by any chance—forgive the pun—the kind of man who wears protective gear to cook?'

'Sadly, no. But Mrs Dawson does.' He opened a drawer and took out a striped butcher's apron.

Georgia accepted it with gratitude and slipped it over her head. Chance took the strings and tied them behind her back, and for a moment they both stood utterly still. His breath on her neck sent a quiver of response streaking through her entire body, until indignant barking from the boot room broke the spell and Chance went off to let the dogs in.

Putting a cold supper together with Chance was a

very convivial experience, both of them talking with
the ease of old friends as they worked. She looked up
from the dressing she was whisking to find his eyes
on hers.

'I'm enjoying this, Georgie!'

So was she. Far too much. 'This is ready now.'

'Good. I'll just cut some bread, open the wine,
and we're there.'

The simple food was perfect, the wine was vintage
champagne, and, no matter who his relations were,
enjoying it with Chance Warner made Christmas
dinner an experience to remember.

'You have the most extraordinary colouring,' he
commented as he refilled Georgia's glass. 'Those
dark chocolate eyes of yours are striking with that
hair.'

'Hair from my mother, eyes from my father—' She
broke off as her phone rang. 'Sorry, I must answer
this,' she said as she took it from her bag. 'It's my
mother.'

Rose and Paul Cooper had heard about the snow
and were so anxious it took a while to allay their
fears.

'I'm safe and absolutely fine,' said Georgia at last.
'We've just sat down to supper, and I'm having a
wonderful time. I'll ring you tomorrow. I love you
too—lots. Goodnight.' She looked up to meet searching blue eyes.

'Did you mean it?' Chance demanded.

'That I'm having a wonderful time?' She paused. 'Yes, I am.'

He smiled slowly. 'So am I, Georgie.'

'Exactly what a gatecrasher needs most to hear!'

He shook his head. 'A gatecrasher is an uninvited guest, Georgie. I asked you to come here.'

'Ordered me!'

'Necessary, in the circumstances. I had to get you to safety as quickly as possible. Next time you fancy getting away from it all try somewhere less isolated.' He paused. 'On the other hand, if you'd done that this year we wouldn't be sitting here together right now.'

'I had an official reason for going to Ridge Cottage,' she informed him. 'Mother left a box of papers there, and only remembered it at the airport as they were leaving. I had the brilliant idea of spending Christmas alone at the cottage and collecting it, but though I searched high and low I drew a blank.'

Chance smiled in surprise. 'If it's a shoebox full of old photographs and so on I actually have it here, Georgie. I found it just days ago, when I finally felt fit enough to make a routine check on the cottage. The letters in it are minus any envelopes with addresses, so the box would have gone to the estate agent after the holidays to wait until claimed.'

'Oh, Chance, that's such a relief!' Georgia smiled

radiantly. 'I wasn't looking forward to telling Mother her box was missing.'

'I'll get it after supper. In the meantime…' He refilled their glasses and raised his to her in a toast, the candle flames reflected in his eyes. 'Happy Christmas, Georgie.'

She held her glass high. 'Happy Christmas, Chance.'

Later, Chance took the famous box from a drawer in his desk in the study, and gave it to Georgia while he made up the fire.

'Would you like me to leave you alone to browse?' he asked.

'Of course not.' She snuggled deeper into her corner of the sofa as she stared at the box. 'I feel a bit like Pandora,' she muttered as she removed the lid.

Chance sat down beside her. 'How about a brandy while you delve?'

She shook her head. 'Not on top of champagne. I know my limitations.' She took out a small bundle of letters tied with pink ribbon. 'I'll just see who wrote these to Mother and put them back.' Georgia untied the faded ribbon and turned the first letter over to read the signature.

Kiss my baby girl for me, with all my love, George.

She blinked hard. 'They're from my father.' She put the letter back and retied the ribbon, then began looking through the photographs. 'That's me,' she said, pointing to a smiling baby hugging a teddy.

'What a charmer!'

'Why, thank you, kind sir.' She smiled tenderly at a formal wedding photograph of a dark-eyed young man in RAF uniform gazing raptly into the adoring eyes of his pretty bride. 'My father and mother.'

'They look so young!'

'They met when my father was stationed at the airbase outside Pennington. My mother was a nurse at the hospital. They were married within weeks, and less than a year later I was born.' Georgia sighed as she put everything back in the box. 'Just after that photograph with the bear was taken my father's plane crashed into a hillside in a freak storm.'

'God, how tragic!' He took her hand. 'What happened then?'

'We went back to Pennington to live in the family home, and my mother got a job as practice nurse in a medical centre.' Georgia smiled reminiscently. 'After my grandparents died Mother and I did everything together, though she never cramped my style if I wanted to go out with Amy or anyone else. While I was at university Mother gave up nursing to work for a hospital charity, and met Paul Cooper at one of the functions she organised.'

'Did you mind sharing her?'

'I'm ashamed to say I did, at first.' She pulled a face. 'I'd been the centre of her world until then. But I grew to like Paul very much. And because my mother had him in her life I was able to enrol with an agency when I graduated, instead of trying for a conventional teaching post.'

'But you miss your mother now she's in Portugal?'

'That I do.' She sighed. 'Once I had the flat I didn't go home to them all that often. But I knew that I could whenever I wanted to. And now I can't.' Georgia turned to look up into his intent face. 'And that's quite enough whingeing from me, Mr Warner.'

He moved closer. 'I can sympathise with a woman who admits to missing her mother. I remember my first Christmas without mine only too well.'

She grasped his hand in contrition. 'Which puts my situation right into perspective. I still have my mother.'

'True.' Chance raised her hand and bent to kiss it.

She gazed, utterly still, at his bowed glossy head and felt something click inside her, as if a missing piece of a puzzle had slotted into place. He sat up, his eyes on hers. Georgia stared back, her heartbeat suddenly in overdrive.

'Georgie, I have a problem,' he said huskily.

'What kind of problem?'

'It started the night of Toby's birthday, when a beautiful girl—'

'Woman!'

He rolled his eyes, easing the sudden tension. 'As I was saying,' he went on, 'the moment when a beautiful *woman* walked into my arms and kissed me by mistake and I wanted to steal her from my brother.'

'But since I don't belong to your brother, or to anyone else, larceny is unnecessary,' she said bluntly.

His eyes narrowed. 'Does that mean you're not against the idea, Georgie?'

She shrugged. 'A friendly kiss at Christmas is harmless enough, surely? It happens under the mistletoe all the time.'

Chance nailed her with a look. 'From our past brief experiences I doubt that any kiss between us would be harmless in the present situation. And the point of all this, Georgie, is that I've brought you here to keep you safe. So, damned hard though it is for me, I'm going to let you go to bed with just a brotherly pat on the hand.'

Georgia burned with mortification. She'd allowed her hormones to get out of hand over a man whose name meant nothing but trouble. 'All right,' she said, and startled him by getting to her feet. 'Goodnight.'

Chance leapt up and seized her hand to stay her. 'I didn't mean right now!'

'I think it's best.' Georgia smiled at him sweetly. 'You've been so kind, the last thing I want is to make things hard for you, Chance.'

'Hard!' He closed his eyes for an instant, and then opened them on hers with a look like a blowtorch. Then she was in his arms, with his mouth on hers in fierce possession which sent her giddy with delight, just like before. She could taste champagne, and aroused man, and she sank into him with a helpless little moan which brought a sound half-groan, half-growl from Chance. He wrenched off his jacket and pulled her onto his lap, holding her against him while his mouth possessed hers with a force which sent such fire flicking along her veins her blood threatened to vaporise. At last he loosened his grasp, and looked down into her dazed, glittering eyes for long, super-charged moments while they both got their breath back.

'Not chocolate,' he informed her at last, a lazy, relishing note in his voice that ignited a delicious quivering deep inside her. 'Right now your eyes are black, molten treacle—with a touch of brimstone.'

'Is that a good thing?' she asked unsteadily.

'No. It's damned dangerous,' he growled, and touched the tip of his finger to her bottom lip, his face taut with a hunger which brought such heat to

Georgia's cheeks she turned away, burrowing into his shoulder as his arms tightened. 'You are so delectable,' he said into her hair, 'that I want to give vent to my inner big bad wolf and gobble you up right now. But I won't. I'm going to find the strength from somewhere—God knows how—to let you go up to bed alone.'

Georgia leaned back, her eyes wide on his. 'Why, Chance? We're two unattached adults thrown together in a situation totally outside the norm. Would it be so terrible to exchange a kiss or two?'

'No. Not terrible at all. Which is the point.' He pulled her closer and rubbed his cheek against her hair. 'I would soon want a hell of a lot more than that, which for me, and for you, would be pure magic. But, Georgie, when I heard you tell your mother you were safe I swore I'd keep you that way.'

The urgency abruptly drained from Georgia, like air leaving a balloon. 'Oh, I see.' She pushed his arms away and stood up, her face set. 'You were born in the wrong century, Chance Warner. No one will know whether we've been as pure as that driven snow outside or not—' She stopped dead. What was she *doing*? Begging a man to make love to her?

'Don't do this, Georgie,' said Chance through his teeth.

'No, I won't.' She raised her chin, snatching back the pride she'd mislaid for a mad moment. 'Don't panic! I won't bother you again. You're quite safe up there on your pedestal.' Her eyes glittered coldly as she turned on her heel to make for the door, but he was there before her, barring her way.

'Georgie—'

'Only my nearest and dearest call me that,' she spat at him.

His jaw clenched. 'Listen to me! The last thing I meant to do was hurt you—'

'Then heaven help me when you do!' She brushed past him, slammed the door in his face, and raced along the hall to run up to her room, desperate to be alone. But her flight was so headlong she tripped on a stair and gave a smothered scream—just as the entire house was plunged into darkness.

CHAPTER FOUR

'GEORGIA!' yelled Chance. 'Are you all right? For God's sake don't move. Where are you?'

She reached out an unsteady hand to touch the banister. 'Halfway up the stairs—I think.'

'Don't move. I'll get a torch.'

Georgia heard the dogs barking as Chance reached the kitchen. Disorientated, she hugged her arms across her chest, shivering from reaction to their quarrel as much as shock from the power cut. But as her eyes grew accustomed to the dark she could see a faint glimmer from the tall Venetian window at the top of the stairs and felt better. She waited a long time before a torch beam cut through the darkness.

Chance sprinted along the hall and up the stairs to her, and would have pulled her close, but Georgia, still raw and hurting from his rejection, thrust him away with a violent hand.

His arms dropped instantly. 'All right, put your claws in. But at least hold on to my hand so I can get you back to the study. Sorry I was so long.' He shone the torch beam on the stairs as they went down. 'I checked on the trip switches in the boot room in the hope that I could just trip them back in, but no luck. There isn't a light visible for miles around, so the power cut is obviously general. And it's snowing again, so no hope of getting it back for a while.'

When they reached the study Georgia burrowed back into her corner of the sofa in relief, grateful for light as Chance made up the fire. He picked up the phone and listened, but shook his head and put it down again.

'Dead. The telephone lines must be down, too.' He shone the torch on the phone he took out of his pocket, and cursed under his breath. 'I spoke to my father twice on it this morning, when I was outside with the dogs, and forgot to put it back on charge. I need to ring the electricity board. May I borrow yours?'

'Of course. It's in my handbag by the bed.'

'Stay there. I'll fetch it.' He got up, the flames throwing the planes and hollows of his face into sharp relief as he looked down at her. 'Is there anything you need?'

She smiled faintly. 'Only something I can't have.'

His mouth twisted. 'Tell me about it! What are *you* hankering for, Georgie?'

'What I always yearn for in a power cut—hot tea.'

'Give me a few minutes and I might be able to do something about that,' he said, surprising her. 'Don't move until I get back.'

On her own, Georgia stared morosely into the leaping flames, cursing her mad idea of Christmas alone in the country. But a white Christmas was such a rarity these days she'd given no thought to bad weather. Never in her wildest dreams had she imagined a situation like this. She'd learned one valuable lesson at least. If it addled her wits to the point where she'd virtually begged Chance to make love to her, she'd never drink champagne again.

He was away much longer than a few minutes. But when Georgia opened the door to his knock later she forgave him for the delay, and everything else, when she found him standing there in the dark, with her handbag slung over his shoulder and a mug of tea in each hand.

She shook her head in wonder as she took one of the mugs. 'How on earth did you manage this?'

His smile was triumphant. 'I went out to the stables to look for my old two-burner gas stove from my camping days and, miracle of miracles, found I still had a full canister of gas from the last power cut. But I had to light the candles in the kitchen before

I could do anything. Luckily I'd left matches on the island.'

Georgia smiled graciously as she went back to the sofa. 'I'm impressed.'

Chance gave her the handbag as he sat down beside her. 'I thought you might need it, but be careful—it's heavy. I put a spare torch in it. You'll find it handy later.'

'Thanks. You were obviously a boy scout.'

'Unfortunately not. Their motto is "Be Prepared". And I wasn't.' He sighed impatiently. 'I've been meaning to get an emergency generator for ages, but I've never got round to it.'

'Did you ring the electricity board?'

'Not yet. The phone's still in your bag.'

She took it out and handed it to him.

Chance dialled, waited, and then shook his head. 'Engaged. Everyone around here must be trying to get through. I'll try again later.'

'Drink your tea first,' advised Georgia as Chance shivered. 'You'd better put your jacket on, too. Were you out in the stables without a coat?'

'No. I slung one on to go outside, but it got damp so I left it in the boot room when I came in.' Chance gave her a searching look. 'Do you feel better now?'

'Yes.' She sipped rapturously. 'I can see why tea was once regarded as medicine.'

His mouth twisted. 'I was actually asking if you'd thawed a little towards me—or do you still want to assault me with the poker?'

'No. The tea saved you from that.'

'If it's any consolation, I'm amazed by my nobility,' he said bitterly. 'As you know damn well, I've wanted you from the first moment we met.'

Georgia eyed him coldly. 'So why did you reject me tonight?'

His hands clenched. 'I didn't *reject* you, Georgie. I meant what I said about having you in my care. And my definition of care doesn't mean taking you to bed to make love to you all night—much as I want to.'

She sighed. 'If you want the truth I was angry because I want that too. Which hardly ever happens for me.'

He moved nearer. 'Why not?'

'Good question. Even in school my peers were having sex all the time. But when a girl in my year got pregnant at sixteen it put me off the whole thing.' She shrugged. 'I had some boyfriends at university, but no grand passions and broken hearts involved.'

'At least on your side.' Chance took her hand. 'I can't imagine any man parting from you willingly. Toby's a case in point.'

'Your brother and I were hardly more than acquaintances. He has absolutely no right to carry on like a—'

'Drama queen?'

She smiled reluctantly. 'Well, yes. I only agreed to go out with him because he caught me at a time when I was feeling a bit low after Mother left. And there was a link, because when he talked about you I realised you were the man my mother and Paul had met while they were renting Ridge Cottage.'

'Where did you first meet Toby?'

'In a café near Amy's shop. It was crowded, and he asked to share my table. Not exactly the romance of the century!'

'Is that what you're looking for, Georgie? Romance?'

She stared into the flames. 'I suppose it must be. That's why all the frenetic coupling around me in college seemed so pointless.' She pulled a face. 'I sound sanctimonious, don't I?'

'No. Just different.' Chance smiled wryly. 'I was the usual hormonal teenage male at university, and enjoyed myself enormously. But I enjoyed sports, too. And—the last straw for most girls—when I wasn't playing cricket or rugby I spent so much time in front of a computer they spat geek insults at me and stormed off when I preferred my kind of games to theirs.'

Georgia eyed his profile objectively. 'I can't visualise you as a geek, Chance.'

'Delighted to hear it!' He swivelled to look at her.

'Look, Georgie, now we're without heat, other than this fire, we need a plan of action.'

'You need a list,' she agreed. 'Batteries, candles, basic provisions, et cetera. Your fridge is stocked up, and I noticed a freezer in the boot room, so everything in there should last for a while as long it's not opened too often.'

He nodded. 'We'll take inventory in the morning, when we have natural light. Who knows? The power might be back by then.'

'What about the dogs?'

'They'll be fine. The temperature in the rest of the house will nosedive very quickly in this weather, unfortunately, but the kitchen is still quite warm. The Aga will keep some heat for a while yet, and I'll put some blankets in their beds tonight. I'll find some for you, too, Georgie.'

She pulled a face. 'A pity I left my hot water bottle at the cottage. I don't suppose you have one somewhere?'

He laughed ruefully. 'Afraid not.'

'Never mind. I packed plenty of socks.'

With reluctance Chance heaved himself to his feet. 'Time I bit the bullet and took the dogs out. I'll check on you when I come back.'

On her own in front of the crackling flames, Georgia counted her blessings. Instead of shivering alone in a cold cottage she was safe in Chance

Warner's beautiful house. Her sole regret at cutting Toby out of her life had been cutting out his all too attractive brother at the same time. But fate seemed determined to throw them together. When she'd opened her door last night to see him standing outside in the rain she'd thought for a moment she was hallucinating. But not only was it Chance Warner in the impressive flesh, the original chemistry between them was still there in full force—and no figment of her imagination, as she'd tried to convince herself. But, chemistry or not, tonight he'd rejected advances she'd never made to a man before. Which was a good thing, she told herself firmly. It would be madness to get involved with a man who had Toby Warner for a brother.

'Wow,' said Georgia, eyeing the laden tray Chance eventually brought in.

'We need to keep warm, and food is fuel,' he informed her, and put the tray on the desk. 'I made a pot of tea for you, but I fancy a shot of Scotch myself. It's damned cold out there, and still snowing like blazes. Ruby was only too happy to get back inside, and for once so was Luther. Did you put more logs on?'

She shook her head. 'I wasn't sure about your supplies, so I just poked the fire a bit.'

'No problem on the log score. I chopped a tree down in the summer.' Chance bent to make up the fire. 'I took a quick look in the freezer and found one section full of bread, by the way, so I took a loaf out to thaw and used the bread in the bin to make sandwiches. Tuck in, Georgie.'

Georgia was amazed to find that even after the dinner she'd enjoyed, and the quarrel later that she hadn't, she was hungry. Chance filled a plate and sat down, leaning back with a sigh of satisfaction as the flames leapt up.

'This roast beef is fabulous,' she said with relish.

'Better with horseradish, but it was too much of a hassle to look for it. Tomorrow I'll get out all the candles I possess.'

'We don't need them in here with the fire.'

'True. And you have a torch to light you to bed. Keep it on hand in case you need to get up in the night.'

'Do you want some tea?'

'No, thanks. I'm warm enough after my Scotch. Tomorrow I'll wear more appropriate clothes.' He smiled at her as she sat down. 'Formality was necessary tonight, to live up to such a beautiful dinner companion.'

'It's only thanks to Mother and Amy that I look like this,' she assured him. 'I wasn't expecting to dine out during my escape to Ridge Cottage...' She trailed off at the glint in his eyes. 'What?'

'You hid your present from your friend pretty sharply. Was it underwear? And are you wearing it now?'

'Yes, it was, and no, I'm not,' she retorted.

Chance smiled as he got up to mend the fire. He rang the electricity board again, and this time got a recorded message announcing that power would be restored as soon as possible. 'Lord knows when that will be. We're a bit isolated up here, and usually the last in line to get power back. I pity the poor guys forced to turn out in this weather to locate the fault.' He turned to look at Georgia. 'Don't worry, I promise to keep you safe.'

'So you've told me. Repeatedly.' She gave him her phone. 'Use it to ring your father if you like.'

He shook his head. 'It's already running low.'

'I was going to put it on charge when I went to bed tonight.'

'Talking of bed, are you tired?'

'Yes. But I do so hate to tear myself away from this fire.' Georgia sighed. 'I did more of a paint job on my face than usual tonight, too, which means a session in a cold bathroom to clean it off. Who'd be a woman?'

He slid nearer and put an arm round her, tightening it when she stiffened. 'Only practical—to conserve body heat.'

Practical, but dangerous. His personal blend of

pheromones had been the culprit the first time they'd met. She'd known she was kissing the wrong man right away, but one touch of that skilled mouth had shorted some circuit in her brain. Since her brain was now working normally, Georgia slid from his grasp. Safety measure, not retaliation, she assured herself.

Chance smiled at her sardonically. 'Nervous, Miss Smith?'

She shook her head. 'It's just practical to go to bed while I'm warm.' She gave him the smile she used on Amy's customers and put her phone in her handbag. 'Goodnight.'

But he was already on his way to the door. 'I'm coming with you, but don't worry—only to light your way and make sure you're—'

'Safe?' she said tartly.

The total darkness in the hall was a shock after the glow of the fire in the study. So was the dramatic drop in temperature. Chance grasped Georgia's hand and shone the torch beam on each tread of the stairs as they went up. Faint light filtered through the landing window as they reached the top.

'Switch on your torch and do what you have to do as quickly as possible in the bathroom, and get into bed,' Chance ordered as they reached her room. 'I'll give you ten minutes tops before I get back with some blankets. I want to see you in bed and—'

'Safe,' she said through chattering teeth.

He let out a crack of laughter and went out, leaving Georgia to make a feverish start on her programme. She ran back into the bedroom after a freezing session in the bathroom and got into her pyjamas at top speed. She added her cardigan and a pair of wool socks, then hung her Christmas Day finery over the back of a chair, put the torch on the other pillow and dived into bed just as Chance knocked and came in.

'Allow me, madam.' He draped a thick blanket over the duvet, and tucked it in on all sides with precision.

'Thank you,' she gasped.

'I'll leave another blanket folded at the end, of the bed so you can pull it up if you need it. Goodnight, Georgie. Try to sleep.'

'I will. Thank you. Goodnight.'

Alone in the dark, Georgia found that the darkness was relative. Courtesy of the snow, faint light showed through the filmy curtains at the windows. Comforted by it, she forced herself to lie still and try to sleep as Chance had ordered. He was good at orders. He'd set about solving their problems with such efficiency it was hard to believe that girls had thrown geek insults at him in the past. Anything—or anyone—less geeky was hard to imagine. She smiled to herself in the dark. It had obviously been the worst insult some sexy female student could think of when he refused to leave his computer to go out—or stay in—and play with her. But even if he had been the archetypal geek in the past—which she seriously doubted—in the present he was a powerfully attractive man. Yet the attraction was by no means just physical. She had been perfectly happy just to be in his company as they'd waded through the snow in the garden, or shared tea and cake in front of the fire. She shivered, wishing she was in front of it right now. If the snow persisted she would ask Chance to let her sleep on the sofa in the study tomorrow night.

Across the landing Chance lay equally wakeful in his wide, cold bed, cursing himself for alienating Georgie so thoroughly. If he'd followed his instincts, instead of his inconvenient and normally more dormant conscience, he could have been holding her in his arms right now, sharing body heat and making the long, freezing night a thing of pleasure. Instead it promised to be purgatory. He never heated his bedroom, so the atmosphere in here was icy. So were his feet. Like a fool, he wasn't wearing socks or anything else—as usual. He should have given himself another blanket. At last he gave up and, by the faint glimmer from the windows, got out of bed and pulled on thick wool socks, tracksuit bottoms, T-shirt and dressing gown, and made for the linen cupboard on the landing. As he felt around in it by touch for a blanket he heard a crash from Georgie's room and shot across the landing, cracking his elbow on the doorframe as he burst into the room.

'Are you all right, Georgie? Did you fall? Talk to me!'

'I'm on the floor, trying to find the torch,' she said irritably. 'It fell off the bed.'

Chance dropped to his knees and collided with a shivering female body. He grasped her elbows and pulled Georgie to her feet. 'Get back into bed. I'll look for it.'

'No!'

'*Yes*, Georgie, you're frozen.'

'I was on my way,' she said through her teeth, 'to the bathroom.'

'Oh. Right. *Hell*!'

'What?'

'I trod on the torch.' Chance bent to pick it up and switched it on, directing the beam at the shivering little figure in striped pyjamas and cardigan. 'Here you are, then.'

Georgia snatched it, and shut herself in the bathroom. When she went back out, Chance was still standing there.

'All right, all right,' she said irritably, 'Just give me a minute and I'll be back in bed—*safe*!'

Chance suddenly cast his conscience to the winds. He took the torch from her and switched it off, then opened his dressing gown and took her breath away by wrapping her up against him. 'Remember that list of the best ways to cope with our emergency? This is top of mine.' He picked her up and carried her from the room.

Georgia collected her scrambled wits. 'Hey. If you're taking me down to the study I can walk.'

'I'm not.' He crossed the landing, guided by the window as he shouldered his way through his bedroom door. 'It's only common sense to share body heat in my bed rather than freeze separately.' He put her down on the side he'd just vacated and pulled the duvet over her. 'Don't move,' he ordered. 'I'll fetch another blanket.'

His instruction was superfluous. Georgia was too cold to do anything but shiver. He came back and threw a blanket over the duvet, then slid in beside her and took her in his arms, holding her there in silence until neither of them was shivering any more.

'Better?' whispered Chance at last.

Georgia nodded fervently. 'Much better.'

'Good. Sorry to ride rough-shod over you, but it's too cold to argue. And you would have argued.'

At this moment, blissfully warm in his arms, Georgia found that hard to imagine.

'I was stupid enough to go to bed commando as usual.' he went on. 'I got up—very reluctantly—to put something on and look for a blanket. I was fumbling about in the linen cupboard on the landing when I heard the crash from your room.'

'Sorry to disturb you.'

Chance tipped her face up to his in the intimate dark. 'You disturb me wherever you are, so to hell with it. Shut up and kiss me!'

Georgia forgot she was angry with him. His lips were warm and firm on hers, and the feel and taste of them was intoxicating even without the faint tang of whiskey she searched out with the tip of her tongue. He growled, deep in his throat, and slid his tongue between her parted lips in a caress which melted her bones. She forgot about Toby and everything else as she wrapped her arms around him fiercely, wanting this—wanting *him*—with every fibre of her body as his conquering mouth took hers and steel-hard arms tightened in a relentless grip which thrilled her to the core.

With a gasp Chance sat up abruptly and began removing their clothes at top speed, his shaking fingers making him clumsy. 'Don't worry, I'll keep you warm,' he assured her hoarsely, and yanked the covers over them to make a cocoon, his long hands splayed against her back as he drew her against him again.

Georgia gave a little groan as for the first time every inch of her naked body came into contact with every hard plane and muscle of his. Her nipples prickled with fire as they pressed against his chest, and her breath hitched and her heart battered against her ribs as his throbbing erection touched the intimate spot between her legs.

'If you want to change your mind about this,' Chance rasped, 'do it now.'

Georgia shook her head vehemently, and lay back as he leaned over her to reach his bedside table. Before she had time for questions she was in his arms again, and his hands were on her breasts and the heat in her nipples exploded in twin points of flame as his clever, inciting fingers and grazing teeth drove her wild. His mouth returned to hers with a demand that heightened her scorching, throbbing pleasure as his fingers stroked the soft, hot petals that protected the secret part of her that until now had languished there unnoticed. Chance found it unerringly, his caress bringing her up off the bed with a gasping cry. He kissed her parted lips, then slid between her thighs in partial penetration, holding still, braced on his arms above her, until she relaxed a little. His breath tore through his chest as he forced himself to wait, then with a final thrust he was deep inside her, and Georgia sucked in a sharp, ragged breath at the lightning bolt of sensation. They lay still, savouring it for an instant, then his caressing hands coaxed her to move with him, inciting her into such hot response their bodies achieved a tumultuous rhythm that propelled them at last to a climax he reached first, and then he held her close until she exploded around him in wild delight.

Georgia lay dazed and still in Chance's arms afterwards, or as still as it was possible to be while her heart thumped. She felt euphoric. Under Chance Warner's expert tuition she had discovered the true joy of making love at last. She had even achieved her very first orgasm, and had fought to control a scream as she'd found out, at last, what other women—or at least Amy—raved about. She shook her head. If she made love with any other man there was no guarantee it would be a regular occurrence. It had only happened with Chance because she was in love with him. Had been from that first moment when she'd kissed him by mistake. Or *had* it been a mistake? Maybe some cosmic influence had sent her into his arms with a purpose that night.

'Why the shake of the head, Georgie?' he asked huskily.

Her train of thought braked to a halt. 'Amazement at how good you are at this.'

'You're pretty damn wonderful yourself, Miss Smith.' He kissed her neck in appreciation, and heaved a sigh. 'I hate to move, but we just have to get some clothes on.'

She groaned. 'You're right. But I'm not looking

forward to it. I don't know where you threw my pyjamas, but they'll be icy by now.'

He laughed into her neck. 'Even in my desperation to get you naked I was clever enough to push them down the bed to keep warm.'

'Clever *and* modest,' she said, giggling.

'Hold on.' He got out of bed and searched for her pyjamas. 'Out you get, then, but hurry up.'

Georgia slid out of bed, glad of the dark as Chance handed her pyjamas over. She struggled into them at top speed, then slid back into bed, straight into his waiting arms.

He kissed her briefly and held her close. 'Now we sleep.'

Georgia's former relationships had not included sleepovers. She was utterly positive she would never fall asleep with a man's hard, warm body moulded to hers. But the various demands of the day, and the heavenly warmth Chance was giving out, soon combined to prove her wrong.

It was just getting light when she woke to an unfamiliar sound. Chance was snoring softly into her neck. She could see the room clearly, so it was definitely morning. She tried to move, but at her first wriggle an arm snaked round her waist and held her fast.

'No, you don't,' said Chance, in a dark early-morning voice, and kissed her ear. 'Good morning, Miss Smith. How did you sleep?'

'Surprisingly well, in the circumstances.'

He pulled her round to face him, heavy-eyed, in need of a shave, and utterly irresistible to Georgia. Oh, Lord, she thought, hiding her face against his shoulder, she'd really got it bad. And she had no idea how he really felt about her, except that she turned him on physically.

'Why surprisingly?' he asked, kissing her hair.

'I always sleep alone.'

'Would you have preferred to sleep alone last night?'

She raised her head to scowl at him. 'Since I wouldn't have slept at all if I had, the answer's obviously no.'

'Are you always this prickly in the morning?'

'Only when someone wakes me up by snoring in my ear.' She grinned evilly at his look of outrage.

'I don't snore! Do I?'

'Yes. But very musically.' She blew him a kiss. 'It was a small price to pay for keeping warm.'

He growled and pulled her close to kiss her hard, then to her disappointment let her go and got out of bed. 'Much as I'd like to stay and debate the matter, I have an appointment with some dogs. But you stay put until I've got the fire going in the study. We'll have breakfast in front of it this morning.'

'I'll cook something, if your gas burners will take a frying pan,' she suggested.

He stopped on his way to the bathroom to give her a look which made her warm all over. 'Does this mean you've forgiven me, Georgie?'

'All things considered, I suppose I must have.' Her smile brought him back to the bed to bend over and kiss her at such length it was obvious where it would have led if the dogs hadn't been waiting.

'I have to go,' groaned Chance, straightening, and brushed a hand over her hair.

Minutes later, when he emerged, teeth chattering, from the bathroom, Georgia watched with appreciation as he exchanged his improvised night gear for boxers, thick moleskins, a wool shirt topped with a Shetland sweater, hiking socks and heavy shoes. He looked up to meet her eyes and grinned. 'You were supposed to avert your eyes modestly.'

'I could do that when you take them off,' she suggested, and grinned back.

'Can't wait,' he said thickly, and started towards her, then shook his head and made for the door. 'You're a dangerous woman! See you in half an hour.'

CHAPTER FIVE

WHEN Georgia reached the kitchen, wearing her warmest layers of clothes, she received a joyous welcome from Luther as well as Ruby.

'You're certainly a hit with my dogs,' said Chance, watching.

'And I much appreciate it,' she said with truth, once the patting and stroking was over. 'I wish I could have one of my own, but it's not possible in my flat.'

'Too small?'

'That too, but in my building pets are forbidden anyway.' She went over to the battered metal box on the draining board. 'Is this the cooker?'

Chance raised the lid to display two burners. 'Now you're here I'll put two pans of water to boil—one for tea, the other for eggs.'

Georgia went over to the windows to look out on an arctic landscape. 'No sign of a thaw, then.'

Chance came to stand behind her, and slid his arms round her waist. 'Are you so anxious to leave me?'

For answer she turned in his arms and kissed him, exulting in the tightening of his embrace as he returned the kiss with interest.

'I'll take that as a no,' he said huskily, and kissed her again.

With snow outside and warmth inside in front of the study fire as they ate breakfast, Georgia felt utterly at peace with the world. Chance had found batteries which fitted his radio, and they were able to listen to music and news reports while they ate. The snow which covered most of Southern Britain, they learned, was due to turn to rain within the next forty-eight hours.

'Good news in one way,' said Georgia, 'but does that mean more flooding?'

'Quite possibly. But don't worry. I'll collect your belongings from the cottage as soon as I can hike down over the common,' Chance assured her. 'Your car can wait until the roads are clear. You'll just have to stay here with me until I'm absolutely sure it's safe for you to travel.'

It was a Boxing Day to remember. When the sun came out later they took the dogs and went down the drive to the main gates, to find the road outside covered with fresh snow and totally free from signs of traffic.

'Not that I would expect much traffic today, anyway,' said Chance. 'I'd better do some shovelling. If the back courtyard is cleared it's easier to haul in logs.'

'I'll help.'

He shook his head. 'I'd rather you curled up by the fire—'

'Nice and safe?' she mocked, and punched him playfully on the arm. 'I want to shovel. Out here with you,' she added, looking up into his eyes.

Chance pulled her close and kissed her, much to Ruby's excitement. 'I suppose you think I'll agree to anything if you look at me like that!'

'Will you?'

'Every time.' He kissed her again, and pulled on the little dog's lead. 'Down, Ruby! She'll have to go in, but Luther can stay outside with us.'

Ruby strongly disapproved of this arrangement. Once she was inside there was so much barking and yowling from the boot room it was audible outside in the garage Chance had converted from stables.

'Ruby's quiet at last,' said Georgia as she pulled on the gloves he gave her.

'Look at the window and you'll see why!'

Georgia laughed when she saw Ruby watching them through the window from one of the countertops.

The day was bitterly cold, but Georgia soon grew warm as she shovelled and swept in her determination to help Chance. She was glad when at last he took away her shovel and broom.

'That's it. Time to pack it in,' he said firmly.

Georgia nodded meekly as she stripped off her gloves. 'OK, boss. Are you coming in now?'

'I'll just tidy up a bit first, and scatter some grit around. Why don't you make a hot drink, and think about what we can eat for lunch?'

Georgia received a joyful welcome from Ruby when she went inside to kick off her boots. 'Believe me, you were in the best place,' she assured her, and surveyed her soaked jeans with resignation. The only place with any heat was the study. She told Ruby to stay, and hurried along the hall. In the study she stripped off the jeans and hung them over the back of a chair, then gave the fire a poke, added some logs and put the fire guard back, then ran upstairs to her room. She pulled on an old pair of denims, slapped moisturiser on her face, and went downstairs to see Chance backing the Ranger Rover into the yard. Wondering why, she surveyed his choice of canned soup.

'Which would he like, Ruby? Wag twice for tomato.'

Ruby wagged a lot more than twice, and with a chuckle Georgia gave her a dog biscuit, then opened a couple of cans of soup and tipped them into a pan, ready to heat. Wondering why Chance was taking so long, she went over to the window. She tensed, her eyes narrowing ominously. He was talking on his car phone. So he'd had means to contact the outside world all along! He was probably on the phone to some female right now. After Toby, she'd had her fill of controlling men.

Eventually Chance strode into the kitchen, the smile on his face fading as he saw her face.

'What's wrong?'

'You kept pretty quiet about the car phone.'

He frowned. 'For a very simple reason, Georgia. Until I backed the car out of the garage to get at the logs I never gave it a thought.'

'Who were you talking to?' she enquired, barely covering her anger.

Chance stiffened. 'There was a worried message from my father on it, so I spoke to him briefly and then returned a message from Tom Hutchings at Ridge Farm. Finally I rang about the power again, but got the same answer. Is there anything else you want to know? If not, hand over your phone and I'll put it on charge in the car so you can talk to your mother.'

She eyed him uncertainly. 'You really forgot you had a car phone?'

'Yes,' he said brusquely. 'I have faults, but lying isn't one of them. While I put your phone on charge perhaps you can finish lunch.' He took the phone and strode out again.

Georgia lit the flame under the soup she had ready. She set the table, cut some bread, then turned with a polite little smile as Chance came in.

'It's ready.'

'Excellent. I'm hungry.' He took the bowl she filled for him and went over to the table, then held out her chair and waited for her to join him. 'Wasn't there enough soup?' he demanded, eying her bowl. 'You don't have much.'

'I'm not as hungry as I thought,' she said brightly. 'There's plenty more if you want it.'

'Good.'

Georgia found it hard to swallow any soup at all past the lump in her throat. How stupid was that?

'You're obviously too tired to eat, Georgia,' he said, eying her. 'Are your shoulders aching?'

'A bit.'

'I was a fool to allow you to help,' he said bitterly.

Her head flew up. 'Allow? I helped because I wanted to do something in return for your hospitality.' Oh, Lord! That had come out all wrong.

'The hospitality comes free of charge of any kind,' Chance said through his teeth. He tossed his spoon down in the dish, splashing hot soup on the table. 'Why the hell are you behaving like this? One minute we're working together in complete harmony, the next you're Miss Frigidaire. I honestly didn't give the damned car phone a thought, if that's the problem. There was no sinister reason for keeping it secret. Not that it matters much. The net result is the same. We wait until the power returns or a thaw sets in— whichever comes first. So what's wrong?'

She reached to mop up the soup with her napkin. 'Nothing.'

'You could have fooled me,' he said flatly, and got up to take the soup bowls. 'Is there enough water in the pan to rinse these?'

'Yes, but I'll do it.'

'No, you will not,' he said in a tone that decided her against argument. 'Read your book in front of the fire in the study.'

She turned on her heel and left the kitchen. She marched along the hall and up the stairs to her room to collect her book, and then went down to the study to poke the fire and add some logs. When they were blazing satisfactorily she curled up on the sofa, but after a minute or two gave up trying to read. She lay staring into the flames, knuckled sudden tears from her eyes, and slid down further, her head on the arm of the sofa, annoyed that she'd let her bad experience with Toby cause her to turn stroppy over the car phone episode. Maybe her first real experience of love—or lust, or whatever—had sent her hormones into meltdown.

She shot upright as Chance came in and handed her phone over.

'You've been crying,' he said softly. 'Why?'

'I don't know. I'm tired, and a bit upset, I suppose. Thank you for this,' she added politely.

He sat down beside her and took her hand. 'Are you still angry with me, Georgie?'

The pet name sent her defences crashing. 'I had no cause to be angry, and you had every right to turn cold on me. But it was a bit hard to take after—after last night.'

'Cold! I feel anything but as far as you're concerned, Miss Smith.' He bent his head and kissed her in emphasis, then took her in his arms as he felt her lips quiver under his.

Georgia pulled away a little. 'I assumed you were putting some woman's mind at rest when I saw you talking on the car phone.'

'And you were jealous?' Chance laughed, and shifted her more comfortably in his arms. 'I was putting my father's mind at rest, I assure you. Now the wilderness years are over we're on good terms these days, Dad and I.'

'Were you such a bad boy, then?' she asked.

He smiled. 'I was the usual tearaway teenager—long hair, leather jacket, motorbike: all the trappings of the rebel. But never drugs. I liked a cigarette and a drink as much as the rest of them when I went out on the town with the lads at the software company, but I steered clear of anything likely to affect my brain.'

'Did you enjoy your work there?'

'Immensely. But after I sold the famous fruit of said brain I found I didn't want to work for a company any more. So I left and went freelance, invested my windfall, and studied ways to make it grow. I was a whiz at maths in school. Numbers fascinate me.'

Georgia frowned. 'But don't you miss working?'

'You mean am I content to rest idle on my laurels for the rest of my life?' he said wryly.

She flushed. 'Yes, I suppose I do mean that.'

'Toby obviously left out telling you of my interest in farming. Ridgeway land adjoins the farm run by Tom Hutchings and his wife. When I bought the house I met Tom in talks about boundaries and so on, and found he was struggling to keep going. He's the fourth generation Hutchings to run the farm, but with fewer men wanting work as farm hands, and no sons of his own to help out, Tom and Nell were having a pretty lean time.'

Georgia's eyes widened. 'So you bought the farm?'

'No. I bought *into* it. Or, to put it another way, I invested some money so Tom can do the modernisation needed to make the farm pay its way, and also offer higher wages to bring in experienced help. I lend a hand there myself on a part-time basis.' Chance grinned at her astonishment. 'I don't get up at dawn to milk the cows. I keep to the arable side and some of the slog, like hedging and so on. But, more important to Tom, I see to the finances and research ways of cutting costs. As I said, I'm good with figures.'

'So that's why,' she said, enlightened.

'Why what?'

'Why you look so fit even after a dose of flu. I wondered if you had a gym tucked away somewhere in the house.'

'Don't need one. Farming is damned hard work; so is keeping a garden this size in check.' He preened outrageously. 'You like my muscles, then?'

She laughed. 'What's not to like? The girls who spat geek insults at you should see you now!'

Chance shrugged. 'Actually, I was pretty much the same in those days—which is why girls got so cross when I wouldn't come out to play. But even then the muscles were the result of hard labour, not a subscription to some gym.'

'What labour?'

'In vacations I took any live-in jobs on farms I could find—corn-stooking, fruit picking. It was an arrangement which suited Elaine perfectly, my father not so much.'

'I'm impressed,' she said with sincerity, and smiled wryly. 'I can't see Toby doing the same.'

'He didn't have to. Elaine inherited family money when he was in his teens, which pays for his flat and his sexy car, and so on.'

'But he still envies you. Which is only to be expected,' she added.

'In what way?'

'Toby's your half-brother, which says it all. He'll never be half the man you are, Chance. I went out with him for a while solely because I was feeling a bit blue after Mother and Paul left for Portugal. Heaven knows why I agreed to turn up at his party.' She shrugged. 'But I'm glad I did—even though it turned my life upside down.'

He tipped her face up to his. 'How, Georgie?

She moved away a little, purposely distancing herself from him. 'It's my turn to make a confession, Chance.'

His eyes narrowed. 'Is it something I don't want to hear?'

'I don't know. I confess—you judge.' Georgia braced herself. 'The reasons I gave you for wanting to come here for Christmas were all true. Missing my mother was top of the list, and, though I could have collected the box any time before January the first, I decided to fetch it at Christmas and stay at the cottage on my own, instead of putting on a brave front at Amy's home. And while I was here I thought I might do a little exploring.'

Chance turned towards her, his eyes suddenly intent. 'Where?'

Georgia looked away into the fire. 'My parents told me you owned a house somewhere near the cottage they'd rented, so I thought I'd do some walking over Christmas and see where you lived.'

'And accidentally bump into me?' he said softly.

She stiffened. 'Definitely not. I thought you were skiing down some Alp, remember?'

'Toby must have told you I wasn't doing that this year,' he said flatly.

Georgia coloured. 'I haven't seen him lately for him to tell me anything. But believe me, Chance Warner, after what happened the first time we met I had no intention of getting involved with you and your family again. Don't flatter yourself that I isolated myself down here for Christmas just in the hope of seeing *you* again.'

His eyes suddenly darkened. 'Is that the truth? Or was Toby right all along? You decided I was a better prospect than a trainee solicitor.'

Georgia stared at him in outrage. 'I don't care about your boring money!'

He gave her a wry smile then which set her teeth on edge. 'Methinks the lady does protest too much.'

She gave up, so full of pain and rage and humiliation she was trembling from head to foot as she jumped to her feet. 'Believe what you like. Thank you again for the rescue. Please look on last night's episode as payment for services rendered—' She stopped as her phone rang.

CHAPTER SIX

GEORGIA took in a deep breath and pressed the button on her phone. 'I'm fine, Mother,' she lied as Chance strode from the room. She reassured Rose Cooper about snow hazards, chatted for a while, then, desperate for once to end the call, said goodbye.

She sat down, staring angrily into space as she pulled herself together. At last she got up to replenish the fire and then toasted herself in front of it for a moment or two. When the ice round her heart had melted a little Georgia closed the door very quietly behind her and went upstairs to the guest room with her book, praying that by morning the electricity would be back, or that the promised rain would have arrived and she could go home. The flat in Pennington wasn't home, exactly, but it would be a whole lot better than staying here under the same roof as Chance Warner.

She dashed tears away angrily as she locked the guest room door. Her first real love affair had been so cruelly short it was a one-night stand. Another first in her life.

Georgia spent a minute or two in the bathroom while she had light, then got into bed fully dressed, and pulled the covers up to her chin. She kept perfectly still, willing her circulation to do its job while her brain went round in circles. Her stupid, unnecessary confession had been another of her big fat mistakes. It was true that she'd hoped to see his famous house during her stay at the cottage. But that had been the extent of her plan. In her wildest dreams she had never imagined him turning up on her doorstep or, wilder still, bringing her here to his house to stay with him, let alone share his bed. Her pulse quickened at the mere thought of the night before, which had been another colossal mistake. But now she had to get through this night. Then tomorrow, even if she had to wade through knee-high snowdrifts, she would go back to the cottage. She could manage there without electricity. There was a log fire big enough to take a small pan of water, she'd left her own supply of food behind there, and her radio had batteries. And the moment the thaw set in sufficiently to move the car she would get back where she belonged...

She shot upright. She could hear an engine of some kind, and raised voices outside. She ran to the window but couldn't see anything. She put her shoes

on, slung a scarf round her neck, and unlocked the
door to steal downstairs. She went straight to the
boot room, where Ruby leapt down from her perch,
barking in welcome.

Georgia saw that the stable was shut, but she could
still hear machinery of some kind. 'Bed, Ruby!' she
said firmly, and shut the little dog in the kitchen.
Georgia pulled on boots and sheepskin and went
outside to investigate.

In the distance she saw the headlights of a tractor
hard at work on the main drive, and Chance shovelling behind it. Georgia fled back into the house and
removed the boots and coat, then returned Ruby to
her lookout in the boot room.

Gambling that Chance would be fully occupied out
there while she was in the kitchen, Georgia heated
water, her eyes brightening as she saw a box full of
household candles on the island. She rapidly made a
ham sandwich and a big mug of tea, then slid a couple
of candles into her jeans pockets and helped herself
to some of Chance's matches.

The fading light was enough to let her reach her
room safely. She put her sandwich and tea on the
bedside table, and stuck a candle in the pottery holder
on it. She struck a match on the sole of her shoe to
light it, and felt a lot better. She locked the door again,
then got into bed to maintain the warmth from her il-
licit trip downstairs. She drank some of her tea while

it was hot, then ate her sandwich as slowly as she could, brightening at the thought that now the drive was clear Chance might drive her back to Pennington tomorrow. She glowered. Of course he would. He was probably rejoicing right now at the thought of getting rid of her. She finished her tea and picked up her book, grateful that it was seven hundred pages long—enough to see her through the night. It wasn't fun reading by the light of a solitary candle, but it was a lot better than lying in bed in the dark, raging over what a fool she'd been to let Chance make love to her.

Georgia banked up the pillows, put her glasses on, and settled down with her book. She was unsurprised when Chance knocked on the door before she'd read even a chapter.

'Georgia? Why the hell are you up here instead of down by the fire? I couldn't find any more batteries, so try not to use the torch too much.'

She turned over a page in silence.

'Georgia! Answer me. Are you all right?'

Just peachy! She smiled smugly as the doorknob turned.

'You've locked the *door*,' he said, incensed. 'Open it. Now!'

He had to be joking!

'Be reasonable; we need to talk, Georgie.'

She sniffed. Two mistakes there, Mr Warner.

'I came to tell you something,' he continued.

Through gritted teeth by the sound of it.

'You can't stay there all night, you'll freeze. And you must be hungry. Come *on*, Georgia. Open the door.'

She turned another page, proud of her concentration on the story under the circumstances. But Lady Julitta, bravely defending her castle from attack while her lord was on crusade, was the perfect role model.

'For God's sake, open this door!' yelled Chance. 'Stop this. You're behaving like a child, Georgia.'

She rolled her eyes. His negotiation skills needed work! She read on in peace for a while, then stiffened as she heard some ominous clicks. To her dismay the knob turned, and Chance Warner stood in the doorway, torch in hand, glaring at her.

'You're reading!'

She nodded serenely. 'I do it a lot. How did you open the door?'

'I picked the lock.' He showed his teeth in a smile. 'Breaking the door down would have meant an expensive repair.'

'Not a problem with your famous money,' she said sweetly, and turned a page. 'Go away, please.'

His jaw dropped in astonishment, pleasing her enormously. 'Look, don't be a fool—'

'If that's your idea of persuasion you'd better try

again.' She held up an admonishing hand as he started to speak. 'We've already established that I was a fool to go to the cottage in the first place, an even bigger fool to fancy taking a look at your house, and the biggest fool of all to let you make love to me.'

'*Let* me?' He gave a sardonic bark of laughter. 'You know it was a hell of a lot more than that.'

'Something I now regret, and will never do again,' she assured him.

'Always supposing you were asked to,' snapped Chance, quite visibly hanging on to his temper. 'I came to tell you that Tom Hutchings had come up in his tractor to dig me out. He brought more candles— which you already know, since you're burning one of them.'

'I thought you could spare just two,' she said, sweetly reasonable.

'If you come down to the study you won't need one.' He took in a deep breath. 'Come on, Georgia. You've made your point. If I was wrong, I apologise.'

If he was wrong? 'About what, exactly?'

'Whatever the hell I said to make you lock yourself away up here in the dark. You can't stay up here until morning!'

She glared at him coldly. 'I certainly can't now you've broken the lock on the door.'

Chance lost patience. He yanked the covers away and stared blankly. 'You've got your clothes on!'

'How observant! I was conserving heat.'

'You won't have to if you come downstairs.' He held out his hand. 'Let's call a truce, Georgia. You won't have to endure my company for long. Now the drive is clear the Range Rover will cope with the road if the snow holds off. If you want I can drive you back to Pennington tomorrow.'

'How kind. I can't wait.'

'But that's tomorrow, and only then if weather permits,' he warned. 'Now, will you please come downstairs and talk about supper?'

'Oh, I see. You require my services as chef.'

'No, I damn well do not!' He took in a deep breath. 'Look, I know I've offended you—'

'A man of perception,' she mocked.

'All right, Georgia. Put your knife away. We can finish arguing downstairs. Now, get your torch, blow out that candle, and come down. Please,' he added belatedly.

She sighed. 'Oh, all right.'

They went down by the light of Chance's torch beam, the silence between them as oppressive as the darkness. Georgia was heartily glad to reach the kitchen, where candles flickered on both the island and the table, giving the room an illusion of warmth. The dogs came rushing to meet them, and to

Georgia's delight Luther made almost as much fuss of her as Ruby.

'They've missed you,' said Chance, and took her torch. 'I'll leave it on the table where you can see it.'

'Fine.' After a quick look in the refrigerator, Georgia took out some supplies and shut the door.

'What do you have in mind?' asked Chance. 'Whatever it is, I need a wash first.'

'While you do that I'll make a start,' said Georgia. 'You like omelettes?'

'I do. As long as you have one, too. You hardly ate anything at lunch.'

'I sneaked a sandwich upstairs before I settled in to the siege,' she admitted.

He touched her shoulder as he passed. 'I wouldn't have known if you hadn't told me.'

She looked up, her eyes steady in the candlelight. 'You're not the only one with a passion for the truth. *I'm* not in the habit of lying, either. About anything,' she added, and felt pleased when she saw her hit strike home. 'Give me twenty minutes or so—but no more than that, please. The food won't keep hot for long.'

Georgia got to work at speed. When Chance came back with minutes to spare she turned out two omelettes, one half the size of the other, from a pair of frying pans.

'Smells wonderful,' said Chance, and moved close to look at the plates.

'I see you've laid the tray ready, so if you'll take that, with one of these, I'll bring mine,' Georgia told him.

'Yes, teacher!' He blew out the candles on the table. 'I'll leave the other pair until I come back.'

Chance put the tray down on the desk in the study and lit the two candles he had ready on saucers. 'Luxury tonight. Heat *and* light.'

'This was how people lived until only a relatively short time ago,' said Georgia, determinedly conversational.

'There speaks the history buff.' Chance handed her a napkin and a fork and sat on the sofa beside her. 'Would you have liked to live in some bygone age, Georgia?'

'No. My main interest lies in the medieval—a time when there were no hot showers and very little hygiene. Women died in childbirth a lot.'

'You want children?'

She shrugged. 'Some day, maybe.'

'This is wonderful,' said Chance indistinctly. 'I'll miss your cooking when you're gone.' He went on eating for a moment. 'I'll miss your company, too.'

She raised disbelieving eyebrows. 'Really? A mercenary gold digger like me?'

His jaw clenched. 'I was rash—caught up in the

heat of the moment. I never thought of you like that, Georgia.'

'Oh, come *on*! You thought exactly that!'

Chance ignored her. 'Your meal is half the size of mine. Would you like some bread, or something else?'

'No, thank you.'

They had finished eating before Chance spoke again. 'Listen to me, Georgia. You wouldn't be the first woman who was only interested in me for my possessions. And I swore to myself I would never be made a fool of like that again. But when I took time to think logically just now it was obvious that no woman would opt for a solitary Christmas for mercenary reasons. It's a contradiction in terms. I apologise.' He got up to take their plates, and stood looking down at her obdurate face for a moment before loading the tray. 'I'll take this out. Would you like tea when I come back?'

'That would be lovely. Thank you.'

Georgia stared into the fire, deep in thought, when he'd gone. Chance was in a conciliatory mood. Her eyes blazed as memories of Toby's scheming flashed across her mind. If Chance was playing nice in the hope of another session in bed tonight he could think again.

It was some time before he returned with the tray. 'While the water boiled I took the dogs out,' he informed her. 'It's damned cold out there, but at least it's not snowing.'

'Good.'

The last time they'd had tea in front of the fire the silence between them had been companionable. Tonight it was heavy with things left unsaid. In the end Georgia put their cups back on the tray and turned to Chance.

'May I ask you something?'

'Anything you like, Georgie.'

'When you thought of finding out my phone number was it just an apology you had in mind?'

'No. My first instinct was to invite you out to dinner, or whatever. But because Toby had told you so much about me I changed my mind.'

'You thought I'd be attracted to the money, not the man?' she said, resigned.

'It crossed my mind. You wouldn't be the first.' Chance swivelled to face her. 'If I were plain Nick Warner, farm hand or whatever, would you honestly have been just as keen to see me again?'

'Yes. But you don't really believe that. And since I'm going home—God willing—tomorrow, you'll never know whether I was telling the truth.' She shrugged. 'Not that it matters. The moment I'm gone you'll forget all about me.'

He shook his head. 'I could never forget you, Georgia—at night in bed most of all.'

'I'm sure you can soon find someone to help you with that.'

He seized her hand. 'I don't want anyone else. Right now I don't care a damn whether you're after my money, or what your reasons were for coming here, as long as you're here right now. I want you bad, Georgie.'

She sighed wearily. 'I thought so.'

Chance stiffened. 'What do you mean by that?'

'Earlier on you had a bit of a *volte face*—became quite conciliatory. So I assumed—quite rightly as it turns out—that you must fancy some company in bed tonight.' She shook her head. 'Well, it's not going to happen.'

He looked long and hard into her eyes, and then dropped her hand and turned away, his face grim.

'Right.' Georgia got up. 'I'll go to bed now.'

He smiled sardonically. 'Aren't you nervous about that with no lock on the door?'

'No.'

'Maybe you should be if you think I'm so desperate to have you in my bed!'

'You mean you'd force yourself on me?' she asked, with such polite interest she thought for a moment she'd risked having her neck wrung.

His eyes blazed. 'I've never forced a woman in my life—never would. And I'm certainly not going to make a start with you,' he said shortly. 'Which you know damn well.'

She smiled kindly. 'Of course I do. As you tell me—repeatedly—my safety is your paramount concern. Goodnight, Chance.'

'Not so fast. I'm coming with you—but only to see you to your room. Laugh if you want, but I just need to know you're safe before I turn in myself.'

Georgia had rarely felt less like laughing. It was an eerie experience to walk up the wide staircase by the flickering light of the candle Chance carried.

'If Ridgeway has ghosts the setting's perfect for them tonight,' she remarked, shivering.

'If you're nervous, forget about my damn rash accusation and come and share my bed, Georgie.'

'Good of you to offer, but I'm cold, not nervous.'

'All the more reason to accept my invitation!' Chance went ahead of her into her room to light the candle on the bedside table.

'No, thank you.' Georgia stood by the bed, watching as the flickering flame threw the chiselled planes of his face into relief.

'Georgie,' he said at last, eyes locked with hers, 'I truly am sorry.'

'Let's not go there again,' she said wearily. 'Goodnight.'

With a muttered curse he pulled her into his arms and kissed her fiercely, then released her and strode from the room, slamming the door shut behind him with a force that almost blew the candle out.

She stared at the door for a moment, then took the candle into the bathroom. Afterwards, unable to face sleeping in her clothes, Georgia changed into pyjamas and fresh socks at top speed, wrapped her dressing gown around her and got into bed to read. But her hand soon grew too icy to keep a grip on the book. With a groan of frustration she pushed it aside, blew out the candle and slid down under the covers, burrowing her head into the pillows. She forced herself to lie still, willing her body to grow warm, but it refused to co-operate.

She heard Chance come upstairs, and stilled as his footsteps halted outside her door for a while, then continued across the landing to his room. Utterly disgusted by her disappointment, she waited, trying to calculate how long it would take him to settle down to sleep, but at last lost patience and switched on the torch. She forced herself to take off her dressing gown, her teeth chattering like castanets, and pulled on her cardigan and put the dressing gown back on top. She draped the blanket from the bed round her shoulders and thrust her icy feet into her slippers, put her glasses case in her pocket, then collected torch and book and stole from the room to go downstairs to the study.

She closed the door behind her with a sigh of relief at the heavenly warmth still given out by the banked-down fire. She took the guard away, poked the logs into life and added more, then lit the candles Chance had left on the desk. Swathed in the blanket, she curled up in the corner of the sofa, put her glasses on and opened her book—and gave a sigh of exasperation as the door flew open and Chance strode in.

Guns blazing again, thought Georgie. 'Hi,' she said, resigned.

'It gave me a hell of a shock to find your bed empty,' he snapped, closing the door.

Her eyes narrowed. 'And how, exactly, do you *know* it was empty?'

'I thought I heard something, so I got up and went to investigate.'

'I came down because I was too cold to get to sleep.' She shrugged. 'I hope you don't mind.'

'I don't mind at all now I know where you are.' He sat down beside her. 'Actually, this is a damned good idea.'

'I know. You should have fetched a blanket.'

He plucked her glasses away and put them on the desk. 'I'll share yours.' He whipped the blanket away, moved close, and wrapped it round both of them. 'Now you'll be warm.'

This was an understatement. Held close in Chance's arms under the blanket she felt hot, not warm. And no matter how much her brain protested the rest of her was delighted to breathe in scents of soap and man and woodsmoke. She could feel her body relaxing gradually, even though his was doing the exact opposite. She could feel him tensing against her, muscle by muscle, and at last he gave a smothered groan and kissed her.

'Don't push me away, Georgie.'

He parted her lips with his caressing tongue, kissing her with a subtle, coaxing sweetness which mowed down her defences, and with a sound half-sigh, half-sob she yielded to the pleasure of his mouth and to the hands that infiltrated layers of clothing to find her breasts. She quivered as he pushed the blanket aside and began removing their clothes. When they lay naked together at last he gave a visceral sigh of pleasure and kissed her with fierce demand, the subtlety gone as heat and passion flared up like wildfire between them. He moved his lips down her throat to breasts which grew taut, the centres hard and quivering, in response to the skill of his caressing lips and fingers, but when the caresses moved lower her brain woke up, and she shook her head in violent rejection.

'*Chance,*' she said hoarsely.

'*Yes,*' he rasped, as he leaned down to reach his dressing gown pocket.

But Georgia gave him a great push that sent him sprawling on the fireside rug.

'What the hell—?' He shot upright, shaking his hair back from his angry face.

'You came *prepared*,' she spat at him, yanking on her pyjamas.

'Would you prefer me to make love to you without protection?' he snapped, and got up to shrug on his dressing gown.

'I *prefer* no lovemaking at all!' she retorted, furious because her voice was unsteady.

His smile set her blood boiling in an entirely different way. 'You're lying, Georgia. Your body was all for it.'

'True,' she agreed, when she trusted her voice to sound normal. 'My body did want you—until my brain told it to back off. Discovering that you came ready to party was a total turn-off. Just like your brother, Mr Warner, you don't cope well with rejection.' Her eyes flashed in the firelight. 'I thought you meant it when you said you'd never had to force a woman.'

Chance raked a hand through his hair—a gesture she was beginning to know. 'I didn't force you. I stopped as soon as you put the brakes on.'

'There was a reason for that.' She thought for a moment, wondering whether to keep quiet or tell him the truth, then gave a mental shrug. After tomorrow it wouldn't matter anyway. She met his intent eyes squarely. 'I fell in love with you the night we first met. I couldn't get you out of my mind afterwards. Otherwise last night wouldn't have happened—'

He smothered the rest of her words with a conquering kiss, and then raised his head, his eyes triumphant. 'You know damn well I fell for you in the same way, Georgie. I couldn't get you out of *my* mind, either. The minute you walked into my arms that night I felt you were mine.'

'Even after Toby said I was a gold-digger, after your famous money?' She pushed him away, smiling cynically.

'I had to wonder, especially after my past experience, but it didn't stop me wanting you,' he said hotly, his eyes blazing as she shook her head.

'Then why didn't you do something about it?'

'I thought you were angry with me for hurting Toby, and that you blamed me for your break-up.'

She smiled cynically. 'If you'd told me that before your accusations I might have believed you.'

He stared at her, the heat fading from his eyes. 'If I could take the words back I would.'

'It's too late now. If you can drive me home tomorrow I'll be grateful. After that, just let me know when the road from the cottage is clear and I'll arrange to have my car collected. You needn't be afraid of unwanted attentions again—at least, not mine.'

'*You* are pushing your luck, Miss Smith,' he said through his teeth.

She nodded ruefully. 'I've had so much luck over Christmas I suppose it was bound to run out some time.'

Chance got up to see to the fire, and then turned to frown down at her. 'So what do you want to do right now?'

Georgia brightened. 'Do you mind if I stay down here tonight, please? I won't use many logs.'

'Oh, for God's sake—use all the damn logs you want,' he said savagely, and strode from the room, slamming the door shut behind him.

Georgia let out the breath she'd been holding and laughed shakily as the dogs, roused by the noise, began barking their heads off in the kitchen. But the laugh soon morphed into sobs she muffled with the blanket so no one could hear. Not that anyone was listening.

The barking had died down, and Chance was still in the kitchen with the dogs. Her breathing quickened as she heard the kitchen door open and close and the sound of familiar footsteps in the hall. But the footsteps went straight past the study door on their way to the stairs, and Georgia, deflated and miserable, fished a tissue from her pyjama pocket to mop her face, and began thumping the sofa cushions. She blew out the candles on the desk and wrapped the blanket round her, and settled down to try to sleep. She'd been right all along about love at first sight. It was a myth. And Chance Warner had obviously been lying about it to get what he wanted.

CHAPTER SEVEN

CHANCE drove back to Pennington by a route which
cut out most of the dangerous side roads, but took
them several miles farther on before they reached
the motorway.

'A lot longer in mileage, but in this weather quicker
and a lot safer,' he told Georgia.

'I hope the journey doesn't take *too* long,' she said
anxiously.

'Why? You have something pressing to get back
for?'

She cast a glance at his face, half hidden by dark
aviators. 'No,' she said evenly. 'I just thought you
wouldn't want to leave the dogs for long.'

'No problem there. I rang Tom Hutchings on the
car phone first thing this morning. He'll get up to
Ridgeway at some point to feed them and take them
for a run.' Chance kept his eyes on the sunlit icy road
ahead. 'He told me that snow ploughs and gritters had

been out today. Otherwise I wouldn't have set out in these conditions.'

'It's very kind of you,' she said woodenly, hoping they wouldn't meet much traffic.

'Are you nervous?'

'I would be if I were driving my car,' she admitted, 'but not in this one. Wonderful heater!'

'A big improvement on life at Ridgeway right now.' He slanted a glance at her. 'Will your friend be at the flat when you get back?'

'No. I rang Amy this morning. The shop is closed for a few days, so she's staying with Liam at his place.' She bit back a gasp as they hit an icy stretch.

'Sorry,' Chance muttered as he steered the car out of a slight skid.

Once they reached the motorway the going was better, though the road was flanked ominously by high banks of snow, and low speed signs were in operation all the way to Pennington.

It seemed such an eternity to Georgia since they'd left Ridgeway that she was surprised to hear a church clock tolling just midday as she gave directions to the flat when they reached the town. To her frustration there was no free parking space near her building, and Chance refused to let her have her belongings until he found a space a couple of blocks away.

'I'll see you safely inside,' he said with finality.

Georgia's teeth clenched. She'd hoped Chance

would take off right away. But common courtesy meant offering him a hot drink before he left. He held her arm in such a firm grip as they negotiated pavements rendered treacherous with slush over ice that Georgia breathed a sigh of relief when they reached the entrance to her building. They went up in the small lift in silence, both of them so constrained by their proximity conversation was beyond either of them. Georgia shot from the lift the moment it stopped, and ran to unlock her door.

'Do come in. Have some coffee before you go back,' she said politely, and took off her raincoat in the tiny hall. 'Amy promised to stock me up with some basics this morning on her way to Liam's.'

Chance's face was expressionless as he put down her bags. 'Thank you.' He followed her into the main room, which to Georgia's relief was reasonably tidy and wonderfully warm.

'I'll just pop to the bathroom,' she said, flushing. 'Do sit down.'

In the bathroom Georgia hastily transferred drying underwear to the airing cupboard, and put out clean towels before she went back to Chance. He turned from inspecting her crammed bookcases. 'All yours?' he asked.

'Mostly. If you want the bathroom it's next door on the left.'

When a search failed to turn up any of Amy's

posh coffee Georgia shrugged. Chance would have to slum it for once. She spun round as he appeared in the doorway. 'No real coffee, I'm afraid. Will instant do?'

'Anything you've got, but not right away.' His mouth twisted. 'I have a big favour to ask. Could I possibly have a shower? God knows when the power will be back in Ridgeway.'

Georgia smiled, taken aback. 'Of course. Use anything you want on the shelf. But be warned—the really hot water runs out after ten minutes.'

He stared, arrested.

'What?' she demanded.

'You actually smiled at me!'

The smile vanished. 'I'll make coffee once you're out of the shower.'

Georgia filled the kettle, put out mugs, and leaned against the small counter to look at the cold day outside. The early sunshine had given way to a uniform greyness which exactly matched her mood. She felt utterly desperate for Chance to get out of the shower and out of her flat.

'Thank you,' said Chance from the hall, jerking her out of her reverie. 'That was wonderful. I tried not to take all the hot water.'

'No problem,' she said airily. 'It will soon heat up again. I'll make that coffee right away. Would you like something to eat?'

He eyed her coldly as he raked a hand through his damp hair. 'I could do with something before I face that journey again, but you're so obviously desperate to get rid of me I won't trouble you. I'll let you know when your car can be moved. Goodbye, Georgia.'

Without another word Chance Warner strode out of the flat, and left Georgia standing speechless in the kitchen doorway as the front door slammed shut behind him. Be careful what you wish for, she told herself bitterly. She went back to the kitchen, and with a sudden hatred of instant coffee made tea and took it to the living room to check the answer-machine. She listened to a message telling her that Maddy had been unwell over Christmas, and asking if Miss Smith could kindly postpone the start of lessons for a week. Georgia let out a sigh of relief as she returned the call. Miss Smith was only too happy to do that. By then she should be in better shape herself.

By late afternoon the promised rain had arrived, and Georgia listened to it beating against the windows, wondering if Chance had made it back to Ridgeway safely. It was pointless trying to convince herself that she didn't care if he had or not. Having waited until now to fall in love, it was depressingly unlikely that she would fall back out of it any time soon.

When the phone rang that evening Georgia seized it eagerly.

'Hi, Georgie. You're home safe and sound, then.'

Georgie swallowed hard on her disappointment. 'Hi, Amy. I was here by lunchtime. Chance Warner drove me home in his Range Rover. Nerve-racking journey even so. I wouldn't have fancied it in my car.'

'Are you all right, love?'

'I'm just tired. The power went off at Chance's house late on Christmas Day, and it hadn't come back on by the time we left this morning.'

'Oh, my God!' Amy screeched in horror. 'How on earth did you survive?'

Georgia explained about log fires, candles and the camping stove, also the obliging farmer friend with a tractor.

'So where's your car?'

'Still at the cottage. I'll arrange to have it picked up when the weather clears.'

'I just hope you don't get pneumonia after all that. You should have come to our place for Christmas, Georgie.'

Amen to that, thought Georgia as she disconnected. But here at least she had light, warmth, and she was clean. Now all she had to do was get on with the life she'd had before she'd met Chance Warner again.

* * *

By her third day back Georgia was beginning to feel it might just be possible. The nights were bad, and sleep only attainable if she read until her eyes refused to stay open, but she was able to fill the daylight hours with shopping to spend her gift tokens, trips to the library, and lunch and a film matinee with Amy while Liam was at the gym. She gave the flat the kind of thorough spring clean hard to achieve when she was working, wrote her thank-you notes, and spoke to her mother a couple of times. Her appetite was the main casualty, but without Amy on hand to nag this was less of a problem than it might have been.

When the doorbell rang on the morning of the fourth day Georgia lifted the receiver to find someone 'delivering flowers for Miss Smith'. Georgia thanked the man and took the great sheaf of flowers into the kitchen, her eyes widening at the message on the card.

With love from Ruby and Luther. We miss you.

Georgia put the flowers in the sink and sank her head into her hands as the entire torrent of tears she'd managed to keep back since her return from Ridgeway streamed down her face. 'Damn you, Chance Warner,' she said hoarsely. 'Don't *do* this to me.'

It took the rest of the day to get back to some form of calm, but by the evening Georgia had managed it enough to eat scrambled eggs from a tray while she watched a film on television. And later she even managed to sleep, after finally finishing the tale of the redoubtable Lady Julitta, whose crusading lord had returned in time to fight off the usurper intent on seizing his castle before he lived happily ever after with his resourceful wife.

Georgia emerged from her shower next morning with renewed determination on her face as she slathered moisturiser on it. She would dress in something special and go out after breakfast. The rain had stopped and it was a relatively fine day. She put on the underwear Amy had given her, added the new sweater and a short tweed skirt, and as the final touch suede boots with heels of the type scorned by Chance. She slicked her hair up into a smooth twist, put her contacts in, and was just getting her coat when the doorbell rang. She sighed impatiently as she picked up the receiver and heard that the postman had a parcel for her. But when she opened the door it was Toby Warner who stood holding a parcel. He was dressed in all his *GQ* glory, a hopeful smile on the face that was so like and yet so unlike his brother's. And right now the last face she wanted to see.

'I intercepted the postman,' he said. 'Let me in, Georgia.'

'No,' she said flatly, and took the parcel from him. 'Go away, Toby.' She would have shut the door in his face, but he stuck his foot in it, wincing as she refused to give way.

'Please. I just want to say I'm sorry.'

'OK,' she said tersely. 'You've said it. Goodbye.'

He scowled. 'Why are you like this? Everything was fine between us until the night of the party.'

She sighed impatiently. 'There was nothing between us, Toby. Ever. We met briefly a couple of times, and against my better judgement I came to your party. But that was it. And whatever it was, it's over.'

The smile vanished as he shouldered the door open and grabbed her by the wrist. 'I don't want it to be over!'

'Nevertheless it is—right now,' said a familiar voice from the landing.

Georgia pushed Toby away, breathing raggedly, and turned on Chance as he strolled through the door. 'I don't know why you're here, but now you are would you remove your brother, please?'

Toby glared in fury at the tall figure standing over him. 'What the hell are *you* doing here?'

'Throwing you out,' said Chance, and he seized his brother by the collar of his expensive leather trench. 'It's time you learned to take no for an answer, my lad.'

'And you're going to make me?' sneered Toby with shaky bravado.

'No.' Chance released him and brushed his hands together. 'Georgia can do that by calling the police to report you for stalking her. Bad news for a trainee solicitor.'

The effect on Toby was dramatic. He turned on Georgia in utter panic. 'No. Please. Don't. I won't bother you again, I swear.'

'Can I have that in writing?' said Georgia bitterly.

Toby deflated like a pricked balloon. 'I wouldn't have hurt you.'

Chance thrust Toby outside on the landing. 'It's time you learnt that when a lady says no she means it!'

Toby looked from Georgia to his brother. 'You want her yourself, don't you?'

'Yes, I do,' said Chance grimly. 'Not that she'll have anything to do with me when I've got *you* for a relative.'

'You needn't be so insulting!' Toby looked at Georgia. 'Do you want *him*?'

'*No!* I just want you both out of here right now,' she snapped, and shut the door on both of them.

Georgia snatched up the parcel she'd dropped, annoyed because she felt so shaken at seeing Chance again. In a heavy suede jacket and rollneck sweater, he'd looked so good he'd not only put his smaller younger brother in the shade, but rocketed her recovery programme back to square one. She sighed and tore apart the cardboard on the parcel to reveal two hardback bestsellers. She'd been waiting for them to come out in paperback so she could afford them—something she'd mentioned fleetingly to Chance. He'd obviously ordered them online. She bit her lip. He certainly knew the right way to a woman's heart—this woman, anyway.

The doorbell jerked her out of her reverie.

She picked up the receiver reluctantly. 'Who is it?'

'Nick Warner. May I talk to you, please?'

Chance's father? Georgia pressed the release on the main door, and then waited in trepidation for the lift to come up. What on earth could he want? When the buzzer sounded she went into the hall and opened the door, then stared as Chance smiled, looking so pleased with himself she felt her heart thaw a little.

'I thought it was your father,' she accused.

'I was rather banking on that. I knew you wouldn't open the door otherwise.' He looked down at her with such warmth and tenderness in his eyes her heart began to melt in earnest.

'Do you want to come in?' she said awkwardly.

'Actually, I hoped you'd come out, Georgie. Will you have lunch with me?'

She hesitated for a moment, then decided against cutting off her nose to spite her face as her grandma had used to say when she was little. She was dressed for the occasion, and she certainly had nothing better to do. 'All right. Thank you. Come in for a moment while I get a coat.'

Georgia left him in the living room and hurried to her bedroom for a jacket. She touched up her face and after a moment's thought unpinned her hair from its twist and combed it loose on her shoulders. She might as well use all the weapons she had in her armoury. She frowned at her reflection. Who was she trying to kid? One look at Chance and she wanted to make love, not war.

He turned as she rejoined him, the heat in his eyes all the reward she needed for her efforts. 'As I've said before, Miss Smith, I never had a teacher who looked like you.'

'Thank you for the flowers and the books.'

'I remembered you were looking forward to reading those.'

'Good memory.'

'Where you're concerned, infallible,' he assured her, and touched a finger to her sleeve. 'I like this.'

'It's trying its best to look vintage 1940s teddy bear, but I bought it at cost from Amy's shop.'

'You look very cuddly in it.' His eyes darkened.

'But I won't think about that right now. I've booked a table at the Chesterton.'

'You were so sure I'd come?'

'I wasn't sure at all. I hoped.' He smiled. 'I thought it would make a change from fry-ups on the camping stove. Though I won't enjoy the Chesterton's finest more than the meals we shared, Georgie.'

Georgia felt uneasy as they walked through the town. She wished vainly that she hadn't told Chance she was in love with him, certain it would make things awkward between them now. She was wrong. The food was good at the Chesterton, the service superb, and gradually she felt just as comfortable with Chance over the lunch table as during their tramps in the snow. But when he helped her on with her coat afterwards he spotted the mark Toby had left on her wrist and, oblivious of anyone looking on, raised her hand to press his lips to it.

'I was going to let him off a good hiding,' he said grimly, as they walked back. 'But I've changed my mind.'

'Change it back,' she said peremptorily.

'Why?'

'Because it will cause trouble, and I don't want my name cropping up again with your family.'

'It will crop up soon enough, Georgie, when I tell them we're together.'

She turned on him in consternation. *'What?'*

'You don't think I'm going to let you get away, do you? How could I explain to Luther and Ruby?' He paused as they arrived at her building. 'I'm coming up with you. We need to talk.'

As soon as the lift doors closed behind them Chance took Georgia in his arms and kissed her, and only let her go when the doors opened on her floor.

Heart thumping, Georgia unlocked her door and went ahead of Chance into the living room. She took off her jacket and dropped it on a chair. 'Would you like to take yours off for a minute?'

'Of course I would.' He laid his jacket alongside hers, then led her to the sofa. 'Now we talk. Or at least I do. And I want you to listen.'

'Am I allowed to talk too?' she demanded.

'Only after I finish,' said Chance firmly, and slid an arm round her. 'This is what I have in mind. Lunch today was just the beginning.'

'The beginning of what?'

Chance silenced her with a kiss. 'If you keep on interrupting I'll just have to keep on doing that,' he said severely.

'I've stopped,' she said promptly.

'You mean you don't want me to kiss you?'

'Make up your mind,' she said tartly, and he smiled and kissed her again. This time the kiss went on longer, but at last Chance tore his mouth away and held her close, rubbing his cheek over her hair.

'We should probably have had this conversation in public over lunch,' he said huskily, and took in a deep breath. 'To cut to the chase: I intend to come courting, Miss Smith.'

Georgia felt a great leap of delight. 'Courting?' she mocked. 'I said you were born in the wrong century.'

'You don't fancy being courted?'

'Oh, I do. Madly. But please go on.'

'I'll do whatever it takes to prove that I'm sorry and convince you that I want you. I shall wine and dine you, and take you to the theatre. You can introduce me to Amy—'

'What as, exactly? Boyfriend?'

Chance laughed and scooped her onto his lap. 'I'm a bit on the mature side for that.'

'My lover, then?' she said matter-of-factly.

'God, yes.' He kissed her gently, then not so gently, and with a groan deposited her back beside him. 'Where was I? Ah, yes. When you're teaching do you get weekends free?'

'Yes.'

'Then I shall drive over once or twice in the week, and you can come to me at Ridgeway for the weekends. And once I've persuaded you to overlook disadvantages such as Toby for a brother-in-law I intend to wed you and bed you and make you all mine—though not necessarily in that order.'

Georgia stared at him in wonder. 'Was that a proposal I heard in there?'

'I've never made one before, so maybe I didn't get it quite right.' Chance raised her hand to his and kissed it. 'That's what courting usually leads up to, my darling Miss Smith.' He fished in a pocket and handed her car keys over. 'One of the reasons why I'm here. But not the most important one.' He sobered, his eyes looking down into hers with an intensity that made her pulse race. 'I came to tell you I love you, Georgia Smith, and to make you admit that you love me.'

'But I've already told you that,' she said breathlessly.

'I thought maybe I'd hurt you so much I'd killed your feelings for me. So I sent flowers and books, and came courting.' He kissed her fleetingly. 'I'll do my damndest never to hurt you again.'

'But tell me, Mr Warner, are you perfectly sure of my reasons for agreeing to your plan of campaign?' She smiled challengingly. 'I could just be lusting after your possessions. Which I am,' she added, startling him. 'At least after two of them.'

'Luther and Ruby!' He shook her gently. 'Georgie, I don't care why you agree as long as you do. Come home with me right now and stay over New Year to celebrate. You'll have to if you want your car,' he added, and grinned as he waved the keys under her nose.

'Of course I'll come.' Her mouth drooped. 'I wasn't looking forward to New Year.'

'You'll like this one,' he assured her, and kissed the smile back on her lips. 'I've been very busy since the power came back on at Ridgeway. Once the thaw set in I went down to the cottage and had a look at your car, then got the local garage to collect it and give it a thorough overhaul—no, don't interrupt. I haven't got to the good part yet. It won't even matter if it snows again. I've invested in a generator at last, so I promise to keep you warm one way or another, whatever happens.'

'Actually,' she said demurely, 'I quite liked the method you used last time.'

His eyes lit with a hot blue gleam she liked enormously. 'That's good to know. I intend to employ that method every night—and part of every day—whatever the weather. Any comments?'

She smiled in such triumph he laughed and crushed her close.

'Why the Cheshire Cat smile, Georgie?'

'My idea of Christmas alone at Ridge Cottage wasn't such a bad one after all, Mr Warner!'

'Because it resulted in the best Christmas of my life, yes,' he agreed, and shook her slightly. 'But make a New Year resolution, Georgia Smith—promise me you'll never try anything like it again!'

'I promise.' She grinned at him. 'But at least I managed half of what I intended with my unusual Christmas.'

'Half?'

'I didn't get peace on earth, but I achieved good-will to all men—even Toby. Because without him I would never have met you, Chance Warner!'

All the magic you'll need this Christmas...

When **Daniel** is left with his brother's kids, only one person can help. But it'll take more than mistletoe before **Stella** helps him…

Patrick hadn't advertised for a housekeeper. But when **Hayley** appears, she's the gift he didn't even realise he needed.

Alfie and his little sister know a lot about the magic of Christmas – and they're about to teach the grown-ups a much-needed lesson!

Available 1st October 2010

Spend Christmas with NORA ROBERTS

Daniel MacGregor is the clan patriarch. He's powerful, rich – and determined to see his three career-minded granddaughters married. So he chooses three unsuspecting men he considers worthy and sets his plans in motion!

As Christmas approaches, will his independent granddaughters escape his schemes? Or can the magic of the season melt their hearts – and allow Daniel's plans to succeed?

Available 1st October 2010

www.millsandboon.co.uk

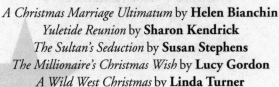

THE *Balfour* LEGACY

EIGHT SISTERS, EIGHT SCANDALS

VOLUME 1 – JUNE 2010
Mia's Scandal
by Michelle Reid

VOLUME 2 – JULY 2010
Kat's Pride
by Sharon Kendrick

VOLUME 3 – AUGUST 2010
Emily's Innocence
by India Grey

VOLUME 4 – SEPTEMBER 2010
Sophie's Seduction
by Kim Lawrence

8 VOLUMES IN ALL TO COLLECT!

www.millsandboon.co.uk

M&B